KAIT BALLENGER

"Non-stop action, pulse-pounding suspense, and red-hot romance… Kait Ballenger's Execution Underground series delivers in spades!"
—Jaime Rush, *New York Times* bestselling author

"Action and romance in one mesmerizing story. A phenomenal start to the Execution Underground series. *Shadow Hunter* will leave you breathless and demanding more."
—Cecy Robson, author of *Sealed with a Curse*

"Taut with action, suspense, and romance that sizzles, *Shadow Hunter* is an evocative prelude to what's certain to be an exciting new series! Fans of JR Ward are going to love the sexy warriors of Kait Ballenger's Execution Underground."
—Kate SeRine, author of *Red* and *The Better to See You*

Also available from Kait Ballenger

AFTER DARK
"Shadow Hunter"

TWILIGHT HUNTER

KAIT BALLENGER

MILLS
BOON

First published in Great Britain 2013
by Mills & Boon, an imprint of Harlequin (UK) Limited,
Eton House, 18-24 Paradise Road, Richmond, Surrey TW9 1SR

© Kaitlyn Ballenger 2013

ISBN: 978 0 263 90420 8

089-1113

Harlequin (UK) policy is to use papers that are natural, renewable and recyclable products and made from wood grown in sustainable forests. The logging and manufacturing processes conform to the legal environmental regulations of the country of origin.

Printed and bound
by CPI Group (UK) Ltd, Croydon, CR0 4YY

To my mom, Jessica Schulz,
for believing in me when no one else would
and for always telling me I could achieve my dreams.
I'll love you always, mama.

TWILIGHT HUNTER

Skinwalker [skin-waw-ker] (n.)—1. A being capable of assuming the identity of an animal 2. God of Norse mythology 3. Shape-shifter

CHAPTER ONE

JACE MCCANNON PALMED the Mateba and clicked back the gun's hammer. The cold grip panels of the modified revolver sat comfortably in his hand. Six silver bullets for a rogue werewolf. Limited shots. But he was feeling lucky.

He gripped the gun with both hands and lowered it to his side, slipping in and out of the shadows. The rank scent of garbage, car exhaust and piss wafted into his nose as he reached the alleyway. Ah, the sweet aroma of Rochester's slums. He ran his tongue over his teeth, jonesing for a cigarette to drown out the smell and steady the adrenaline buzz creeping through his veins. Damn, he wanted to find this son of a bitch.

Resting his back against a brick building, he paused and glanced up. The white moon stared down at the Earth, calling him. Heat prickled beneath his skin.

He wrenched his gaze from the tempting sky and forced himself into the moment. Inhaling deeply, he rushed around the corner and scanned the area, pointing his gun into the darkness. No one. No werewolves, no hobos. Damn, not even the prostitutes were roaming.

Not that he blamed them. Regular killings weren't anything to call home about—happened all the time. But this was different. Innocent women being found with their organs slung around their corpses, Jack-the-Ripper style. The worst part? Jace had no idea where to find the sick fuck responsible, and the thought of the young women's pain sent his blood boiling.

He explored the alley, gun still at the ready and eyes searching for any sign of movement. A rustling noise hissed from around the next corner. Jace held his gun tight and sneaked down the narrow passage toward it. The sound grew louder, and he quickened his pace. When he reached the bend he stopped, listening closely. He threw himself around the corner, gun ready and his finger on the trigger.

A plastic bag caught on a Dumpster swished in the light wind. He cursed under his breath. Maybe he wasn't so lucky tonight. He pushed his fingers through his hair. The cell phone jammed in the pocket of his jeans vibrated. He pulled out the annoying piece of shit and read the screen: David.

He jabbed his thumb into one of the buttons, hoping it was the right one, and shoved the phone to his ear. "Yeah?"

"Meeting in an hour." David's deep voice rumbled over the line.

Aw, hell. Jace shook his head. "Don't toy with me. I've got business."

"I'm not shittin' you, J. One hour, and you better show or Damon's gonna rip my head off. I told him I'd get you here."

Jace frowned. He hated being forced to carry a damn cell phone. He didn't enjoy people contacting him whenever they pleased. "It's nearly the full moon, David. This is my prime time. You know that."

"You don't have to preach to me. Damon's the one riding your ass like a Grand Canyon donkey, not me." David paused for a moment. "He's gonna want a report tonight."

"Yeah, yeah, I hear ya. I'll have something."

"Sure you hear me, and I like to dress up in tutus while my girl spanks me and calls me Big Daddy."

Jace smirked. "Hey, if that's what gets you off…"

"Shut it," David said. "You've gotta report tonight or Damon will go postal. So what are you gonna tell him?"

Jace glanced into the empty darkness surrounding him. "Same thing I told him last time—jack shit. I'm not opening my damn mouth until I've got their packmaster bound and chained, or, preferably, I'm carrying his head on a silver platter courtesy of my bare hands."

David let out a frustrated sigh. "I thought you said you had something."

"I do." Jace lowered his voice. It didn't matter that he was alone; some things he couldn't say aloud if he wanted to keep his sanity. "I've got a scent, and it's familiar, so I smell it everywhere. Trailing this monster's stink is about as much fun as shooting myself in the foot."

"It's something."

"You better believe it's something. But what do you expect me to do, David? Tell the whole damn division their werewolf hunter happens to be so good at his job because he's a friggin' half-breed?"

Silence answered him from the other end of the line. Another rustling sound blew through the alley, but Jace ignored the noise. "Look, I'll deal with this, all right? Forget about it. I'll be at the damn meeting with bells on and a smiling face, but let me do it on my own terms."

"Yeah, fine. I better see you there or the next time I'm around, I'll have a long rope and it'll be coming straight for your neck."

Jace huffed. "Talk to you later, Big Daddy."

"Yeah, you too sugar."

With a small click, the line went dead. Jace shoved the phone in his pocket again. The swishing sound continued, the noise growing. Jace rolled his eyes, ready to ball up the grocery bag and pitch it. He eyed the plastic.

Shit. The wind had stopped. The bag wasn't blowing.

The faint sound of footsteps echoed, and the rustling quieted. Jace lifted his revolver from his side, launching himself down the alley and around the corner. He held his gun tight, prepared to shoot.

Streetlights illuminated what lay in front of him. He stopped midrun and stared at the horror.

He gaped, all his breath escaping in one large rush. "Shit."

Blood. There was so much blood. Splattered everywhere. The light from the overhead lamps framed the corpse like spotlights at a play starring an innocent, mutilated victim. The girl's head hung crooked, touching her shoulder, mouth open and eyes lifeless. Her features were contorted in a look of pure terror. Her arms lay limp at what had once been her sides, and her legs were spread wide, with her pants and underwear wrapped around one ankle. The middle of her body had ceased to exist, ripped to shreds by what Jace knew were large canine teeth.

Anyone with a weak stomach would have tossed his cookies at first glance. Despite all the crazy shit Jace had seen in his years as a hunter for the Execution Underground, even *his* gut did a flip. What the hell was wrong with this guy? *Guy?* No, this killer wasn't a person. This sicko was subhuman, and not because he was a werewolf. This was beyond evil.

Jace fought the urge to punch his fist into the

brick wall beside him. His rage overcame him, and the beast inside him longed to emerge. He growled, releasing the tension, and tried to calm himself. He needed to examine the body, and fast. If the police got here, he was screwed six ways to Sunday.

He knelt by the corpse. Bruises marred her forearms and neck. Based on their colors, they had definitely been made pre-mortem. She'd been dead at least thirty minutes. He breathed in, and underneath the overpowering smell of blood, the scent of sex lingered. She'd been raped before her death.

Power. That was what this freak was all about—power. He attacked young women, humans in their early twenties, who were no match for his supernatural strength. *He preys on victims he knows he can take with ease. Deep down, he's a coward.* And from the carnage of his attacks, this wasn't just about stealing women's sex or overpowering them. With this kind of blood display, these attacks were either personal or passionate, and Jace would bet on the second.

A sexual sadist. *Anger excitation.* It wasn't the sex that got this bastard off. It was the pain of these innocent women. Intestinal damage and blood loss: a slow death, so his victims suffered in front of his eyes. *He attacks them as a wolf and violates them in human form as they die.* The familiar anger built inside him again.

Jace pulled a pack of Marlboro Reds from his

leather trench coat. He slipped one from the box and lit up. The smoke rushed into his lungs, the nicotine calming him instantly. This shit was going to kill him, but most days he didn't care.

A small amount of guilt rose in his chest as he stared down at the victim. Here he was, clearly not giving a rat's ass about his health or his life, with no family left to give a shit if he died. But he was living and breathing, while this innocent girl, who'd had a full happy life ahead of her, lay at his feet, violated and murdered. She'd had something to lose, people who would miss her.

He stared into the open cavity that had once been her chest. No heart. *He eats their hearts when he's finished. Consumption shows a desire to keep part of the victim with him. No remorse.* Jace grabbed the flask that always resided in his pocket. He unscrewed the cap and downed a long gulp of Bushmills Irish Whiskey. The liquor trickled down his throat in a warm rush. If this was any sign of how the night was going to go, he would need a lot more than the contents of the flask to keep his demons at bay.

He glanced at the dead girl again as he crouched at her side. He wracked his brain for any possible clues he could have missed. Careful to use only his sleeve and not leave a fingerprint, he lifted her hands and peered underneath her fingernails. No skin or fur. She hadn't put up much of a fight. Maybe the killer took her by surprise? Given his cowardly choice of weak victims, Jace wouldn't be surprised.

He would report to the Execution Underground and then leave things to his fellow hunters. Shane could use the voice distorter he'd rigged up to call in the crime, if need be. Jace had what he needed for his report, but he couldn't notify the beat cops himself, not until he was certain he wouldn't need to recheck the body. And it would take them a while to find her in the back alley like this, if they ever did.

As he stood, ready to go to the damn meeting, another scent came to him on the wind. He paused for a long moment.

What the...?

Spinning so fast the world blurred, he had his gun out and the trigger pulled within seconds. A werewolf peeked its head out of the darkness as the bullet sped straight toward its head.

The wolf dodged the ammo and bolted from the alley. Jace dashed after his target as his cigarette fell from his lips and landed next to the girl's body. A werewolf's speed outranked a regular human's any day, but his boots clashed against the pavement as he tailed the monster with ease. The werewolf skidded sharply to the left with Jace on its heels, his pace never faltering. Adrenaline shot through his veins, charging him like a live wire.

He tapped the trigger of the Mateba and, aiming while he ran, he fired wide with purpose in mind, intentionally missing and using his silver bullets to herd the wolf. If he fired right, it turned left. He was careful, making each bullet count and ensuring he had one left for the kill.

One of Jace's shots ricocheted off the ground near the werewolf's feet. It jumped with a loud yelp and bounded into an alleyway. But he was prepared; he knew these back streets. He sprinted after the wolf. A smirk spread across his face as the monster ran into a dead end. It spun toward him and growled.

Right hand bracing his gun, he reached with his left and removed his silver dagger. When the wolf's golden eyes locked on the weapons, it backed into a corner, and Jace swore he heard it whimper before its growling continued. Stalking like a predator, he moved forward, ready to thrust the blade into the monster's heart. All his muscles tensed as he prepared for the animal to lunge at him. His whole body longed for a fight.

And damned if he wouldn't give this rapist mongrel the fight of its life.

CHAPTER TWO

FROM THE MOMENT he pulled his gun, Frankie Amato knew what he was. A hunter. She'd stumbled onto a hunter. She stared down the barrel of his gun with fear and adrenaline pumping through her veins. A large lump crawled into her throat.

The rumors are true.

What had she gotten herself into? They'd murdered her kind for centuries, but as civilization progressed, their numbers had dwindled to near extinction, or so she'd thought. Shit. She hadn't expected this. A hunter in Rochester—on her turf. How could she have been so oblivious?

In the past few months, several lone wolves who'd refused to join her pack had been murdered. As Alpha of the Rochester Pack, it was her job to protect her people and keep them out of harm's way. But the protection she guaranteed didn't extend to the rogue wolves, and she'd given no more than a fleeting thought to the rumors that they'd died at the hands of a hunter. Now the voices of gossip and the murmurs of trouble, which had spread like wildfire throughout her clan, smacked her in the face with a major reality check.

And son of a bitch, he'd backed her into a dead end. She'd let down her guard, and the bastard had cornered her.

She bared her canines, growling from deep within her throat. The hunter strode closer. Shadows covered his face, and his gun pointed at her head. The silver dagger he'd pulled from his coat flashed in the moonlight. Her heart pounded in fear, knowing the fate she would be subjected to if she didn't fight fast.

Frankie's tail hit the wall; she hadn't realized she'd backed away in the first place. The hunter maintained the upper ground, holding the fighting advantage. Even if she lunged for him, his dagger would pierce right through her chest. Anger and rage filled her, and she snarled, dying to rip his throat out. But her sense of logic prevailed. She would shift into human form, wait until the right moment, when he thought she was weak, then speed-shift—her specialty—back into a wolf.

A shiver ran down her spine as her limbs and muscles contorted. Pleading wasn't her style, but it was worth a chance. A loud howl escaped her lips, slowly transitioning into the cry of a woman as she shifted. She fell back against the brick wall behind her and slid to the ground, bare flesh scraping the pavement.

The hunter stepped closer. His gun barrel held steady. A streak of rage rushed through her. She hated herself for being such a moron. Why had she gone looking for the killer when she was off her game? Damn her sense of pride. She'd overestimated her ability.

On the average day, she could handle this, but now she was knee-deep in trouble and shit out of luck. Damn estrus always clouded her judgment. Hell, she'd even warned her pack against doing anything stupid. And topping the list of stupid things to do, hunting a supernatural serial killer while in her Call ranked number one by far.

She scanned the alley. Sheer brick walls, a couple of Dumpsters too far away to offer protection, and nothing amongst the garbage she could use as a weapon. Nothing that would help her escape, and there was no way in hell she could dodge around him when she was cornered like this. He'd proven he was a good shot when he oh-so-successfully corralled her into a dead end.

She lifted her hands and held them up, palms out. She wasn't below milking the helpless-female card. Not if it saved her ass.

Draw him in. Pretend you're weak. Then shift, finish him off and get the hell outta Dodge.

He hovered in the near shadows, a massive black silhouette, nothing visible but the width of his body and the gun still trained on her. Yeah, there was no missing that.

"I don't know who you are," she said. "But I'm not your enemy."

A rough sound escaped him. Had he just scoffed at her?

"I'm serious," she insisted. "Look at the evidence. That girl was mutilated and raped." She gestured to her own body. "I'm not covered in blood. I'm weaponless, and I don't have the…uh…right equipment to do what was done to that poor girl."

Frankie held her breath as she waited for him to reply. The silence was deafening. Please let him care about her being innocent. Granted, hunters traditionally stuck to troublemaking rogues without a pack, but that didn't mean he would spare her. Hunters were reputed to be ruthless, and he might not take pity on her. She thought of the rogue several months ago who'd been attacking random innocents just for the hell of it. She'd killed the son of a bitch personally. But even though her goal of controlling rogues aligned with his, she'd seriously played her cards wrong by coming here tonight, even if it got her out of the damn mating ceremony.

Tonight, during her estrus, she was supposed to "choose" a male to mate with, confirming him as her destined mate. Something she did *not* want to do. Call her sentimental, but she didn't want an arranged mating, even though her mate had been chosen for her when she was a child. Since Alejandro was the strongest pack male and her closest friend, her parents had chosen him for her. Better Alejandro than any other pack member, she supposed, but either way, she didn't want this mating, even though it was required of her as packmaster. Being caught by a hunter would be one hell of an excuse for skipping the ceremony, not that her current situation was preferable.

Blood rushed to her head, pounded in her ears. She opened her mouth, not really sure what she was going to say.

He took a step closer, and his scent flooded her nose.

She sucked in a deep breath. "Uh…look, you smell…" His tantalizing scent washed over her. Man, he smelled delicious. "You smell…normal. There's no blood on you, so I know you didn't kill her. That means we're on the same side. We're trying to catch the same monster."

He didn't speak or move. She waited several agonizing seconds.

"Stay still," he finally muttered. "Don't make any sudden moves." His deep voice washed over her, and the thought of him saying her name sent a wave of heat boiling under her skin.

Damn it all to hell. Her friggin' estrus cycle was one of the few things she hated about being a werewolf. How the hell could she be thinking about him like that when she was staring down the barrel of his gun?

His huge, black boot broke into the pool of light. Her gaze traveled up his frame as the moonlight illuminated his face. She struggled to breathe. A simmering heat rushed down her spine and lodged itself between her legs. She was suddenly aware of how very naked she was as she stared up at the heavenly hunk before her.

His raw glare penetrated her. The color of lily pads, his eyes belonged to something vibrant, complex and daring—and, if she didn't know better, something supernatural, not a human hunter. Strands of his chin-length, auburn hair fell into his face, accenting his sharp, masculine features. His overall demeanor screamed of danger and a rough life, but his face was flawless, perfect—he looked like a model dressed in a ragged assassin's clothing. And his body…where did she begin?

He towered over her, well over six feet, and his physique matched his height in enormity. Muscles strained against the sleeves of his trench coat, and she bet that rock-hard abs were hidden underneath the coat. An image of her kneeling in front of him in submission settled in her mind. Whoa. She'd never wanted a man to take control of her. But as she lay on the ground, sprawled naked before his eyes, the vulnerability of her situation excited her, and the thought of him having his way with her sent a rush of wet heat between her legs.

He opened his mouth, and his voice was like a

growl in his chest. "Get up," he said, his tone gruff and angry. His gun remained still.

Frankie gaped, frozen in a mixture of desire, anger and fear.

"That was an order, not a request," he barked.

She inhaled a slow breath, found her footing and rose to her feet. Her hands shook at her sides.

"What's your name?"

For a moment she couldn't remember; his nearness muddled her mind. Her logical side reared its head, and her stomach churned. This man was a hunter. If she told him her name, he would know exactly who she was, and even though she wasn't a rogue, killing the Rochester packmaster might be too sweet a temptation for a hunter to resist. She swallowed the large lump in her throat and said the first name that came to her mind.

"Francesca. My name's Francesca." Her mother's name, from which her shortened version had originated. She prayed the half lie would save her. Whether now or later, if he found out who she really was, she was totally in for it.

"Turn around."

She circled to her right and trembled harder. She imagined him taking her from behind and choked back a gasp.

"Hands behind your back."

"What?" she asked without thinking.

"You heard me, hands behind your back."

No way was she going quietly. "No, let me go."

He scoffed. "Not gonna happen. You can cooperate or I can make you."

He drew closer, and his warmth seeped over her bare skin. To hell with her traitorous body. She was going to rip him to shreds, so he couldn't get to her first. She would let him think she was going to cooperate, then catch him unaware. She shoved her shaking wrists behind her and concentrated on her breathing. She wasn't going down without a fight.

Now.

She spun around and lunged for the hunter's ankles. She threw him off guard by hitting lower than he expected as she speed shifted into wolf form. He crumpled to the ground. His elbow jabbed into her side as he fell. She yelped before she sank her canines into the muscled flesh of his forearm. He let out a guttural yell.

In a sudden reaction to the pain, his grip on his gun loosened, and the weapon fell from his hand. But Frankie didn't care if he was temporarily disarmed, if he'd lost his advantage. The asshole deserved to be ripped to shreds for killing her kind, even if they were rogues.

Shaking her head from side to side, she continued to rip at the hunter's arm. Without warning, he shifted onto his side and slashed his knife through the air. The blade hit her skin. She released his arm as another yelp ripped from her throat. Her fur bristled as adrenaline shot through her.

Scrambling across the pavement, she bolted down the alley. He grabbed his gun and sprinted after her. She needed to gain some distance, so she could turn and get a running start to lunge again, get her momentum going back in his direction. But shit, he was fast—too fast.

The hunter threw himself through the air, landing on her back. Her nails scraped the pavement as she tried to claw away from him.

In a moment of luck, she wriggled her way free. Turning on her attacker, she jumped for his throat. Her paws hit his chest, and he slammed into the ground from the weight of the blow. She growled and snapped at his neck, but he caught her by her scruff and tossed her aside as if she weighed no more than a child's doll. She skidded across the pavement, her skin rubbed nearly raw. A shiver ran down her spine as her limbs and muscles contorted. Damn it, because of her estrus she couldn't hold her shift, not with her emotions running the gamut, from anger to arousal. A loud howl escaped her lips as she slowly changed back into human form.

Before she could process what was happening, he climbed on top of her. His body was flush against hers, but she continued to fight. They rolled out of the alley and into the orange glow of the streetlights. With superior strength, the hunter pinned her to the ground and shoved the sharp blade of his knife against her throat.

JACE'S BREATH POURED from his lungs in one quick rush. Adrenaline rattled his senses, and he fought to ignore the searing pain piercing his arm. The damn she-wolf had bitten him before she'd shifted back into human form. He held his knife steady at her throat, waiting for her to respond. He had to make sure she was subdued. She lay beneath him, unmoving. With him on top of her and the knife at her throat, she wasn't going anywhere. His nerves began to calm. He stared down at her face.

Gorgeous. Absolutely gorgeous. His cock stood at attention, throbbing and hard in a full-on salute. He salivated like a starving man as his eyes scanned over the silky, golden-brown skin of the beauty lying beneath him. What the fuck was wrong with him? A female werewolf had just tried to rip his ass to shreds, and now he was checking her out?

If that didn't take this fiasco to a whole new level of clusterfuck, he didn't know what did.

She was naked, every inch of her flesh bare. His eyes feasted on her body, and man, she was exquisite. As petite as she appeared, her legs stretched for miles, defined with strong yet feminine muscles. Her long ebony-black hair shone in the streetlights, barely covering a pair of high, full breasts, and he knew from his earlier view that she had a fine round ass just begging to be squeezed.

His dick twitched at the thought of those legs wrapped around his waist as he pounded into her, fisting her hair as she yelled his name with those perfectly full lips of hers. And man, did Princess have a set of eyes. But there was a look of pure fight underneath the chocolate-brown surface as she glared at him, the look of a female warrior.

A warrior who'd taken a nice big bite out of his arm with her canines and nearly escaped him twice. With his half-wolf blood, he healed pretty quickly, but given the strength of her teeth in wolf form, that bitch of a wound would take a lot longer than usual to heal.

He inhaled a deep breath. He needed to get hold of himself and clear his head, erase the burn pulsating through him. She was a werewolf, and he knew very well that whether she was an Alpha or an Omega female, she was nothing but trouble and seduction. The first female he'd encountered in all his years of hunting—his attraction to her shouldn't have been a surprise, right? This must be how it had been for his father when he'd met the female werewolf who'd proven so irresistible that he'd left Jace's human mother for her. It was meant to be.

The image of his mother's tearstained face crossed his mind. She was sitting at the kitchen table of their shabby apartment, her head buried in her hands. He heard the boiling pot on the stove hiss as the contents overflowed. Potato soup. One of the only things they could afford after his dad walked out.

His father was weak, and there was no way in hell he would let himself follow suit.

Jace's mind snapped to the present, and his gaze narrowed into a thin glare. "Don't even think of trying to escape again."

Slowly he eased off her, hand on his gun and knife still at the ready. Between the woman, the weapons and the prospect of her shifting into a wolf again, he seriously had his hands full.

"Get up," he said. "Any sudden movement and a bullet is coming straight for you."

She carefully rose to her feet, and the few shadows cast on her naked frame disappeared, revealing an even better view of her beauty. Jace kept the gun aimed as he stepped behind her.

With his knife held to her throat again, he holstered his gun, though his body screamed for him to caress her. He gripped her shoulder and drew her toward him.

Jace swore under his breath. His eyes had been treated to a prime-time view of her sweet behind, and his palm itched to touch her. He swallowed the large lump in his throat and tried to control himself. She was a damn werewolf. What was wrong with him?

He reached to his belt clip and pulled out a pair of silver cuffs. He always carried them, though he'd never needed them until now. "You know the drill. Hands behind your back, before I change my mind and kill you."

"You're lucky I didn't rip your throat out, asshole." She thrust her hands behind her, careful not to lean into his knife at her throat.

Despite her words, his dick jerked again as her smooth, feminine voice hit his ears like the call of a siren.

"This is ridiculous," she growled.

No argument there. *Ridiculous* didn't even begin to cover it. *Fucked up beyond comprehension* was more like it.

He slapped the cuffs on. She groaned in pain as the metal rubbed her skin. Jace's heart panged at the sound of her agony, but his anger and frustration spiked, and self-loathing filled his mind. Aside from the fact that he didn't hurt women, why was he being so merciful?

He shifted his dagger to his left hand. Stepping toward her, he lifted the blade to her throat and grabbed her around the waist, pulling her to him. But as his hand made contact with the skin of her stomach, every instinct in him fired. An electric charge surged up his arms and through his whole body.

Instinctively, he held her closer, and her fine ass pushed against him, nearly sending him over the edge. A low growl drummed in his throat. He tilted the knife farther, leaning her neck into him until he buried his face in her long hair. The smell of gardenias flooded his nose, and he couldn't hold himself back from wanting her.

ROBERT LINGERED IN the shadows of the alley amidst the Dumpsters and the trash left behind by the resident lowlifes. He slipped through the darkness with the subtlety of a skilled predator. When he'd finished carving his latest masterpiece from his worthless slew of whores, he'd stuck around, and not just for his usual grind with his pale-faced pussy.

He stared down the alley. His gaze locked on to Jace and the werewolf bitch. He watched as Jace tightened the silver handcuffs he'd slipped on her wrists. What the hell was Jace's problem? Why hadn't he killed her yet? Robert's blood simmered, and an impatient grin crossed his face as he waited for the moment to come. Would Jace take her like *he* took his whores? There were few things he would love more than to see Jace bloody his hands. The image of the mutt's blood soaking Jace's clothing as he loomed over her mutilated body crept into Robert's mind, and he felt his dick stiffen. She would be so sweet lying cold and still beneath him.

Long moments passed, and Robert waited in anticipation. Still nothing. What sort of game was Jace playing? After several more moments, when the weak bastard didn't even give the bitch so much as a paper cut, a feeling of annoyance passed through

Robert. He frowned as Jace led her from the alley. Jace was weak, pathetic. Nothing but another crying, bleeding heart.

Fine. If Jace refused to serve as his added amusement for the evening, something else would.

Once Robert heard the hunter and the were-bitch retreat, he wandered through the alley until he found what he was looking for: the bitch's scent. For fourteen blocks he followed her smell, finally ending up at a nondescript apartment building. He picked the lock with ease, a trick his father taught him when he was five. He strolled nonchalantly up two flights of stairs until he reached an apartment door that reeked of her too-sweet stench. The smell infected him, seeping into his skin like an airborne poison. After unlatching the door with his pick, he slipped inside and flipped on the lights.

A small one-bedroom apartment: nothing but a four-poster bed, a bathroom, a tiny kitchen and some random pieces of furniture. He walked over to a nearby desk and gazed at several of the pictures. He picked up one of an older middle-aged couple posed together with a young girl in front of them, smiling for the camera. The bitch and her family.

Just fucking heartwarming.

He dropped the picture and watched the glass scatter across the floor. He picked up one of the shards and pressed the flesh of his thumb against the point. A sharp pain pierced his skin, and he savored the feeling as he admired the drop of blood emerging from the wound.

Nothing interesting in this apartment, not even…

He caught sight of a flashing red light. He turned to find an old-style answering machine attached to a landline. He pressed the play button.

"You have one unheard message. First message," said the automated female voice.

The voice was quickly followed by a momentary rustling before a man's voice came through the line. "Frankie? Frankie? It's me. Please, pick up." The voice paused. *"Ay dios.* Our mating ceremony was supposed to start an hour ago and…"

Robert stopped listening as a slow grin spread across his face. Frankie? He let out a low chuckle at his sheer luck.

Rochester's packmaster. Jace really was playing games after all.

CHAPTER THREE

JACE WAS SCREWED, so totally screwed. He slammed the door to his black H3 and moved to the driver's side of the Hummer. Reaching for the handle, he silently cursed himself and wondered what the hell his problem was. Catch and kill. That had always been his philosophy when it came to hunting. Never once had he let one of those monsters live. Until now.

He climbed into the car and closed the door behind him. Glancing in the rearview mirror, he saw her wiggling in the backseat, naked breasts swaying as she fumbled against the cuffs. He shifted his weight, and his erection pressed against his pants. As much as he wanted to succumb to her beauty and the electricity that flowed between them when they touched, he knew better. He'd already thought too much with his lower head tonight.

She was right about the evidence. With no blood on her, no weapons and a different scent, there was no question she hadn't killed that girl. But either way, letting her live was a betrayal of his job and his fellow hunters. And damn it, he sure as hell wasn't about to change his convictions for a sweet lay. Werewolves were his enemies and always had been. He slammed his fist onto the steering wheel. The whole situation was bullshit. She hadn't done anything wrong, so he wasn't sure he could bring himself to kill her, but shit, she was a wolf.

He revved the engine and glanced in the mirror one more time. Her jaw clenched, pure frustration evident on her face as she continued to struggle with the handcuffs. Princess was seriously pissed off. Ripping his eyes from her gorgeous body, he pulled away from the curb and floored the gas pedal. Damn meeting started in fifteen minutes.

He patted his pocket, searching for his cigarettes, and slipped one out. He fumbled with his lighter until he finally lit up, then exhaled the smoke with the cancer stick still in his mouth.

A feminine cough sounded from the backseat. "Just because you want to destroy your lungs, doesn't mean I want to ruin mine."

Jace lifted the cigarette from his lips and blew the smoke into the air. "Rather demanding for a captive, don't you think? Besides, we both know it isn't going to kill you. You werewolves are pretty damn indestructible when it comes to drugs and alcohol." He fought back a near laugh. He knew that all too well, didn't he?

"I'm no one's captive." She glared at him in the rearview mirror.

Jace raised a single eyebrow. "Then what do you call those cuffs there?"

A deep scowl crossed her face, and even with an angry frown, she was still beautiful. "I'll get out of here, and the first thing on my to-do list will be ripping your throat out with my teeth."

"Feisty much?" He blew out more smoke before lifting one side of his mouth into a half grin.

"Kiss my ass."

"Gladly." He smirked. "Though I'd prefer to feel it first, if you don't mind." He checked the mirror; a blush bloomed across her high cheekbones, strong enough to show through her golden brown skin. His heart jumped, revving to life like his car's engine.

His fingers whitened against the steering wheel before he slammed his fist into it again. He needed to focus. *Meeting...meeting...meeting...man, those big brown eyes.*

"Damn it." She was killing him. She'd been around maybe twenty minutes, at the most, and already he regretted every decision he'd made thus far.

Why didn't I shoot her in the head? Boom, problem solved.

"What's *your* problem?" she asked. An electric shock zoomed down his spine at the sound of her voice.

"Captive, remember? That means you're supposed to be quiet."

"I won't shut up until you gag me."

"That can be arranged." He puffed harder on his cigarette, filling the car with smoke.

"Try it," she taunted.

Nothing he felt like trying, he thought. He would likely lose a finger or two in the process.

She coughed again. "Could you roll down a window or something for hell's sake?"

He flicked the ashes out the window. "You've got a really big mouth, don't you?"

"The better to rip your throat out." She smiled, and in the rearview mirror he saw her long canines. He ran his tongue across his teeth—he had a pair of his own.

Sexy.

The word ran through his mind before he could stop it, and he instantly hated himself all the more. He thought of his mother's face: the purple and yellow bruises that marred her porcelain skin and the wrinkles around her eyes as she sobbed. That was the night *he* walked out, leaving her unable to provide for her rapidly growing son, and slamming Jace with a life-long curse. Damn. He wasn't right in the head, fantasizing about sex with one those monsters.

And as if his self-hate wasn't enough, her voice taunted him, poking fun at his agony by driving him wild.

"You know, I—"

He stomped on the Hummer's brakes, and the car jerked. Princess toppled halfway into the front seat, and only his death grip on the steering wheel stopped his forehead from colliding with the dashboard.

"Ow! What the—"

He turned to her, eyes narrowed in anger. Her mouth snapped shut when she met his gaze. As he spoke, his beast's rage overtook him.

"Enough. Let's get something straight. Unless you want a forty-caliber lodged in your skull, I suggest you keep your mouth zipped up nice and tight. Got it?"

She shook her head, the movement almost imperceptible, so it looked like she was trembling. Maybe she was. Shit. She peeled herself off the floorboard and retreated back to her spot without another word. He hit the gas again and sped toward the council's warehouse four blocks away.

The small sniffle he heard behind him ripped at his heart. He tried to ignore it and focus on driving. Another sniffle. He couldn't help himself. He checked the mirror.

Tears were streaming down her cheeks, staining her perfect face. Her legs were hunched up to her breasts, and she was staring at the floor. His heart ached, threatening to explode. She was naked and vulnerable, and he'd just issued her a death threat. A wave of guilt shot through him as he thought of how he'd roughed her up in the alley. He really was a worthless bastard. He'd sworn to himself that he would never be like his father, never hurt a woman, but in the end he was no better than his asshole dad. Did it matter that she was a werewolf? She was still a woman. The angel and devil on his shoulders duked it out. He wasn't quite sure which one was calling him a jackass. Maybe both.

Speeding around a final corner, he spotted the abandoned warehouse where the council held its meetings. He drove to the entrance and parked the H3, glad he had tinted windows. Before he chanced doing something stupid, he twisted the rearview mirror away from him, so her reflection wouldn't tear him apart.

He stepped out of the car and glanced back at her. "This car is alarmed. Open a door, shatter the glass, fuck with the wiring, and the noise will wake the dead. That'll bring me and three other supernatural-hating sons of bitches running." His gaze raked over her nude form. "Unless you want that kind of attention…"

He slammed the door and walked toward the warehouse. Never in his life had he wanted to attend a council meeting so badly.

JACE STRODE INTO the rusted, run-down warehouse as he pulled yet another Marlboro from his trench coat and stuck it between his lips. Looking up from his lighter, he glanced at the three other hunters. Damon was sitting at the far end of the table, his hands folded together on his lap as he shot daggers at Jace with his ice-blue eyes. The usual warm fuzzy welcome.

The massive building was empty save for the single table, several overhead drop lights and the mounds upon mounds of old crates they'd put in to make the place seem more like an actual warehouse. Someone would be hard-pressed to find the switch that opened the door to the hidden room that held the Rochester division's headquarters, unless they moved a hell of a lot of wooden crates. Even if they located the keypad, they would still be faced with the code and the body scanner.

Damon spoke. "You're la—"

"No." Jace held up one finger, cutting Damon off. He took a long pull on his cigarette, exhaled, then glanced down at his watch with a smug grin on his face. "*Now* I'm late."

Damon's face hardened into a frozen mask, but Jace knew the overwhelming anger that lay beneath that cold, impassive stare. Jace felt rage—it was in his blood—but Damon took angst and made it into a lifestyle. Head of the council and the fiercest vampire slayer Jace had ever seen, Damon Brock never smiled, and he sure as hell couldn't take a joke.

"Sit down," Damon ordered.

Jace flopped into one of the hard, metal chairs and propped his dirt-covered boots on the table. David sat at Damon's right side with his large hand covering his black goatee as he snickered.

Jace nodded in his direction. "How's it going, Big Daddy?"

"Not too bad, sugarplum." A smirk crept across David's face, reaching all the way to his black eyes.

Jace had never seen a woman who didn't give David the "look" as soon as she met him, taking in that dark hair shaved close to his head, near-black irises, golden skin and chiseled features, scanning up and down his tall, massively built body, lingering on his massive shoulders and irresistible grin. But the entire time Jace had known him, David had had only two things on his mind: toasting demons and banishing their sorry asses back into hell, and All-sún, a girl he would never have again.

Jace and David exchanged smirks. David may have kept Jace in check and coming to meetings, but he wasn't beyond goofing off a bit to grate on Damon's nerves. Damon always responded as if they were undermining the entire division, making it almost impossible to resist fulfilling his paranoid expectations at least occasionally.

A grim look crossed Damon's face. "What have you two been doing in your spare time?"

Jace fought not to roll his eyes at the predictable question. Damon was always suspecting him and David of conspiring over something. "Getting more action than you, that's for sure," he said. As a matter of fact, he could think of a very naked, gorgeous woman he would like to get some action with at that very moment. He shook his head. Now was *definitely* not the time. "Of course, none of us is getting as much as Shane over there. Ain't that right, kid?" He winked.

"I don't know what you're talking about. And if you mean sexual intercourse, then no." Shane fiddled with the buttons on his dress shirt. Though he was dressed to a nerdy tee, as usual, behind his gold-rimmed glasses and shy attitude there was a fighter in there, and Jace knew that if Shane would just ditch the specs and let loose, his problems with women would be cured.

"Come on, Shane. One of these days you'll need to get familiar with the ladies." David lightly punched Shane's arm.

Damon frowned. "If all of you would stop goofing around, we've got a bunch of mutilated dead girls to talk about."

Like he would ever forget that vicious mess he'd encountered in the alley, Jace thought, and pulled hard on his cigarette. "Mutilated dead girls—way to spoil the mood."

Damon's eyes narrowed into thin slits, his permanent grimace still in place. "Mouths shut and weapons in the bin. You know the drill. McCannon, you first."

Damon grabbed a plastic bin from the floor, placed it on the table and pushed it forward. All weapons went into the bin before anyone was allowed to enter the HQ room. Standard protocol given the scanners they had to pass through in order to enter.

Jace pulled out his gun and unsheathed his dagger. He slapped both on the table and pushed them toward Damon.

Damon shot him a glare. "All of it."

Jace frowned. He reached toward his ankles, feet still on the table, and removed two more daggers. "There."

"David, your turn," Damon said.

David stuck his hand down his shirt and pulled out a large Star of David necklace. He set it on the table before he emptied the contents of his pockets: multiple vials of holy water, a small collection of gold religious relics, several knives and finally a bag of salt. Rochester's premiere demon exorcist, David Aronowitz, was more likely to be found wandering heavily armed through the city's underground scene than wearing a yarmulke and keeping kosher. Unknown to the tiny ninety-five-year-old grandmother he adored, David regularly filleted demons Rambo style for a living.

David leaned his elbows on the table. "That's all I got, D." He shot Shane a glance. "You next, buddy."

Shane pulled his basic nine-millimeter handgun from its holster on the side of his dress pants and carefully placed it on the table. He grinned for a moment, like he was finished, before he put his hand up. "Oh, sorry, I forgot—just one second." Twisting in his chair, he unsnapped the flap of the messenger bag hanging from the back of his chair. With a loud boom, he dropped a massive book on the table.

Jace chuckled, and David belly-laughed right along with him.

David rested his head in his hand as he continued to laugh. "Shane, how many times do we have to tell you that a book is not a weapon? The scanner won't even pick it up."

"I beg to differ. It's actually a very powerful tool. This book contains mounds of information about the rituals of pagan religion. It comes in quite handy when…"

He continued rambling while Jace stubbed out his cigarette. Dr. Shane Gray specialized in all things occult and studied the nastier ends of human society. But while his multiple Ph.D.s proved he had a lot of brains, he'd acquired jack shit in terms of street smarts.

"If you look at this page here, it shows you the diagram of the—"

Jace plucked his flask from his pocket and unscrewed the cap. "Come on already. If the kid thinks the damn book is a weapon, let him check it. He's gotta have something other than a gun. It proves he's got brains. That's one hell of a weapon in my opinion." He took a swig of the whiskey and felt the burn slip down his throat. With the way the evening was going, he would need a lot more alcohol to drown out the nightmares. Damn things had plagued him nearly every night since his dad left, and on the nights when his inner beast surfaced, it was nearly impossible to find any peace. That, combined with his thoughts continuing to wander to the divine woman in the backseat of his car, who happened to be a werewolf… well, best to start drowning the beast now if he had any hope of sleeping tonight.

Damon banged his fist on the table. "Would you all quit chatting like schoolgirls and get a move on?"

Jace dropped his boots off the table. "Why're you in such a hurry?"

"Efficiency," Damon said. He slapped a stake, a crucifix, two daggers and a handgun on the table, before he unsheathed a short but sharp steel-bladed sword from a holster on his spine.

Jace raised a brow. "Overkill much?"

Damon shot Jace a look of annoyance. He quickly placed all the weapons into the bin, taking special care with the sword, the knives and the glass vials. Everyone stood from the table and walked, with Damon leading the way, to the far side of the room, where David moved aside several large wooden crates, revealing a small switch in the wall.

When Damon flipped the switch, a small section of the metal-panel wall slid open. A small keyboard popped out, and Damon punched in the code. There was a swish as a compartment opened, and then

Damon lowered the bin inside. Once the weapons were secured, the hidden entrance on the warehouse wall folded open. Damon stepped inside, then stood stock-still as the laser scanner ran over his body.

"Cleared," an artificial voice said.

Damon moved past the portal, and the other men took turns following him through the scanner. When they finished, all four of them descended the basement staircase into the control room at the heart of their operation. Multicolors flashed across the array of screens connected to the computer database. The Execution Underground bosses never skimped on their tech budget.

Damon's expression was all business as he took his regular seat. "We need to focus our efforts on the case of these mutilated women."

Damon's voice droned on, and Jace fought to pay attention. What if she got loose? He would be screwed. She would tell the local packmaster that he had moved into the area, and then all the damn monsters would be on the lookout for him.

"Jace, get your head out of your ass and focus," Damon barked. "This concerns you more than anyone."

Jace looked up and frowned, but he managed to keep his mouth shut. Someone needed to teach Damon a lesson in manners.

After several long seconds of glaring, Damon turned back to the group. "As I was saying, the deaths started nearly three weeks ago, and that's just here. It could've been going on in other cities around the state or even the country for months, even years. The frequency is escalating, which means we've got to end this, and soon. Not only for the sake of the victims, but to save our own asses, as well. We can't have HQ breathing down our necks and finding out how infested this city is with supernatural scum. Four young women, mutilated and dead, means—"

Jace sighed. "Five."

Damon closed his mouth and the room fell completely still. Jace stood and leaned against the nearest wall.

"Right after David called me about the meeting, I found her in an alley. Same M.O.—ripped to shreds and then raped while she bled out."

Damon's hands clenched into fists. "You've had three weeks. Three weeks to find this son of a bitch, and yet innocent girls are still being murdered on your watch."

The anger Jace directed toward himself and his rage at the killer combined with his current frustration and bubbled beneath his skin. Had the Mateba been clipped at his side, a bullet would already have zoomed straight through Damon's smug face.

David and Shane glanced away from the argument in progress, uncomfortable with the skyrocketing level of anger on display. They busied themselves pretending to multi-task. Shane started scribbling notes on his paperwork, and David fiddled with the items surrounding his computer as if counting paperclips was an extremely important task.

Jace pointed straight at Damon. "You can't pin this on me. You aren't out there every night trying to track this monster down. I'm the only one working this damn assignment."

"Because it's *your* area of expertise," Damon said.

Jace pushed away from the wall and straightened to his full height. "Just because the guy's a werewolf, that doesn't make it solely my problem."

"What if he *isn't* a werewolf?" Shane interjected.

Jace's head whipped in his direction. "What the fuck are you talking about?"

Shane ignored his pissed-off tone and continued. Sometimes the kid had more guts than Jace gave him credit for.

"I mean, have we really considered the possibility that this could be something else? Maybe that's why you've had such difficulty catching him?"

"Shane has a point," David said. "Have we really thought about it? We need to keep our minds open. For all we know, it could be some bastard who likes to pretend he's the new and improved Ted Bundy. He could be human."

Jace slammed his fist against the wall. "I *know* this is a werewolf, all right?"

Shane piped in again. "But how can you be certain if—"

"I've never been so certain in my damn life. The way this shithead rips open his victims isn't possible with human hands or human weapons—or human teeth. So unless he's siccing a pack of rabid dogs on these girls after he rapes them, then there is no damn way this is anything other than a werewolf attack. Everybody got that?"

David moved to stand at Jace's side and slapped a hand on his friend's shoulder. "Why don't you call Trent tonight and see if he'll check it out? Maybe it's some other kind of shifter. He'd know. We can talk to him and Ash when they get back from helping the Brooklyn division catch that ghost shifter. They'll be at the meeting tomorrow morning."

Jace gritted his teeth together and kept his jaw clamped shut. He thought of the female wolf out in his car. What the hell was he going to do with her? He pulled at his sleeve and hoped to hell that the blood from his wound wasn't seeping through his trench coat. At least the wound was starting to knit itself back together. He could feel it.

"While we're at it, why not have Shane take a look, too? Maybe this has to do with the voodoo stuff he likes so much," David said. "I'll go with you, Shane."

Shane smiled from ear to ear. He didn't get to do much out in the field, and Jace could tell he was stoked. "I can examine the scene for any possible evidence of occult ritual activities. But you know, rarely is there actually a—"

Jace let out a low growl. "The cops have probably stumbled across her by now. Though even the beat cops avoid those back alleys, so who knows, maybe you'll get lucky and find her the way I did—legs spread, heart missing and organs thrown around like fucking confetti over the asphalt. So once you've all taken a good long look and made a spectacle of this poor girl's corpse, why don't you give me a holler so I can say I told you so?"

Damon glared at Jace, his high cheekbones casting shadows across his features, hollowing him out like a dead man. "If this *is* a werewolf, you have one week from tomorrow before HQ takes over the investigation and I have to replace you on grounds of incompetence. They're breathing down my neck as it is, and they're not going to sit back and do nothing if civilians keep dying."

"That isn't gonna happen. I'm the best damn werewolf hunter on the East Coast, and you know it, Damon. Don't give me that shit."

"Please, Jace, no reason to use so much humility." Damon wrenched open a drawer and pulled out a large stack of papers. "This meeting is over." He turned away from Jace and glued his gaze to the pages. "All of you fill out your damn paperwork so HQ can have their damn signatures, then scan it into the computers and go home. David, I need the updated report on that Vetis demon possession, and someone call Trent and tell him to get his shit together and give me some notes on the influx of shifters. I want to know why the hell, on a regular basis, we're being overrun with freaks who shift into alley cats. And while you're at it, tell Ash I need a report from him on the haunting in that old psych ward."

Jace fought hard not to put his fist through one of the computer screens. "Why the hell did we have a damn meeting if it's only going to last ten minutes? You could've picked up a phone if all you wanted was to verbally ream my ass."

Damon didn't look up. "Perhaps it would have lasted longer if you hadn't pissed me off."

Without another word, Jace strode out the door, and back up the stairs.

David called after him. "J., I'm—"

The large metal entrance to their haven slammed in its frame, cutting him off. The cold air of the unheated warehouse hit Jace hard. He exhaled and watched his breath swirl in the overhead light, like steam from his anger. His thoughts flashed through the night's events, and he frowned.

Mutilated dead girls, a pissed-off werewolf hunter and a naked vixen. Not a good combination.

DAVID SAT DOWN at his desk and stared at the back of Damon's head after Jace stormed out. Another meeting, another "my dick is bigger than yours" contest between Jace and Damon. They might as well pull their cocks out for everyone to see so they could settle the battle once and for all. Damon's constant harping on Jace's every move was getting old.

David crossed his arms over his chest. "Why do you have to bust his balls like that? You know it only makes him want to challenge you more."

Setting down his pen, Damon looked up from his paperwork. "David, it would serve you best to keep your mouth shut."

David threw up his hands in surrender. Man, was Damon good at overreacting. "Look, I'm just trying to promote some camaraderie here."

Damon turned and glared at him with his piercing, ice-blue eyes, then returned to his reports. "When I want your input, I'll let you know."

David frowned. He swore Damon lived with a permanent stick shoved up his ass. It would explain the pissed-off attitude 24/7. But pissed off or not, there was no way he was about to let Damon dismiss him that easily. "HQ encourages all hunters to form alliances with each other. We're an international net-work, not a bunch of loosely affiliated individuals. Their words, not mine."

Damon threw his pen onto his desk, his jaw clenched tight. He turned to David again. His eyes narrowed with a look of sheer annoyance. "I suggest that unless you want to join Jace on the fast track to losing your job, you shut the hell up while you're ahead."

David gripped the edge of his chair. He was willing to put up with a lot of bullshit, but leader or not, no one talked to him like that, and no one threatened his job.

Standing, he pointed at Damon. "Don't think that just because I'm not as rebellious as Jace that means I'm gonna sit here and take your shit. If that's the game you wanna play, then so be it. But *my* ass is covered. I've never stepped a foot out of line, and you know it. Can you say the same?"

"Are you implying that I don't follow protocol?" Damon asked.

David shook his head. "I'm not implying anything. I'm saying that a hunter who does everything by the book is a good hunter. A hunter who throws the book at others like it's the damn Torah is covering up his own mistakes by pointing out others'."

David walked toward the door and paused, then glanced back. He couldn't let Damon's threats go any further. He'd taken it one step too far this time. "I'm calling your bluff, Damon. You can't and won't fire Jace, because he really *is* the best damn werewolf hunter on the East Coast. We all know he's not exaggerating when he says that. It's pure fact, and if you take him off the case just to prove your own stupid point, you're a fool and those girls' blood is on your hands. And you won't fire *me,* either, because where are you going to find another demon hunter with my kind of experience? When you find someone who has known how to summon demons and sense demonic possession since they were five, you let me know. Then I'll start being afraid of your threats."

David turned to Shane and nodded for him to follow. "Come on. We'll go examine the crime scene again, since our leader here can't trust the judgment of his expert hunters."

Shane's eyes widened. Without a word, he snatched his messenger bag off the back of his chair and hurried after David.

Damon didn't bother to say a word.

FRANKIE THREW ALL her body weight against the H3's window. Her shoulder hit the glass and sent pain surging through her torso. She maneuvered her hands onto the handle one more time and pulled. Nothing.

"Damn it," she said into the silence.

She rested against the seat, the leather sticking to her naked skin despite the cold temperature. She let out a loud huff. Locked up in a hunter's car, and every escape route she'd tried thus far hadn't worked.

To think, this morning she'd been bitching about how quickly her hair and nails grew during her estrus. Normally she loved going to the salon for a mani-pedi, but having to do it every couple of days got old fast. She was eternally ungrateful to her werewolf ancestry for saddling her with the problem. That had been her worst concern during the day. Well, that and the whole Alpha-mating thing. Boy, had that come back to bite her in the ass.

A small pang hit her chest. Alejandro would never forgive her for skipping out on their arranged mating ceremony. It wasn't his fault he'd been chosen to be her mate. He hadn't chosen it any more than she had, but she knew he was a stickler for tradition, and leaving him at the altar had shamed him in front of the pack. She hated to think of such a strong warrior, her closest confidante, being hurt by her betrayal. She and Alejandro had grown up together. She felt she owed him more than that. But how could she take him as a mate, a husband, when she loved him only as a friend?

Pushing the thoughts from her mind, she willed her body to change. In her wolf form, these shackles would slide from her wrists, and she could launch herself at his throat with three-inch canines the moment he opened the door. Unfortunately, that opportunity had passed some time ago, quite literally, with the clock ticking past midnight. Changing now was nearly impossible with her body's yearly estrus period, her mating cycle, kicking into gear. Not that she would have been likely to manage it anyway, not with the silver cuffs on her wrists.

But damn, she had to try something.

Think, Frankie. Think.

Trying every handle and unlock button—no easy

feat while handcuffed—hadn't yielded any luck, either. The hunter hadn't lied—there was no way in hell she could get out of this gas-guzzler unless he allowed it.

She kicked the window out of sheer annoyance. Though it had proved impossible to break earlier, she had to keep trying. Her foot slammed into the glass. The release of tension calmed her, and she side-kicked harder, finally leaving a solid crack, but the window refused to shatter. It had to be bullet-proof.

Tomorrow. She would escape tomorrow. When the mating call had passed and she was back to her full power, she would take the bastard down. She would be in top shape. Already the knife wound and her scrapes had healed, despite the weakness associated with her mating cycle. But until then, she was stuck. Damn.

"Stupid. Handsome. Kidnapping. Psycho," she grumbled, timing a word with each blow. Cracks splintered across the glass, but it still refused to break.

"What the *hell* are you doing to my car?"

She peered into the front seat. The hunter was back, so quiet and stealthy, she hadn't heard him arrive.

He twisted the rearview mirror to watch her. "I thought I told you there was no point in wasting your energy?"

"I had to try. You could've been lying."

The car's engine purred to life. He shifted into Drive, and they sped away from the warehouse. "I am *not* a liar." His words sounded like a growl.

Frankie's eyes widened. Apparently she'd jabbed a soft spot. She fought to keep a smirk off her face as she realized the advantage this could give her. She thanked herself for paying attention in psychology way back in high school, before dance became her focus.

"Well, if you're not a liar, that must mean you're not a bad guy, right?"

"What are you getting at?" he said, his voice as gruff and angry as before.

"I mean to say, if you're not a bad guy, why bother taking me captive? You're not going to kill me or you would've done it already."

"Are you sure?"

The pit of her stomach shimmied like she was teaching one of her salsa classes. She wasn't sure. But she had to take the chance. She wanted him to be good. Needed him to be good. Her life depended on it.

Right now, Mr. Hunky Hunter saw her as an object, a monster, exactly like his job told him to. She needed to humanize herself.

"You know, I'd really like some clothes. I had some stuffed in a backpack near where you caught me. I'm a normal person. I don't usually walk around nude."

"You do when you're with your pack." He pulled out another cigarette and lit it. "If you're even part of a pack."

She coughed, trying to take in as little smoke as possible. He smelled beautiful, but the smoke drowned out his natural scent. The man seriously needed NicoDerm CQ. He blew out more smoke, and she swore she could already feel her lungs shriveling into black prunes.

"Are you? Part of a pack?"

She stayed silent. Would he hate her more if she belonged to a pack or if she were a rogue? Considering the recent DOA rogues, she would bet on the latter.

"A rogue, huh?" He glanced at her in the mirror.

Her heart pounded faster as she stared into the reflection of his luminous green eyes. She cleared her throat. Damn hormones. "I'm in a pack."

Her pack. Even after functioning as packmaster for three years, she still struggled to absorb the idea. But through her blood, she had birthright, and since her mother and father's deaths, she had fulfilled her duty. No brothers, no sisters, no cousins. Just her. She was the only one left, and now the first Alpha female ever to run Rochester.

He turned to the road again, and she leaned into her seat. "Where are we going?"

He didn't answer her. His gaze was focused on the road ahead of him with an intense concentration. A strand of his silky auburn hair slid across his headrest, and her fingers itched to reach out and touch it. Ruggedly handsome, the hunter looked as if he'd strolled out of one of her most intimate fantasies, and the image of her hands running over his strong, muscled shoulders shook her.

The car stopped, and her whole body jerked forward. The hunter hurried from the car. A cold burst of air rushed into the vehicle as he opened the door beside her. He leaned in close and pushed the barrel of his gun into her lower back.

"You know the drill. Don't say a damn word."

She clamped her jaw shut and didn't move.

"Good girl. Now get out of the car."

Slowly she stepped out of the Hummer, praying for someone to see her and call the cops to report her for indecent exposure. Man, would she love to see a cop right now. Her captor grabbed hold of her arms and led her onto the sidewalk toward a nearby brownstone. He marched her right up to the entryway before he paused and entered the door code. As soon as the green button lit up, he pushed her inside and paraded her up the stairs.

They climbed two flights and finally reached a shabby wooden door sporting a pitted brass number six hanging a little too far to the right. He pulled a key—hanging on a chain like a dog tag—from inside his shirt and jammed it into the lock. The tumblers clicked, and he hurried Frankie into the run-down apartment.

Bleak. That was the one word to describe the small space. A flattened, faded, brown couch sat in the middle of the room, facing a T.V. From the dust on the screen, it was rarely, if ever, used. A small gas stove, a refrigerator, and of course, every man's best cooking pal, a microwave, sat against the far wall—no division between the living room and the makeshift kitchen. An open door stood across from her, leading into what appeared to be his bedroom. The faint scent of cigarette smoke hung in the air.

"Nice place you've got here," she said as he herded her farther into the apartment.

He ignored her sarcasm and used his key to lock the door behind them. "It locks from the inside, so don't try to get out." Standing there handcuffed and naked, she watched him wander into his bedroom, peel off his trench coat and throw it onto the bed.

She wiggled her wrists around, fighting against the handcuffs to no avail. She could already feel the silver beginning to burn her skin. What the hell was she supposed to do? Just stand and wait? She glanced up again, and her breath stopped short as the hunter turned and met her gaze. A warm flush crept through her, and a flood of heat emanated from her core. His appeal in the alleyway was nothing compared to the handsome, rugged man who stood before her now.

In the light, his dark auburn hair glistened and the vibrancy in his emerald eyes took on a life of its own. With the trench coat gone, he sported a pair of faded jeans and a black T-shirt that conveniently hugged his muscular body in all the right places. She slouched in on herself, trying to hide her bare breasts. The thought of his hair brushing against her cheek while he laid her down crossed her mind.

She lowered her stare to the floor. "Um…can I have some clothes, or at least something to cover up?"

When she looked at him again, all the air rushed from her lungs. His eyes ran over her body, and she would have sworn his irises flashed a hint of gold, the familiar color of a wolf's eyes. But that couldn't be right. He *hunted* her kind. She shook her head.

Friggin' Stockholm syndrome!

"What's wrong?" he asked, his voice rough.

"Nothing. My mind is just playing tricks on me, that's all." She paused. "The clothes…uh…please?"

He looked at her for another long moment before he walked into his room. He returned with a white dress shirt extended in his hand.

She rattled her handcuffs. "A little help would be nice."

He stalked behind her, his gait smooth and graceful like an animal's. Yanking her closer to him, he worked at the cuffs. She stumbled and bumped into him. Her whole body froze. She clenched her thighs together as a wave of desire rolled through her, leaving her core hot and ready from the feeling of his arousal pressed against her.

JACE FOUGHT TO keep his breath steady and avoid panting like a rabid dog. He wanted to bend her over and take her right there, just like that—enter her hard and deep, reaching places where she'd never been touched. He unhooked the cuffs and held out the shirt. Princess slipped her arms in the sleeves. He stared at her with hunger in his eyes, his hands aching to run up her arms, over her shoulders and down onto her beautiful breasts.

Man, he was one sick pervert. He'd dragged her here in handcuffs, and now he was eying her like she was his own walking pin-up girl.

She finished buttoning the shirt, and he pointed to the bedroom. "Bed. Now."

"Wh-what?" The word sounded as if she were straining for air.

He pointed to the gun still holstered at his hip. "Don't make me repeat myself. Bed. Now." He gave her a small nudge between the shoulders, and she shuffled toward the bedroom. He wiped his hand off like she was contaminated. Every time their skin touched an electric current jolted his body, leaving him with a strong, powerful feeling, like a freshly recharged battery.

Princess froze when she reached the mattress.

He placed his hand on his gun, ready to draw. "What the hell are you standing there for? Get on the bed."

Without warning, she spun around and charged him, knocking into him full force and toppling them both to the ground. Shit, he should've put the cuffs back on her. She threw a punch and hit him square in the jaw. He grabbed her fist and pushed her away. Damn, she packed a punch. She struggled against him, holding her own better than many male werewolves he'd fought, but he shoved her hard. He had his own supernatural advantages. From the startled look in her eyes, she hadn't expected his strength. She scrambled into a crouched position and paused just long enough for him to pull his gun.

He pointed the barrel straight at her head. "What the hell are you thinking? I told you not to try anything," he growled. "Make this easier on both of us and do as I say."

She stood as he simultaneously rose to his feet, gun still pointed straight for her. "Get on the bed. I swear, if you do anything else, I will put one of these bullets right through your skull. Don't make me do anything we'll both regret later."

Her eyes grew wide as she inched toward the mattress, her hands up in surrender. "You're not going to—"

He sighed. "I may be holding you captive, but I'm no rapist. I spend my days hunting and killing werewolves, not sleeping with them. Now, get on the damn bed. Just because I won't take advantage of you doesn't mean you won't be first on my shit list if you don't cooperate."

She climbed onto the bed.

"Wrist," he mumbled. She lifted her arm and he slapped the cuff on, hooking it to the headboard to chain her in place. "Don't try anything stupid while I get the other one."

He wandered into his closet and retrieved his only other set. When he returned, he caught her pulling against the cuffs. "I thought I told you not to try anything stupid."

"I think sitting here and doing nothing would've been more idiotic. You can't expect me not to fight." She stopped fiddling with the cuffs and shot him a glare. "You're so lucky I can't shift."

"Why do you have to be so uncooperative? Usually, following the orders of someone who's threatening to kill you is a good idea, but you still keep challenging me."

"At the moment you're not threatening to kill me, you're just standing there."

His eyes narrowed. "Don't push my buttons. I don't have time for your crap." He walked to the other side of the bed. Grabbing her wrist, he cuffed her free arm to the other side.

She writhed and fought against the restraints in between breaths. "And you think *I* have time for this? I have a *life*. Unlike you, I spend my time doing constructive things rather than hunting down innocent people."

Jace strolled over to his trench coat and dug his flask out of the pocket. "Innocent? I found you at a murder scene. Your innocence is somewhat questionable."

"We both know I didn't do it. I was looking for the killer," she said. "I told you. No blood, no weapons and no male equipment."

He meandered into the "kitchen." "You think I don't know that? If I thought you did it, you'd already be buried six feet under." The Bushmills sat at the front of the cabinet. He grabbed it, poured some in the flask for later and then carried the whole bottle back to the bedroom. "You may not be the killer, but how can I trust that your goal is the same as mine?"

"My goal *is* the same. Why else would I have been in that alley? If you know I didn't do it, why the hell are you holding me?"

"To get to the Rochester packmaster."

Her eyes widened, and she blinked several times. "You've got to be kidding me."

He took a swig from the whiskey bottle. "No, I'm not. That son of a bitch Frankie Amato has got another think coming if he thinks I'm gonna take care of business for him. Every night I've been patrolling, looking for the sick fuck who's hurting these women, and are any of his men out searching? No.

There should be werewolves prowling everywhere, if not to help, then at least to cover his ass. Because if I didn't know any better, I'd say someone in the Rochester pack is doing this."

"Well, maybe if you weren't so biased and hateful, you'd realize that Frankie is trying his best. I volunteered to search for the killer." Her nostrils flared as she exhaled a long breath. Her anger reminded him of an animal in fight mode—powerful and stubborn.

He scoffed. "Oh, so he sends a lone female werewolf to do his work? Where are the rest of you?"

"Maybe he doesn't want to endanger his pack members." Her full lower lip quivered and contradicted all the fire in her eyes.

"Better werewolves than innocent people."

She froze as if he'd stabbed her in the chest. Her cheeks flushed as her shock boiled into rage. "How can you say that? We *are* people."

Jace gulped more whiskey. "Infected people."

"We're not infected. We can't turn anyone into—"

"Maybe not someone who's already been born. You can't infect *them,* but a fetus, you sure can. What about all those freaking babies that you harness with your curse from birth, huh?"

The image of his father haunted his mind as he spoke—his old man's handsome features, which resembled his own, twisted and snarling with anger as he slapped Jace's mother around. But the worst: after all the abuse the bastard had forced his mother to endure, he'd strolled out the door and left them with nothing but scarred memories and broken lives.

Jace lowered his eyes to the floor; he could still smell the summer rain mixed with the city's scent from the night his father left.

"You have no idea what it's like to be one of us. How do you know it's a curse? Some think it's a gift." She tugged against the cuffs, her face filled with raw pain.

"How do I know?" He started to laugh and brushed his fingers through his hair. *"How do I know?"* He set the bottle on the ground and stalked toward her, his gaze fixated on her large, chocolate-brown eyes. She pressed closer to the headboard as he leaned onto the bed and positioned himself over her. A shiver of power shot down his spine, and he allowed the beast to take the reins. "Because it's my curse to bear."

She gasped as his green, human irises transitioned to golden wolf eyes and reflected in her gorgeous stare.

CHAPTER FOUR

DESIRE BILLOWED THROUGH Frankie as she stared into the hunter's wolf eyes. *This can't be happening.* He wasn't human? Shit. The flash of gold she'd seen in his eyes earlier hadn't just been a trick of the light. She hadn't seen *that* coming. A hunter with any supernatural abilities or bloodlines was completely unheard of. How could she have anticipated the familiar pair of wolf eyes staring her in the face? And if the hunter wasn't human, which clearly he wasn't, then he needed to get the hell away from her before her estrus cycle hit full force. Once that happened, like it or not, they would both be more than ready to do the horizontal tango. He didn't even know her real name—and, more importantly, she didn't know *his* name, either—but if he stuck around she would be sleeping with him. She needed to get him out of there—now.

"Get away from me!" She pulled against her restraints.

He leaned in closer, his body hovering centimeters over hers. "What? Does your own infection disgust you?"

Damn it! I thought you were human! What the hell could she do to get him to stay away? This uncontrollable need to mate with the nearest Alpha male was exactly what she'd been trying to avoid earlier in the evening.

Another tsunami of heat and longing overcame her, and she arched her spine, gritting her teeth. No wonder she'd been so attracted to him, because no matter how small his werewolf heritage might be, he wasn't completely human, and all her body needed to detect and prepare itself for an Alpha male was the slightest trace of a bloodline. Neither of them would be able to stop it. "Absolutely not, and it's not an infection, it's a gift. A gift that's going to hit you like an oncoming bus if you don't listen to me."

"What the hell are you talking about?" He pulled away and left her on the bed. Her skin prickled against the rush of cool air as the heat of his presence disappeared from her skin as quickly as it had come.

She sucked in a sharp breath. "It's the full moon, and tonight I would have been forced by my pack to choose a male to begin the mating process with. I already knew who I would be choosing, but only because my parents arranged it before their deaths to ensure that the strongest bloodlines continued. I'm not in love with him, so I ran to avoid the ceremony."

He grabbed hold of the whiskey bottle again and raised a single brow. "And I give a shit, why?"

"Because I'm in my mating cycle. It's my time to

choose a mate, and you may not be a full werewolf, but you're not completely human, either."

How was he not making this connection? She watched his grip tighten around the bottle. Maybe she *was* getting through to him. All she could do was appeal to his sense of reason.

"I was out hunting for the killer because I was trying to escape my mating ceremony. I thought I'd have a couple hours of strength to hunt before my cycle hit full force. When you captured me, I thought you were a human, so you were immune. I thought that tomorrow, when my strength came back, I could easily take you down and escape—and, lucky me, mating ceremony avoided for one more year in the process. But when 3:00 a.m. rolls around, between the full moon, the supernatural hour and the mating call, you're not going to be able to control yourself around me."

"Stop feeding me bullshit."

She tore at her handcuffs to no avail and gritted her teeth. Her anger at his ignorance skyrocketed. Why wouldn't he listen to her? "It's not bullshit. It's fact. I'm a werewolf, asshole. While human, my body is also wolf—"

"Son of bitch!" he interrupted.

She knew he didn't like what he was hearing, but he needed to know, so she ignored him and kept going. "It's a natural estrus cycle. Once a year. It's not like I can control it. I've been taking extended vacations around this time since I was fourteen."

He swore again. "So what? It's just my fucking luck you decided to stick around this year?"

Her eyes hardened. "I told you to let me go. You still can."

He frowned. "Look, I don't care what you think you know about me just because I'm a half-breed, all right? The truth is you don't know a damn thing. I've never once acted like one of you animals my whole damn life and I'm not starting now." He turned away.

She wrenched against her restraints, and the wood of the bed frame groaned beneath her strength. "On the night of the full moon, do you feel its pull, like something living is crawling underneath your skin, threatening to burst out?"

He froze.

"I bet you get the same feeling when you're angry. You constantly fight to control your emotions and hide your identity from the other hunters. When you're hunting and you smell a female werewolf, it turns you on more than a human woman ever could, doesn't it, and you hate yourself all the more for it."

He remained silent, his body language speaking volumes. The muscles in his back flexed, and rage radiated off him like a nuclear bomb.

"And right now I'm making you angry," she said, pushing him to his limits. "Because every mention of your true nature pisses you off. You'd rather loathe yourself your entire life than embrace what you really are. You've probably never even shifted."

Silence answered her, as powerful and forceful as if he'd screamed.

He needs to know this, she reassured herself.

"How can you hunt your own kind?" A pang of sadness hit her in the chest. A part of her felt sorry for him because she was challenging all his preconceived notions about himself.

"I'm not one of you."

Tears welled in her eyes, and she bit her lower lip. This wasn't happening. "You are."

He spun to face her, his face flushed and his hands clenched into fists. "I am nothing like him!" he roared.

Frankie jerked against the headboard as his eyes flashed wolf-gold again. A young, untamed and angered wolf, even a half-breed, was impossible to control, and she didn't even have hands to fight with.

He knocked over a nearby table, which crashed to the floor, one of its legs splintering. "I would never abuse my wife because I couldn't deal with my own nature and the anger that comes with it. I would never walk out on my family because of some fucking mating call, and I would *never* kill an innocent human being."

Walking to the bedside, he stared her square in the face, and Frankie saw the resolve in his gaze.

"I'm nothing like *you*."

He was so close to her that she could feel the heat pulsating from his body. Clenching her thighs together, she tried to ignore her undeniable need. She inhaled a sharp breath, balling up her courage. "You can't hide from the truth forever."

He broke eye contact and stalked into the kitchen, grabbing the whiskey as he went.

"And for future reference…we're not all monsters," she called after him. "I had a family once, and I never would have betrayed them."

He continued walking toward the front door. He pulled out the key, turned it, then opened the door and stood clutching the knob.

"Even if you don't believe me, at least tell me your name." *Since we're going to be together tonight.* Her stomach churned with nerves.

"McCannon. My name's Jace McCannon," he said, before he slammed the door shut behind him.

JACE CHARGED THROUGH the hallway, bounded down the stairs and bolted into the street. The cold winter air slapped him in the face, sending a deep chill through his bones. What the hell was he going to do? What if she was telling the truth?

Shit.

He paced back and forth in front of the building, his massive combat boots thumping against the ground and his heart pounding right along with them. He'd never been so on edge in his life.

He glanced up at the sky. The moon was shining down on him, and a sharp heat prickled beneath his skin. Damn it, how did she know all those things about him?

Because you're one of them, his mind taunted.

He pounded his fist on the hood of the Hummer, leaving a large dent. The car's alarm sounded, piercing his ears with its high-pitched noise.

"Damn." The alarm drowned out his curse. He considered walking back upstairs to get the key, but he couldn't go back up there. Not, for the sake of his own sanity, just yet. He would have to wait for the alarm to shut off on its own. He clutched his hair, feeling the need to rip it from his skull—something, anything, to bring him back to reality.

Reality? He laughed. He hunted werewolves for a living. The real world was harsh. In true reality, evil consumed, and he was longing for ignorance. He stared down the street and saw a young couple entering another apartment building. They shot irritated glances his way as the car continued flashing and screeching. What would it be like to be them? To be clueless about the supernatural scum blending in with society? Jace stood there for several minutes until the alarm finally gave up and shut off.

Just when he thought he might have a moment of peace his phone vibrated in his pocket. He pulled it out without looking at the screen and held it to his ear. "What?"

"Uh…hi, Jace."

"Who the hell is this?"

"It's Shane."

He sighed, and his shoulders slumped. Just great. If there was one thing that always made him feel like even more of an ass, it was being pissy with Shane. It was like kicking a damn puppy.

"Sorry, kid. I'm having a rough night. What can I do you for?"

"David and I are at the crime scene right now."

Jace waited for him to keep going, but only silence came from the other end of the line. "And you're calling to tell me…what?" He glanced down. An ant crept across a crack in the sidewalk. He ground his boot into the pavement and squashed it.

"David wanted me to let you know…"

Jace tapped his foot, his patience already running short. "Spit it out."

"We think there is evidence that's suggestive of demonic or cult activity," Shane said in a cautious voice. The kid exhaled a slow, heavy breath into the phone, as if he anticipated Jace ripping him a new one.

Jace stayed silent, processing what Shane had said. "Kid, you care to tell me why that is, when it's clear that only an animal is capable of creating that much carnage with its teeth?"

He heard Shane inhale deeply, gearing himself

up for a long-ass speech. "The hearts have been re-moved. You see, the heart is a symbolic organ and—"

Jace's grip on the phone tightened until he thought it might break. "Get to the point." He stared at the apartment building. She was up there, lying on his bed. Naked. The thought of Princess's smooth, cara-mel skin made his mouth water, and he saw himself running his tongue along her hot, pink slit.

Man, he was a sick freak.

Shane's voice snapped him from his thoughts like a broken rubber band. "—it's actually used in many demonic and satanic rituals, so the removal suggests motive."

The anger that had already settled inside Jace's chest boiled. "David put you up to this, didn't he?"

"Um…"

"He thought I wouldn't be angry if *you* called, huh? Let me talk to him."

"He said—"

"Put him on the damn phone, Shane."

A rustling noise crackled through the receiver be-fore Jace heard David's deep voice. "Listen, J. I th—"

"No, *you* listen. Did you look at that poor girl's body? Something ripped her to pieces, and you can't tell me a human is responsible." He jabbed his fin-ger in midair, then dropped it, remembering David couldn't see his anger.

"I believe you, J. But some demons can shape-shift into animals, and—"

Jace slapped his palm into his forehead. "Is the kid near you? Can he hear me?"

"If you keep on screaming, yeah."

"Then walk away for a minute." He heard David take a few steps. "I *told* you I got the scent from it. So you wanna tell me how the hell I'm wrong?" he whispered.

"Damon said if there were any signs of demonic or cult activity to let him know. I thought *you'd* want to know, too. We've got to keep our options open."

"Screw Damon." Jace clenched his jaw and battled to hold a string of profanities inside.

"I'm following orders, man. I'm not saying you're wrong. Damon's just trying to get this solved, and getting to piss you off in the meantime is just a bonus for him."

Jace paused. The vein in his temple throbbed. "What are you talking about?"

David sighed. "He's placing everyone else on the case, J. One more strike and he's taking you off as lead hunter."

"No, no, no. Vote to overturn that shit and problem solved." Jace shook his head. This was the last thing he needed.

"I can't."

"What do you mean, you can't?"

"If I challenge Damon, from here on out he'll start giving me the same crap he dishes out to you.

I can't have that. At least one of us has to be in his good graces," David said.

"So you're hanging me out to dry, then?"

"I didn't say—"

"Doesn't need to be said. Message heard loud and clear." Jace jabbed the off button and considered chucking the device into the middle of the street.

Shoving the phone back in his pocket instead, he exhaled a long breath. The chilly February weather transformed his breath into something visible, and he imagined his body steaming with rage like the smoke stack of an old train. Everything was peachy—just fucking peachy.

"DAMN. THAT SON OF a bitch hung up on me." David shoved his phone into the pocket of his leather jacket and frowned. Jace was one hell of a hunter and a good guy, but man, did he have the temper of an angry bull on steroids. And David had just taken a cattle prod to the bull's ass.

Shane stood from where he knelt by the body and cleared his throat. "Jace has had it rough lately."

David shook his head. With Damon harping on Jace's every move and the massive blows his self-esteem had been taking from not being able to catch the damn killer, rough was a massive understatement. "You don't need to preach to me about it. I cut him more slack than anyone."

"I wasn't implying you didn't. I guess I just feel

bad for him." Shane paused and glanced at the ground before he turned to David again. "Do you think Damon's right? Do you think Jace should've caught the guy by now?"

"Damon needs to keep his friggin' mouth shut, that's what I think." David frowned. "Jace is the best werewolf hunter I know, and I've worked with quite a few over the years. If he hasn't gotten this guy yet, there's a reason." He zipped his jacket closed as another gust of cold Canadian wind blew through the city. With weather like this, he needed to put in for a transfer to Honolulu. "It's colder than a witch's tit out here."

Shane shoved his hands in his pockets. "So you think it's not a werewolf, then?"

"No, I trust J's judgment. If he says it's a werewolf, I believe him." He would be an idiot not to, knowing Jace's darkest secret.

Life would be so much easier if they could tell the Execution Underground management the main reason why Jace was so damn good at his job. But hell would be made of flowers and candy before Damon would let a half-breed be a part of his team.

David ran his fingers through his hair. "For the sake of these girls, I can't close my mind to other possibilities." He gestured to the body. A shiver ran down his spine as he looked at her one more time. Rigor had set in, and her already lifeless form had become all the more still. The blood had dried around her in a pool of black, and the remnants of the crimson on her skin crusted over. He shook his head. A normal human wasn't capable of this kind of carnage.

"Do you think there's any significance that all the victims are attractive women? Well…at least as far as we can tell, anyway." Shane's eyes darted around the alley.

David shrugged. "That's a hard call."

Shane met his gaze for a moment before his eyes fell to the ground again. "I think it has some significance."

"How do you figure?" David asked.

"Look at the details." Shane bent next to the body and pointed at the victim's face, her heavily shadowed lids and red-tinted pout. "From the crime-scene photos, all the other victims wore heavy makeup like this." He gestured to the hair hanging over the girl's shoulder. "All of them had their hair done nicely, and from what's left of their clothes, they weren't dressed casually." He stood and stepped back from the body.

"All right, then. What are you thinking?"

"My theory," Shane said, "is that he isn't blitz attacking them on the streets. He's picking them up, like at a club or a bar. That would explain the age range, as well—college girls. A lot of them look around the age of my students at U of R."

David nodded. "I'll be damned, Shane. Where do you come up with this stuff?"

Shane shrugged. "I pay close attention to detail."

David stared into the girl's frozen face. She was so young, and if she didn't look exactly like Allsún—large wide eyes veiled by thick lashes, heart-shaped face, head full of curls, and the look of a small pixie—she was close. But no girl would ever be as beautiful as Allsún, not in his eyes. The thought of her lying there like this poor girl sent his stomach reeling, and a sharp pang hit his chest.

But how would he know if this girl really looked like her? Other than quick glimpses, he hadn't seen Allsún in years. He shook his head, trying to fight off the thoughts. What he wouldn't give to bury his face in her neck, kiss her one more time, hold her and know that she was safe. He closed his eyes and buried the painful memories in the back of his mind, where they belonged. "Only one problem, though," he said.

"What's that?"

"This girl doesn't look like she's twenty-one yet. If she's not drinking age, either your theory is wrong or she was trying to pass as older."

Shane frowned. "I wish I had my phlebotomy kit. I'd love to run a test of her blood-alcohol content."

"Too bad there's no I.D."

Shane bit his lower lip and rested his chin on his fist. Only a few seconds passed before his eyes lit up. "I have an idea," he said.

David grinned. "I'm not surprised."

Shane pulled a handkerchief from his pocket. He unfolded the dark blue material, revealing a pattern made up of the constellations. He bent next to the body and used the handkerchief to lift the girl's hand before he glanced up.

David raised a single brow and nodded toward the handkerchief.

A deep blush ran across Shane's cheeks. "The constellations have a lot of meaning in the occult. Besides, my grandmother gave it to me. I have to use it or she'll get her feelings hurt."

David chuckled. "I can't very well fault a man for caring about his grandma. If mine gave me a pink flowered jacket, you better believe I'd wear it just to please her."

Shane fought back a smile as he rubbed the handkerchief across the girl's hand.

David's eyes widened. "What are you doing? Shane, you can't tamper with the crime scene."

Shane ignored him and continued wiping at the girl's skin. "Trust me." Once he managed to clear most of the blood off, he said, "Look at this, David."

David walked forward and crouched down beside him. The faint outline of a black X was visible on the top of the victim's hand.

Shane stared at him with a sad look in his eyes. "That's what they put on your hand at a club if you're under twenty-one, so then the bartender knows not to serve you. It looks like she tried to wash it off."

He shook his head. "Someone hurting a young girl like this makes my blood boil."

David nodded. "Me too." He stood to his full height and turned away. He didn't know how much longer he could stand looking at this poor girl. In his field, he didn't often deal with dead bodies. Demons used their victims and then usually left them as catatonic shells of what they'd once been. Rarely did they take the time to kill their targets. He wasn't sure which was worse. "You have everything you need for the report?"

Shane sighed. "Yeah, I do. We can go ahead and… Hey, what's this?"

David turned around to find Shane holding the butt of a cigarette. The butt of a Marlboro Red. The two of them exchanged glances.

David let out a low growl. "You've gotta be kidding me."

Shane bit his lower lip. "Should we just throw it out? The cops haven't found it yet, and they won't if we dispose of it, so there's no harm done, right?"

David shook his head and mumbled another string of profanities. "We have to turn it in. I already texted the picture of the crime scene to Damon. If he sees that in the shot, all our asses will be hung out to dry."

The shit just wouldn't stop piling up for Jace, would it? David shook his head. If he thought the phone conversation had been like pissing off an angry bull, he sure as hell didn't want to be around when Damon got hold of Jace.

JACE MARCHED INTO the building and up the stairs. He reached his door and pressed his ear to the aged, splintery wood. Silence.

The huge knot in his stomach unraveled a little as he opened the door. Princess was still sitting on the bed, staring at him with those big brown eyes. The knot tightened again, and his stomach churned.

"Jace?" Her voice was soft and breathless—the sound of a lover's whisper.

A jolt of electricity zipped down his spine, and his cock strained against his jeans. He loved hearing her say his name, and he longed to take her hard, claim her as his. He used every ounce of strength he possessed and forced himself to turn away. He closed the door without locking it, then walked into the "kitchen," so he wouldn't have to see her.

"Who were you talking about when you said you were nothing like 'him'?" she asked.

He grabbed the whiskey again and chugged a few gulps.

"Jace?"

"Why do you care?" he barked, his words sounding more defensive than he'd intended.

"Can you just answer the question?"

He blinked several times, stunned at her boldness

and her lack of fear. "How about you don't push it further? All right?"

When she didn't respond a sense of relief cleared his heightened nerves, but the knot in his chest kept on squeezing.

What was it about this woman that drove him mad, but made him feel like such a dick for wanting her? There couldn't really be something to that whole mating bull she was talking about, could there? He frowned.

She's a werewolf. She's a werewolf. He repeated the mantra and focused on the image of his father, seared into his brain.

Over the years he'd envisioned the face of a werewolf seductress. With the bat of one eyelash, she'd stolen his father and ended his mother's abuse, but left their family shattered. He squeezed his eyes shut and imagined Princess as that woman, that temptress. But the light in her warm eyes ruined everything. He wanted to hate her, but every instinct pushed him into her arms.

"McCannon. Is that Irish or Scottish?" The question wrenched him into the moment.

"What?"

"Your last name, is it Irish or Scottish?" Her voice carried from the other room with ease—loud and forceful, but still feminine.

"Why the hell does it matter?" He opened one of the cabinets and rummaged around, even though it was virtually bare. A can of soup. Some ramen noodles.

"I'd like to know."

He settled on some bread and pulled a few slices of ham from the refrigerator. "Why in the world do you want to play twenty questions with a man who took you captive and now has you chained to a bed?" He slapped together a sandwich and bit into it.

"According to your alarm clock, we have ten minutes until the supernatural hour. It would make me a bit uneasy if I didn't get to know you before we start…well, you know…."

"I don't know what the hell you're trying to sell me, but I ain't buying." He finished the last bite of the sandwich, eating at light speed.

"Suit yourself. Believe me, I'm not seducing you, and if it were my decision, you'd walk out of this apartment or let me go. It would spare us both a lot of unpleasantness. But since you don't believe me, you'll have to see for yourself."

His stomach growled. Ignoring her, he sifted through the cabinets again.

She sighed. "You could humor me a little. If I'm wrong, what will it hurt?"

He paused and gripped the cabinet handle a little too hard. "Irish."

"See. Was that so difficult?"

He gritted his teeth. "Don't push it."

"If you'd like to know, I'm Italian."

"No, I wouldn't like to know." His jaw clenched tighter.

"I, however, want to tell you. As I said, my name is Francesca. I'm Italian, born and raised here in Rochester. I own a dance studio, and when I can, I teach salsa classes myself. My favorite color is red, but I look best in blue, and I hate long walks on the beach."

"A salsa-dancing werewolf?"

"Yes, an award-winning, salsa-dancing werewolf," she said.

He leaned on the counter and rested his head in his hands. He thought of how she would look in one of those skimpy little dance costumes, her hips swinging, the flashy red beading on her round behind shaking, her leg muscles flexing as she moved in her spiked heels. His cock hardened, and his longing escalated. No other woman had ever driven him so crazy.

She's a werewolf. She's a werewolf.

A beautiful smell, like sweet gardenias, wafted into his nose and broke his resolve a little further. He was imagining this. Could the smell of her hair, her skin, literally reach out to him? Good Lord, his dick ached. He slammed his fist onto the countertop. A liquor bottle fell from the top shelf with a crash and shattered. The contents splashed over the counter and onto his shirt. Whiskey trickled onto the floor.

"What was that?" she called. Her voice rang in his ears like a melody, a siren's call. What the hell?

She's wrong. I'm not one of them.

"There is no fucking mating cycle, and it has nothing to do with me," he muttered.

He paced from the kitchen to the living room and back. His shirt clung to his skin, sticky and damp. He lifted it over his head, ready to chuck it into the laundry bin. He turned around and froze.

She was sprawled across his bed, her spine arched and her chest rising with her quick breaths. A small moan escaped her lips as her eyes ran over his frame. Gold flecks blossomed in her irises as the darker side of her took control. A fire ignited under his skin, and he couldn't stand it.

Unbuckling his leather belt, he stalked toward the bed. She spread her legs wide, and there was no mistaking what she wanted. For the first time in his life, he let the beast take hold.

BURNING, WHITE-HOT NEED.

Frankie's core grew warmer, and she felt herself slicken, preparing for an uncontrollable orgasm. The red digits of the clock screamed the inevitable. 3:00 a.m. She was going to have wild sex with a man she barely knew, but she didn't care. She wanted Jace inside her, his hands and lips and tongue exploring her.

Another wave of longing rolled through her as she admired him. A large masculine torso with ample amounts of muscle tapered down to a tight, firm ass. His chest alone was better than any fantasy she'd ever imagined. He prowled across the bed and joined her.

Her instincts reached out to him, and everything froze.

The electric current that shot through her whenever they touched spiked higher, leaving her wet and ready. Their eyes locked, and she admired the beautiful, gold flecks in his. The sound of the bed frame creaking sent her heart racing. His eyes filled with the hunger of a wolf.

He knelt over her, and her gaze traveled to his massive erection.

Good Lord Almighty.

Well-endowed didn't even begin to describe it. He lowered himself over her, his hands on either side of her head. He ground his arousal into her hips, and she gasped.

"You just couldn't keep quiet, could you?" He shoved harder against her. "You were begging me to screw you."

"I—" Her voice was half moan, half whimper.

"And you knew I'd oblige." He balanced himself on one hand and slid the other to her lower back, pulling her closer. He lowered his head to her ear. "You're lucky I didn't take you in the middle of that alley."

Blazing heat radiated from every cell in her being, and she teetered on the edge of climax.

"I could make you come for hours." He positioned his fingers outside her entrance. "Just like this." He stroked between her legs, and her body seized.

She rode a release so intense her stomach muscles burned from the strain. She'd never come so quickly—and whether it was Jace, the mating call, or both, she didn't care. All she wanted was him.

"Look at me." He turned her chin, forcing her to meet his eyes. "I can leave you chained or I can free you, then tie you back up. Whatever I want." His lips grazed hers. "Do you know what that means?"

She inhaled sharply, incapable of forming words.

He let out a low growl. "I asked you a question."

"No," she panted.

He slid his face across her collarbone, his warm breath tickling her skin. "Ask me what it means." He ran his tongue over her skin.

She gulped. "Wha…what does it mean?"

He nipped her earlobe. Her mouth opened, but she couldn't even gasp.

He grabbed her hair in his fist and ran his canine teeth over her neck. "It means you're gonna take everything I give you."

JACE'S HANDS TRAILED from her hair to her smooth thighs. His cock throbbed. He admired her pink slit.

His eyes wouldn't leave her body, and he rubbed two fingers over her most sensitive flesh. Princess was gorgeous. She twitched beneath his touch, and he inhaled the smell of gardenias on her skin, mixed with the scent of her sex. His mouth watered, and he anticipated her taste.

He snaked his hand up her stomach and under her shirt, then slipped it over the delicate bones of her rib cage until he squeezed her tit. He rolled her nipple between his fingers. She gasped, and while she was distracted he sucked her between his lips and ran his tongue around her clit. She moaned and pushed her hips forward. He slid his tongue inside her, and her sweetness ran down his throat.

Damn. He couldn't get enough.

He flicked his tongue with quick, precise movements that sent her breath racing. Covering her tender spot, he suckled her until she cried out. She quivered, slowly rocking her hips forward and spreading her legs even wider. Her taste poured onto his tongue, and he let out a deep-throated moan. Delicious.

He released her, stared up the length of her body as her lips parted from pleasure. He wanted to kiss her soft red lips, feel her warm breath. He slipped a single finger inside her, and her walls pulsed. When he removed his hand, her eyes widened as he savored her sweetness off his finger.

A devious grin spread across his face. She was hot, and so fucking wet. His cock stiffened with a painful urge. He would devour her, eat her alive. But he would draw out the moment. She would be screaming his name before he finished with her.

With his massive hard-on standing at attention, he was ready and very willing to serve her. But he intended to make both of them wait. He was going to take his time.

Crawling on top of her, he unbuttoned the dress shirt with painful slowness. He loved how she looked in his shirt, but he loved her even more when she was naked.

When he'd popped open the last button, he ripped the material from her body. Her chest heaved while she caught her breath, and he feasted his gaze on her large, round breasts.

He smirked, and a light blush blossomed across her skin.

Beautiful.

He lowered his head, brushed his tongue over those hard, pink nubs. She shuddered, yielding and submitting to him. Her hips rose. Yeah, he wanted that, too, but not yet. With a control he didn't think he possessed, he grazed his teeth across her glistening nipples, lightly pulling against her skin. She moaned with pleasure as his fingers encircled her peaks again. He tortured her with slow circular motions, paying equal attention to both her perfect breasts. He kneaded one as his mouth claimed the other.

She trembled with each lick. He damn near lost his mind when she whimpered. The urge to take her hard and deep was overpowering. His dick pulsed with eagerness, and he shoved her up the bed until her shoulders hit the headboard, releasing the tension tugging at her wrists. He wrenched at the handcuffs. The wood of the bedposts creaked, and he squeezed until the metal broke.

Holy shit.

He let go of the broken handcuffs, impressed by his own strength. He glanced at Princess and paused. Shit. She could fight him now and he would be totally off his game. Without a word, she wrapped her arms around him, not even bothering to try to escape. All his stray thoughts disappeared, and he focused on dominating her. If she needed pleasure so badly, he would give it to her. God help them both.

Jace grabbed hold of her thighs and dragged her down the bed. Moving with languid speed, he flipped her over and her body hit the mattress. He gripped the curves of her hips, then slid his hands up her sides.

He lifted her so her back was flush against his chest, gripping her throat with one hand. "Say you want it."

Nothing but a pleasured groan escaped her.

"Tell me you want it."

Her heartbeat was rapid but steady; his own heart matched the same pulsating rhythm.

"I want it," she whispered.

Nuzzling into her neck, he inhaled her luscious scent. He caught sight of her delicious breasts, the pink tips shining where his lips had taken them. He pushed her onto the bed again, reached beneath her and massaged her right breast. He ran his thumb over her nipple, and she gasped. He pulled her ass closer to his hips and bent over her.

"Louder."

Her spine arched, and her muscles tensed in anticipation. "I want it."

"Like you mean it." His fingers dug into her sides, and he slid his cock between her thighs. He ran the length of his shaft over her warm center. She writhed and ground her ass into him.

"Fuck me." She was breathless, panting.

"What was that?" He rubbed across her slit again and chuckled as she moaned.

"Please," she gasped. "Jace, fuck me."

"You better hold on to something, Princess."

She grabbed the sides of the mattress, and he thrust into her in one stroke, filling her to the max. She fit around him perfectly; her core hugged him in all the right spots.

Holy hell.

She was tight. A sexual hunger more intense than he'd ever experienced raced through him. He had to take her. Hard. Fast.

Without warning, he pounded into her. With each loud smack, the heat rose and they both teetered on the edge of ecstasy.

Her muscles tightened around him, and the bed creaked underneath the blows. Her legs shook as she started to climax. He clamped his hands tight on her hips and stopped moving.

"Jace…"

He ran his hand over the curve of her behind, scanning the view of him sheathed inside her. His cock was held tight and bathed in her wetness. "Don't come until I tell you to."

"I can't stop. I—"

He let out a low growl. He wanted to flip her over, pull her against him and nip at her collarbone, but pleasuring her while watching her gorgeous behind, seeing the curve of her back arch in ecstasy, was too sweet. "You *will* stop, and you'll be thanking me later and begging for more."

He slammed into her, and even with his hands holding her sexy hips, she staggered underneath his strength.

"More, Jace."

Running one of his hands down her side, he groped her ass and she slickened.

Damn, fucking her was sweet bliss. Her legs and ass vibrated against his hips. With one large hand, he cradled her in place. His pace and force increased with each move.

"Jace," she panted. "I…I can't…"

"Tell me what you want."

"I…"

He exhaled a long hiss. "Tell me what you want and I'll give it to you."

"Oh…I…make me…" She moaned and shoved her hips into him.

"All right, I'll settle for that."

He pulled out of her and flipped her over on the bed. Wrapping her legs around him, he slipped deep inside her. Heat flowed from her core. His cock throbbed, and he strained as he held himself back from explosion.

"Come for me," he growled.

At his words, her body shook. Waves of ecstasy rolled over them both. His warmth rushed into her, and he bent down and kissed her hard. Her hands ran down his shoulders, and the sugary taste of her lips made him groan. He couldn't get enough. It would never be enough. He wanted all of her, and now that had her, he needed her like he needed air.

"Say my name, Jace." Her words came out as a breathy moan.

When he broke away, her golden eyes filled with a craving for more than just sex.

His heart jumped, and his stomach flipped. "Francesca," he whispered. A large lump crawled into his throat.

Damn it. He was so fucking screwed.

ROBERT SIPPED THE first few drinks of his Bombay Sapphire martini as he scanned the sea of worthless bodies filling the club. The multicolored strobe lights flashed through the room, and the bass beat thumped in his ears as a crowd began to gather.

A blonde whore whose hair color and tan both looked like they'd come straight out of a bottle flipped her long locks around while one of the DJs poured water over her body. The crowd of mostly twentysomething males howled and yelled. The bitch smoothed her hands over her shirt, making sure to plaster the white T-shirt to her surgically enhanced chest and show off her hard, cold nipples. Robert took another sip of his martini.

Cold. Exactly how he liked his women.

Turning back toward the bar, he eyed two females a few seats down. A pretty little brunette and a long-legged redhead. They giggled as they leaned over their drinks. A grin spread across his lips. He'd seen wide, happy eyes like that before. The eyes of young girls. They were new to the club scene. Very fresh meat.

He slipped off his bar stool and snaked his way toward them. Long-legs smiled at the bartender and yelled over the music, "Hey, can I get a masturbating butterfly?"

The girls laughed as the bartender said, "Coming right up," and winked at them.

The server walked away, leaving Robert with ample opportunity. Time for the show. He plastered a charming smile across his face and positioned himself next to the redhead. This would be all too easy.

He propped himself against the bar. "Could I buy you ladies a round of drinks?"

He saw the brunette roll her eyes. "Why don't you just go—"

Both women turned toward him. The look in their eyes transitioned from annoyed to intrigued as soon as they saw his face.

The wonders of being an extremely attractive man.

Their eyes scanned the length of his body, moving from his chestnut hair to his handsome face and ice-blue eyes, then raked over the thick muscles of his abdomen. He couldn't help but grin. Women made it all too easy—wanting him as soon as he made eye contact.

After several moments, he cleared his throat. "So, about those drinks?"

"Oh." Long-legs turned to the brunette. They both giggled incessantly. "Sure," she said. "I've already ordered my drink, though."

The bartender returned at that precise moment. "Here you are, miss." He passed her a drink.

Robert slipped a hundred-dollar bill onto the bar before she had time to protest. "These ladies' drinks are on me."

The bartender nodded and took the bill. He hurried to the cash register.

"Thank you." The redhead batted her eyelashes as she sipped her drink.

He held out his hand. "My name's Robert."

She lightly shook his hand. "Monica."

"And how about you?" Robert glanced at the petite brunette.

The girls broke out into another fit of giggles. "My name's Jill," the brunette said.

Robert faked a smile. "Well, may I get you something, Jill? I'd hate to leave you out."

Jill bit her lower lip, and several stray strands of hair fell into her face. She hooked her arm through Monica's.

Skin like porcelain on both of them. They would both look stunning drenched in red.

Jill glanced at Monica. "I don't usually drink."

Monica nodded. "She hates the taste of alcohol."

Robert drank more of his martini and stepped closer to them. "Well, I just so happen to be an ex-bartender," he said, lying through his teeth. "I bet I could find something you like. Little to no alcohol taste."

Monica gave Jill a small nudge with her elbow.

"Sure," Jill said. She met his eyes.

Hazel brown—they would be gorgeous as the light faded from them. The thought sent a shiver down his spine, and his dick stiffened. "I bet you'd like something sweet and feminine, something with vodka, whose taste can be easily masked." He stepped toward her and took her hand in his. Her eyes widened as he laid a kiss on her skin. He inhaled her scent. Vanilla perfume.

"I know just the thing." He let his warm breath linger before he pulled back and flagged down the bartender. Robert nodded toward Jill. "This pretty woman would like a chocolate martini. Equal parts vanilla vodka and crème de cacao. And if you could add just a dash of Godiva liqueur after you've mixed it, it would be greatly appreciated."

The bartender nodded and stepped away.

"How do you know I'll like that?" Jill asked.

He smiled at her. "You smell sweet, like vanilla. It seemed like a good guess that you'd like the taste, as well."

The girls exchanged excited glances.

Robert set down his empty glass. "How about this? If you don't like the drink, I'll buy you another. Anything you like. But if you do like it, you'll agree to dance with me. Just one song."

Jill nodded. "Deal."

The bartender came back and handed Jill her chocolate martini. She lifted the drink to her soft pink lips and tasted. Her eyes widened, and she glanced from Monica to Robert. "That's delicious."

Monica's jaw dropped, and she touched Robert's arm. "You've done the impossible. I've never been able to find a drink she likes."

Robert smiled and held out his hand to Jill. "You owe me a dance."

Her grin spread from ear to ear. She gave Monica her drink to hold and placed her hand in his, letting him lead her onto the dance floor.

He could tell already that this was going to be a great night.

CHAPTER FIVE

AFTER HER LONG night with Jace, Frankie stared at the ceiling of the apartment and sighed, sinking into the old mattress, which enveloped her like a huge cocoon. She glanced to her right, where Jace lay next to her, sleeping. He was an Alpha, a warrior in every sense. But when he slept his chiseled features softened. She stared at his peaceful face, and her heart melted. The hard stare he normally wore, filled with overwhelming anger and suppressed rage, had disappeared.

She relaxed into the comfort of the bed and thought of the burning fire that had blazed behind his eyes when they'd been intertwined. He was good—damn good. Those large muscular arms, his silky auburn hair, and those toned abs he'd put to such good use... She'd peaked faster and harder than she ever had. His touch had sent ecstasy coursing through her veins, and she'd ridden on a natural high for so long she hadn't been able to think of anything but him.

He stirred, and her whole body tensed. Rolling over on his side, he flopped on the mattress, his deep sleep unbroken. She bit her lower lip. As much as she longed to stay by his side, she knew better. Her loyalty lay with her pack.

I can't leave them.

This could be her last chance to escape.

Placing her feet on the ground, she slid off the bed. The hardwood floor squealed underneath her, and she froze.

Nothing. He didn't even twitch. She snatched his shirt off the floor and pulled it on. The smell of the material wafted into her nose—cigarettes, whiskey, musky cologne and the woodsy scent of his skin. She clutched the shirt to her body without buttoning it.

Tiptoeing to the door, she grabbed the handle and it creaked open. Thank goodness he hadn't locked the door from the inside again after he'd stormed back up last night. A sliver of light from the hallway crept in. She paused and considered turning around. A large lump filled her throat. The way they'd made love had been so intimate, so personal. But now she was leaving, without him even knowing her real name. She swallowed past the pain and hurried out the door before she could change her mind.

The latch clicked, and she rushed down the stairs. Her spine cracked into place, courtesy of Jace's inventive positions. She couldn't even count how many times they'd done the horizontal mambo or a variety of other dances that burned up the sheets. She grinned, but the wave of sadness caught back up with her, washing her smile away. She jogged from the building, the cold night air nipping at her hot skin.

She scanned the area. How would she get home? Streetlights tinted the concrete orange. Cars, trash cans and buildings. No people.

Hot-wire a car or shift?

She eyed the Hummer, then remembered that it had an alarm. Glancing over her surroundings one more time, she stripped off the shirt, knelt to the ground and concentrated on the adrenaline buzz.

The burn erupted inside her, and she winced at the feeling of her bones snapping, her appendages ripping apart. The excruciating pain led to relief when her fur sprouted into place, blocking out the cold air. The usual heightened smells and sounds barreled over her senses. She let out a breath and collected herself, then bolted down the road. The calluses on the pads of her paws scuffed against the pavement.

She ran for blocks, until her muscles strained. The thought of her home, her warm bed, soft sheets and silky nightgown comforted her. She wanted to fall onto her mattress and curl up into a ball, but she had something to do first. She rounded the final corner, then dashed down the alleyway. The backpack sat exactly where she left it, untouched. She had to move quickly in case the cops were nearby, checking out the body. One whiff and she knew she was in the clear, but that could change.

Moving behind the Dumpster, she crouched down

on her hind legs. Her wolf form filled her with adrenaline, and she thrived on the energy. She focused on the calm in the eye of the storm and allowed herself to shift into her human skin. She fell against the wall of a bakery, exhausted.

Exhaling a long breath, she grabbed her clothes, and pulled on the jeans, tank top and jacket. She left her jewelry and lingerie in the backpack. She didn't give a shit about a bra.

Home. Bed.

That was all she wanted. There she could escape the sadness and anxiety balling up in her chest. Why had she slept with Jace?

A one-night stand?

She wasn't that kind of girl. She'd worked hard not to be.

She threw the bag over her shoulder and sprinted down the road toward her apartment. It wasn't far. When she reached the entrance, she jammed the key into the lock and fumbled with the handle.

She scrambled up the stairs, then strode down the hallway to her door.

Finally.

Her muscles weakened, threatening to collapse. She pushed the door open and stopped. Her keys hit the floor.

"No. No. No. This isn't… No." Her eyes locked onto the phrase painted across her wall. Bile rose up in her throat, and her stomach flipped.

A LOUD BATTLE CRY rose above the sounds of clashing swords, drowning out the noises of the surrounding forest. A large man decorated in the skins of a wolf towered over the beautiful woman standing before him. His weapon pushed against hers. Despite his size, she shoved against his blade with the strength to match his.

"Just give up, you Valkyrie whore. You'll never beat me, Freyja."

As she spun with her sword in hand, golden hair swirling around her shoulders, Freyja's sword collided with the man's shield. "The Brighasmann is mine and mine alone, Loki. I'll be more than happy to kill you for it."

A sneer crossed Loki's face, and a deep growl ripped from his throat. "If you so much as wound my flesh, I will destroy your precious warriors one by one."

Freyja let out a scream so loud and shrill the ground beneath them shook. "You won't be able to touch them. They're too powerful to destroy." She gritted her teeth and slashed her sword across his body. The edge of her blade bit into his arm.

He stumbled back, clutching his wound. Blood gushed from the tear. "I am the God of Mischief. I can't destroy them, but I will wreak havoc in their lives until they destroy one another." He grinned, then began to chuckle hysterically. "Look into my eyes and see for yourself."

Freyja met Loki's gaze. Reflected in his eyes, Jace lay in the middle of a pool of blood while the light faded from his emerald pupils.

JACE JOLTED AWAKE. Cold sweat poured over his skin as he snapped upright, and he fought to calm his breathing. Fuck. The dreams had gotten the best of him again. He flopped back down onto the bed with a sigh, eyes closed. He wracked his brain to remember the names of the man and woman. Damn. The image of himself lying dead and bloody invaded his thoughts. It was so vivid. If he could just get back to sleep… Without nightmares.

He rolled onto his side and tried to let sleep reclaim him, but it was no use. He lay there, still groggy, until his bedside alarm blared like a damn foghorn. He cracked one eye open and glared at the clock. 3:00 p.m. He smacked at the buttons until he hit the right one. Why the hell had he set the alarm to go off this early in the afternoon? A nocturnal creature in all senses of the word, he waged an ongoing war against the sun, vowing to ignore its existence.

He sat up and stretched, his muscles tight. What the hell had he done last night? He ran his fingers through his hair and glanced down at his morning wood.

Shit.

He'd fucked a werewolf. His vision spun.

He slid off the bed and stumbled into the kitchen.

Whiskey. He needed whiskey. Yeah, his head would clear after a swig.

Placing his hands on the countertop, he looked up at the top shelf. What the…? A small prickle of pain cut into his hand, and a droplet of blood pooled on his pinkie finger. Broken shards of glass and sticky, dried liquor covered the counter. Shit. The last bottle had broken when he'd…

His cock throbbed. She was so tight, and she'd ridden him like a pro. Those full breasts and those sweet, pink nipples had jumped like mad as he slammed into her. He could run his tongue over her all night long. He cracked a smile.

Hot damn.

Princess was like his personal nympho. He'd had her in every way he wanted. She'd…

Wait…

He wandered into the bedroom again. Nothing but his tangled sheets lay on his bed. He let out a groan.

"Well, I'll be damned." She'd hit it and quit it.

He grabbed his leather coat off the couch and pulled out a Marlboro. Slipping it in his mouth and lighting up, he looked at the bed again. Never once had a woman left him behind before.

The nicotine billowing into his lungs calmed him, and he mulled over the night's events. Her dark brown eyes had shimmered with flecks of liquid gold as she embraced him, and her long, black hair danced around them. A burn erupted in his chest. He rubbed his hand over the area. Heartburn? Yeah, he hadn't eaten much the night before.

After a short shower and a quick shave, he brushed his teeth and yanked on his clothes, then threw on his leather coat. His phone buzzed. A text from David telling him it was time for yet another bitch-fest meeting. Grabbing his keys, he hoofed it out the door and down to the street, where the sunlight hit his eyes, momentarily blinding him. Squinting, he jogged to the Hummer, grimacing at the cracks spanning the back window, evidence of Francesca's fight for her freedom. With a disgusted sigh, he hopped into the driver's seat, revved the ignition and sped off. He cranked up the radio and drowned his thoughts with the sound of classic rock. Anything to block out memories of last night. The last thing he needed to be thinking about was her.

When Jace entered the Execution Underground's downstairs corridor, he wasn't sure whether the headache throbbing in his temple was an unexpected hangover or a preliminary response to the sound of Damon's voice. He stepped into the control room, as prepared as he was ever going to be to hear the usual spiel. David and Trent were sitting at their desks talking to one another in hushed voices, while Ash and Shane stood conversing over coffee. When Jace stepped inside, their heads all turned in his direction and silence blanketed the room.

"What?" He glanced at each of their faces in turn, looking for some explanation.

They all refused to meet his eyes.

Jace gritted his teeth. It was too early in the damn day for this. "David, what's going on?"

His best friend glanced up momentarily before his eyes returned to the floor.

Trent finally cleared his throat. "I hate to say it, J, but you really choked this time." His Jersey accent thickened to the point that he sounded like a cartoon character. His face was nearly hidden beneath his usual baseball cap, which he wore to conceal the severe scar across his left eye, earned in a fight with a crazed shifter "I was going to try and help you on the case, but I'm thinkin' that possibility's been blown outta the water."

Ash Devereaux sat down and leaned back in his seat, brushing his fingers through his silky blond hair. "I have no idea what ya'll been up to. Someone wanna tell me what's been going on?" he said, his good-ol'-boy Louisiana drawl ringing clear and true. He had the pretty-boy face of a male model, but he'd never felt comfortable with the fast-paced life of the big city. Half the time he moved at snail speed, but Jace knew better than to fall for it. In a fight Ash was quick on his feet and deadly in his rage.

"You mind if I take a hit off your flask, Jace?" Ash asked. "Damn ghosts have been killin' me lately, keeping me up all night talking. I need some sleep real bad."

"Knock yourself out." Jace reached in his coat and handed him the liquor.

Ash chugged a few gulps of the whiskey before he passed it back to Jace. "Thanks, man. I still ain't used to so much talkin'. There are a lot of ghosts in New Orleans, but they're all pretty quiet, even the ones that died partyin' during Mardi Gras. But ya'll Northerners speak too loud and too fast, even when you're dead and gone."

Laid-back and relaxed, Ash Devereaux put the dead to rest and ensured they moved on to whatever lay ahead of them in the afterlife. But after years of seeing the dead and hearing their desperate pleas, he attempted to drown out their voices in any way he could. Jace couldn't fault the man for desiring some peace. Hell, he'd been drowning his own demons for years.

"You want to tell me what the hell is going on here?" Jace asked him as he slipped the flask back out of sight.

"I'm not gonna be the one to deliver the news," Ash said.

Jace walked to his desk with a frown on his face. "Somebody better tell me." He glanced down at a stack of papers as tall as it was wide. "And what the hell is this?"

His answer came in the loud clank as the door to

the weapons room opened and Damon's steel-toed footsteps made their way into the room. His hand slid into view on top of the stack of papers.

"This," he said, "is the steaming load of shit you get for being so incompetent."

Rage coursed through Jace's veins as he looked up at his boss. "You mind elaborating?" The ice that filled his voice rivaled Damon's own coldness.

"You have to ask? That's pathetic."

Jace stood and stepped forward, his hands balled into fists. David and Trent grabbed him, fighting to hold him back. His whole body shook from anger.

"What were you thinking?" Damon roared. "You could've blown our entire operation." He reached inside his pocket and flicked a cigarette butt onto Jace's desk. A Marlboro Red.

Damon snarled. "You left that at the crime scene where any cop could've found it, tested the DNA and followed the trail right back to you. You're lucky we were there first."

Jace fought back a string of profanities that would have made a sailor wince. Adrenaline pulsed through him. But screw up or not, no one talked to him that way.

"You need to back off," he said in the calmest voice he could muster. He stared Damon straight in the eye, daring him to continue. But Damon never knew how to stop when he was ahead.

"The only thing that needs to be done around

here," Damon said, stepping toward him, "is you need to get your act together—" he leaned in until he and Jace were nearly nose to nose "—or get the fuck out. You're on probation. You're not on this case anymore, and this is your last warning before I feed you to headquarters. Fuck up and you're done for," he snapped. "Now take your homework and get out of my sight."

Jace didn't need to be told twice. Without a word, he picked up the stack of papers, stormed out of the underground control room, through the warehouse and out to his car. When he reached the Hummer, he stopped and forced himself to breathe.

Shit.

He had royally fucked up. Dropping his cigarette butt at the crime scene because he'd spotted Princess in her wolf form?

Damn rookie mistake.

The image of her beneath him crept into his mind, and he let out another curse. Why wouldn't the thought of her leave him? How many women had he been with who he never even thought twice about the next morning? But something about her lingered with him.

He glanced at the workload in his arms. He wanted to throw the papers into the air, watch them scatter across the street. That would be the final fuckup, but damn, it would feel good. He cursed. As much as he hated having his balls busted, this was the only job he knew, and no matter what Damon said, Jace knew he was a damn good hunter, and he wasn't about to lose his job. He got inside the Hummer, revved the engine and burned rubber.

After driving for several blocks, he parked the car outside a liquor store and stared out the windshield. He wasn't even fifty feet away from where he'd found Francesca last night. "Damn it all to hell."

He got out of the car and immediately detected the trace of her scent. He strode down the nearest alley. His bitch fest with Damon had scraped at his already raw nerves. He'd been punished over a stupid mistake—and damn if he hadn't done the same thing to Princess. He couldn't blame her for running away at the first chance she got. He really was a worthless bastard.

He followed her scent for several blocks and paused. He told himself he just needed to be sure she was safe. That was all. But his heart jumped in his chest at the thought of seeing her again.

Hung up on a werewolf? God, help him.

HE STARED UP at the building and repeated his mantra of curses.

He was a complete idiot. He'd stooped to a new level of stupidity with this one, and he was past the point of no return.

Digging around in his coat, he found the lock pick he always carried and let himself into the building.

He waltzed in like he owned the place, right past a bewildered-looking family. They eyed him up and down, and the mother squeezed her baby just a little closer as they hurried past.

The door slammed behind them as he walked toward the stairs. "Nothin' to worry about, folks," he said under his breath. "Just your friendly, neighborhood werewolf executioner."

He sniffed the air. The smell of her perfume lingered, mixed with something he couldn't quite identify, but the familiar trace tormented him. He followed the scent of gardenias up two flights and to the second apartment on the left.

Was he really going to do this?

He knocked hard. "Francesca?"

He listened for a long moment, but no one answered. He let out a loud sigh and pounded on the wood again. "Hey, Princess, you in there?"

He rocked back and forth on his heels, praying she would answer the door and make it easy on him. With all his senses on edge and his adrenaline pumping, he knew she was in there. But there was that other scent mixed with hers. The rank smell of...

Damn it.

Jace smashed open the door and burst into the room with his Mateba pulled and ready to fire. The door hit the wall in an echoing bang. He charged through the entryway and tightened his finger on the trigger. He would blow the fucker's head off.

A small sniffle came from the middle of the room and Jace's eyes locked onto the woman he already thought of as his. She was sitting on the floor with her legs tucked underneath her, and she was clutching a broken picture frame. The shattered glass cut into her hands, and drops of her blood speckled the hardwood.

Holy hell.

He holstered his gun and stood at her side. "Are you okay?"

She gave a small nod. Clutching the broken frame tighter, she glanced to the wall and back to the mess around her.

The apartment was trashed. Pieces of broken glass, torn fluff and splintered wood from the furniture were scattered everywhere. Jace walked to the wall and saw what she'd been looking at. Dried blood. He'd written the words in blood. *Take it like a bitch.*

Taped underneath was a professional, full-length photograph of Francesca with two people whose faces had been scribbled over with a permanent marker, blacking them out. Pasted over her photographed body were pictures of torn flesh, the killer's way of making sure she knew how she would look after he got hold of her. After her death. Jace ripped down the picture and examined it more closely. He knew whose bodies had been pasted over hers—the women that sick fuck murdered.

He stared at Francesca sitting on the floor, a look that was half defeat, half rage contorting her face. Though she didn't fit the usual profile, he was sure she knew she was the next victim. He'd made a huge mistake in so many different ways by taking her back to his apartment. He had a feeling that was exactly why she'd been targeted. He needed to fix this. He would not let that psycho destroy any more lives. Especially hers.

"Was the room like this when you showed up?" he said.

Her hands trembled as she nodded.

Jace's anger peaked, like a bomb ready to explode. *No one hurts my girl.*

Where the hell had that come from? He shook his head. No, she wasn't his.

"He's not going to hurt you, Princess. Not even over my dead body. I'll rise from the grave just to drag his ass down to hell. You got me?"

Her eyes widened, shining with unshed tears, and all the color washed from her face. But then her mouth drew taut with underlying anger. His arms itched to wrap around her. He wanted to torture the SOB who'd done this.

"My parents…" She opened her mouth to say more, but nothing came out.

His attention captured, he asked, "What about your parents?"

"The photograph." Raising her bloodied right hand, she pointed to the picture he was holding.

His palms clenched into fists, and he swallowed down a feral growl. "Where are they? Did that damn psychopath go after them, too?"

"No, my...my parents were murdered three years ago." She stopped trembling, and some of her color returned to her cheeks. Her eyes glazed over, masking her emotions as she collected herself.

"I'm sorry."

"Don't be. They wouldn't want to be the object of anyone's pity, and don't be sorry for me, either. I don't remember much of that night. The pack shrink says I'm lucky that my mind blocked out the memory." She stood and walked toward him, still clutching the frame. Her gaze returned to the picture. "He ruined my only portrait of us, all three of us, together as a family."

She stared at the photo with such calm resolve, her sadness dissipating and shifting into another emotion he couldn't quite identify. The silence hung thick in the air, suffocating him.

"I don't know what to say. I'm not used to dealing with..." *Living victims.* "Do you... Is there somebody I can call for you?"

She shook her head. "No."

Jace raised a single brow. "You're sure? You don't have anyone?" He regretted the words as soon as they escaped his mouth, and he wracked his brain, try-

ing to think of something to say. Preferably something that didn't make him sound like an insensitive
moron.

"I don't want to put anyone in danger," she said.
"All I want right now is to find this low-life piece of
shit and tear him limb from limb." Her volume escalated until she sounded powerful and firm.

He cringed as her hands tightened on the broken glass, not a single trace of pain on her face. He
reached out and cupped her hands in his. An electric
jolt shot up his arm and down his spine. She jumped
and pulled back.

"Whoa. If you want to rip him apart, then you
better stop cutting up your hands. You're going to
need them." He rubbed his thumbs in gentle circles
on her skin until her hold loosened.

Taking the frame from her, he placed it on the
ground. Shards of glass protruded from her smooth
skin.

"Sit on the bed."

Without another word, she walked to her swanky
four-poster, slow and lifeless like a zombie, before
resting her hands on her lap.

He scratched his head, not really sure of his next
move.

*What would I do if she were another hunter? What
would I do for an ally? First aid?*

"Do you have any peroxide?"

"There's some under the bathroom sink." She gestured to a door on the other side of the one-room apartment.

He rushed into the bathroom and stepped around the mess. The brown peroxide bottle had rolled behind the toilet in the midst of all the vandalism.

Snatching the bottle and some spare toilet paper, he hurried back out. If Princess was anything like him, her werewolf genes would kick in and she would start healing in no time. The glass needed to be pulled out pronto, before the wounds started healing around it.

He knelt in front of her, and she stuck out her hands.

"Ready?" He looked her in the eye.

She gave him a single nod, and he plucked the first piece of glass from her palm. She winced.

"You okay?"

She inhaled sharply. "Just get it over with."

Trying not to be too rough, he picked the shards from her skin one by one and tossed the bloodied pieces onto her bedside table. When her hands were glass free, he screwed the cap off the peroxide. "This may sting a bit."

She gave him a rueful grin. "I know."

Jace poured the liquid over her flesh. The chemical sizzled and popped as soon as it hit the wounds. She hissed in pain, but her gaze didn't falter. She took it like a pro.

"You do this often?" he asked.

A little smile curved her lips. "More than you'd think."

"No offense, Princess, but you don't really seem like the fighting type." He paused as he patted the toilet paper across her skin, cleaning off the blood and excess peroxide. "You've got the attitude, but you just don't look the part. I'll have to see how you handle yourself in a fight."

She cocked her head to the side and eyed him up and down. "You're not going to pull the whole 'I'm a big bad wolf' and 'I don't need any help hunting this monster' crap?"

"Don't get me wrong, I don't need any help. But considering you want revenge and someone needs to be by your side protecting you, I think taking you with me is the best solution."

Her eyes lit up, a beautiful burn behind them like when they'd…made love? Was that what they'd done? His stomach dropped down into his feet, and he looked away. Son of a bitch. "Although, who am I to make your choices for you?"

"Un amante." Her voice barely registered above a whisper.

Jace froze. He didn't speak Italian, but he sure as hell knew what that meant. *A lover.* His mouth went dry, and his stomach churned as if someone had grabbed his insides and twisted his intestines into knots. He released her hand.

Rushing to the other side of the room, he searched

through his trench-coat pockets for his cigarettes. "You mind if I light up in here?" He pulled one out and stuck it in his mouth before she could answer.

"I guess I don't really have a choice, do I?"

Flicking the lighter, he puffed out his sweet smoke. *Shit. Shit. Shit.* He glanced in her direction and his stomach flipped again. *Just a quick bang, that's all it was.*

He burned halfway through the cigarette, sucking the gray fog into his lungs. The smoke gave him just enough calm to keep his cool. A bucket of ice dumped over his head would have been better.

He took another drag. "Pack your bags. We need to get out of here."

Her head snapped toward him, her eyes wide-open and attentive. "We're going hunting *now?* Don't you think that's a little stu—"

"Don't get your panties in a knot. We need to get our shit together first. But we can't talk here. We need to be prepared before we go at him, and because he's a sexual sadist and gets off on all this, it's likely he'll come back here to..." He shrugged.

She walked over to her wooden wardrobe and sifted through the clothes. "To what?"

Jace sighed. "Flog the bishop."

Her long hair whipped through the air as she spun to face him, gaping like a waterless fish. "You can't be serious?"

"Who knows what this bastard is capable of?

You've heard of crimes of passion? There isn't much that's more passionate than sex, and everything this guy does is so he can yank his own chain. Much as I'd like to camp out here and stake him out, we'd be just as likely to trap ourselves. We do this, we do it right."

She bent down to grab something from the bottom drawer, treating Jace to a prime-time view of her tight, round ass squeezed into a pair of low-cut jeans. His cock jerked, bulging against his pants.

Damn.

He ripped his eyes away and shook his head. He was a sick pervert for ogling her in the middle of a crime scene after she'd been traumatized by a serial killer. He scanned the room. The sound of Damon's voice mocking him earlier that morning pounded in his head.

"That's disgusting," she said, interrupting his self-loathing.

He shifted and rearranged himself. The last thing he needed was for Princess to think he was some creep who got his jollies off scared women. "You bet. Now grab your things and let's get outta here."

When she finished stuffing everything into a purple backpack, she threw the bag over her shoulder.

He nodded to the door. "Let's go."

She headed out, but paused near the entryway, stopping by a photo the sicko had knocked askew on the wall during his rampage. She took it down, and he looked at it over her shoulder. The big grin she wore in the photograph highlighted the beauty of her features—he'd never seen her smile like that. The man next to her wore a puffy white shirt, like the ones on the covers of the old romance novels his mom used to read. But whoever the pansy was, he was holding Jace's girl in his arms.

He indicated the photo. "Who's he?"

She stared at the image, and a small smile crept onto her face. "That's Alejandro."

"He your cousin or something?"

A blush blossomed across her cheeks. "No, he's a member of my pack…and my partner."

Jace's jaw clenched, and he ground his teeth as he contemplated punching the wall.

A RUSH OF heat prickled underneath her skin. Frankie ran her thumb over the edge of the snapshot. A member of her pack, a strong Alpha male, her salsa partner and a very good friend, Alejandro Miguel Diaz was everything she *should* have wanted in a man. She'd long ago accepted Alejandro as her fate and convinced herself she would eventually come to love him, to want him. But her decision to hunt the killer, followed by Jace kidnapping her, had saved her from the long-arranged mating, and she'd never felt freer.

Without another word, Jace brushed past her and stormed into the hallway. She straightened the photo and trailed after him. His face looked strained, his mouth drawn into a thin line. She could tell he wanted a fight—and soon.

Her brow furrowed as she watched him stomp down the stairs. What was his problem? She hurried after him, following him to the Hummer while ignoring the searing pain in her hands as she gripped her bag strap.

The drive back to Jace's apartment was long, tense and awkward as hell. Jace stared at the road with extreme tunnel vision, his fingers white on the steering wheel. His tension was suffocating in the small, enclosed space. Frankie didn't know what caused his sudden shift in mood, but from the angered look on his face, she wasn't about to ask. Yes, Alejandro was her dance partner. So what? She'd told Jace that she loved Alejandro only as a friend. Had their mating really made him this ridiculously possessive?

When they finally pulled up in front of the apartment complex, she leaped from the car, eager to escape the toxic atmosphere. Jace followed more slowly, stalking from the vehicle to the door. Short of steam coming out his nose, everything about him reminded her of an angry cartoon bull, ready to charge. He punched in the combination and headed up the stairs. She jogged after him, admiring how swiftly he moved despite his massive frame. She remembered the sculpted muscles hidden under his trench coat shifting beneath her hands as she lay underneath him.

She swallowed the huge lump in her throat. She needed to stop this. Even though Jace was gorgeous, masculine eye candy, even though his ferocity and passion matched her own, and even though he rocked her world in bed, he hunted his own kind.

She did the same thing, in a way, but she only hunted rogue wolves, killing them to preserve the safety of her pack. But Jace… She couldn't help wondering whether he would kill *her* if he knew her true identity.

They reached the door with the crooked number six, and Jace stopped midstride. The door was cracked, but no light came from inside. He unclipped his gun and prepped his aim. Carefully, he nudged the door open farther and glanced inside. He slipped in, and she followed close at his heels. A loud creak echoed from the bedroom, someone stepping on a floorboard. As Jace crept forward, she inched toward the makeshift kitchen. There was no way in hell she was fighting anyone unarmed, not while she was in human form. Any old knife was better than nothing.

The sound of a large boot hitting the hardwood sent a chill down her spine as the invader stepped out of the bedroom. She hit the light switch, unsure of whether Jace's night vision was as keen as hers.

A man as large and intimidating as Jace stood in the bedroom's door frame. He had a wild look in his eye and a gun at his side, and Frankie's heart paused at the sight of him.

"Who is *she?*" The trespasser's gruff, rumbling voice shook her to her core as he pointed in her direction.

What?

Frankie's eyes shot to Jace. "You know this guy?"

Jace lowered his gun and clipped the piece back in place, but he ignored her and answered the man's question instead. "She's none of your business. What the fuck are you doing in my apartment, David?"

"What do you think I'm doing? I'm looking for your sorry ass. Damon's been blowin' up your phone nonstop for the past hour with no answer."

Frankie eyed the man from head to large leather boots. With buzz-cut dark black hair, a coat that could hide a load of heavy artillery and a silver Star of David around his neck, there was only one thing this man could be: a hunter. He had to be another hunter. Her head spun. She remembered Jace mentioning others before, but she'd passed it off as a bluff. Two hunters in her territory, while she was already chasing after a rogue werewolf. She wasn't quite sure how much more she could handle.

"I never got a call." Jace patted his pockets in search of the wayward phone. "Damn it. I must've dropped it."

"Well, losing that phone has got you in some deep shit." The hunter named David gestured to the blood on his clothing. "There's been a double killing."

Jace groaned. "You gotta be shitting me."

David shook his head. "No B.S. involved. The bodies were dumped less than a mile from the warehouse. Damon's gone ape-shit looking for you. I came by here to warn you."

Jace frowned. "I don't need any warning about Damon. He can kiss my ass. And what does he want me for? He took me off the case, remember?"

David lowered his eyes to the floor and cleared his throat. "Your name was carved into their forearms, J."

CHAPTER SIX

FRANKIE STEPPED BACK and placed her hand on the kitchen counter, gripping the edge for support. The anger rolling off Jace triggered all her primal instincts. Goose bumps rose on her arms, and even though he was directing his rage elsewhere, her body urged her to shift into defense mode. His hands shook at his sides, and his jaw clenched.

David cleared his throat. "Damon thinks there's a possibility you may be involved. He put out the word that any hunter who encounters you is supposed to bring you in for questioning. And you don't need any extra attention from HQ or the risk of your bloodline being revealed."

Jace practically growled. His rage made her jittery. She wanted to help him, but she suspected that her help was the last thing he wanted.

David sighed. "Look, man, I'm sorry but—"

The door burst open, and the bang as it hit the wall echoed through the small apartment. She jumped. Screws and wooden splinters from the shattered wood scattered across the floor. The man who stepped through sent chills down her spine. She backed away before she could stop herself. Cold blue eyes seared into Jace's, and she was glad she wasn't on the receiving end of that stare. Her stomach churned.

Two other men stepped in behind the latest intruder, one with golden-blond hair, the second with his face shadowed by a Mets cap—the muscle to back up Mr. Ice Eyes. Frankie eyed Ice up and down. Not that he needed any backup muscle with his massive biceps and natural scare tactics.

"You just can't stay out of trouble, can you? Every time I turn around you've fucked up again, and now I've got no choice but to hand you over to HQ as a suspect. You're a disgrace to the division."

Jace let out a harsh snarl, unable to control his anger. His eyes burned with a golden fire and he flashed his canines.

"Holy motherfucker," Blondie said in a slow, Southern drawl.

The Mets fan's jaw dropped. "Damn it, Jace. You're a fucking shifter?" he said, and she heard traces of a Jersey accent in his voice.

David stepped forward. "Look, Damon, it's not what you think."

"Shut up, David, and move out of my way or you're going down with him as a traitor." The muscles in Ice's throat strained and his fists clenched as he stared Jace down. "I didn't want to believe it, but you haven't left me any choice, you sadistic, woman-beating whoreson. You just signed your own death warrant, you werewolf piece of shit. Those dead girls can all trace back to you, and now I find out you've got the same mutation as the killer you've supposedly been hunting."

Frankie yelled before she could stop herself. "Stop!"

Ice turned toward her. The power pulsating off him was staggering. Her breath caught. She fought not to step back and show her weakness. There was no backing down now. She shoved her fear aside and concentrated on absorbing the anger that hung thick in the crowded apartment air. It would make it easier for her to shift.

She willed herself to stand straight and stare him in the face. She told herself she could take him. "You can't kill him. He didn't murder those women."

"Who the hell is *she?*" Jersey shouted.

Frankie shot him a glare. "You shouldn't be asking *who,* you should be asking *what.*" She bared her canines and the wolf-gold flashed through her eyes, her pupils narrowing to thin slits.

"Just perfect. A piece-of-shit half-breed and his loyal bitch." Ice's jaw clenched so tight she thought his teeth might shatter.

She let out a low, feral growl. "He may be a half-breed, but I'm full-blooded, and you'll be screaming like a girl when I rip out your jugular."

Jace straightened to his full height and pointed a single finger at Ice. "Go on. Give me an excuse to tear you limb from limb." His voice was disturbingly calm, but rage flew off him like darts, with Ice as the bull's-eye.

Ice turned to Jersey. "Take the dog outside while I deal with this."

Frankie swallowed her anxiety in one large gulp. She knew the drill. "Bring it. We'll see who the real bitch is."

"Take care of her, Trent."

"Don't make me do this, Damon," Jace said to Ice. "We're on the same side."

Ice—Damon—ripped a gun from inside his coat. Hooking his finger around the trigger, he aimed straight for Jace's head. "You lied about your identity from the very start. You were never on our side."

Before Damon could fire his first shot, Jace grabbed hold of his wrist. He twisted the other, then swept him to the ground. The gun fell to the floor as the two men battled. Damon kicked Jace in the stomach, knocking him off balance. He stumbled back as Damon crawled toward the gun.

Jace drew his knife and threw the weapon across the room with the accuracy of a well-aimed bullet. The blade pierced Damon's flesh between his collarbone and his shoulder. A wet stain blossomed across his black shirt, and several drops of blood hit the floor as he clutched the wound. Frankie's adrenaline kicked into overdrive.

"I don't beat women," Jace said through clenched teeth. "And no one calls my mother a whore." He threw himself forward at the other hunter.

As Frankie stared, she felt a large, iron-tight hand grab her elbow. She tore her eyes from Jace to find she was staring into Jersey's pissed-off face. A surge of adrenaline pumped through her, and she flung her head back, using the momentum to head-butt him full-force. Pain shot through her skull, but the bruise would disappear within the hour or, if she shifted, even sooner. Jersey stumbled back and bumped into the wall. His cap fell off his head and onto the floor. She crushed it under her tennis shoe. "This is Yankee country, asshole."

"You bitch!"

"Mind your manners."

Deep inside her chest, her inner animal shifted as it fed off the adrenaline. She had to do something fast or Jersey would charge her. She might have him in the brains department, but even with her wolf strength, he was still twice her size and packed a whole lot of muscle. They would be an equal match. She clenched her jaw. She could beat him.

She kicked off her shoes and crouched to the floor. A look of recognition crossed Jersey's face, and he shot forward, determined to stop her from shifting, but he was too late. Speed-shifting was her specialty.

Her clothes ripped to pieces as she went from woman to wolf.

A deep snarl ripped from her throat. They stared at each other, unmoving. He stopped midstride, and Frankie seized the moment. Diving for him, she sank her canines deep into the flesh above his ankle. The nasty iron taste of human blood filled her mouth, but she held on. She jerked her head from side to side in an attempt to snap the bone.

Jersey howled in pain before he kicked her off. His boot collided with the side of her stomach, and she yelped as all the air rushed out of her lungs. He unhooked a silver chain from his belt loop and swung it around.

"You're going to like this new necklace. I picked it out just for you."

Frankie's paws slid against the hardwood. She scrambled away and tried to bolt for the hallway, but Jersey threw himself on top of her. Flipping onto her side, she writhed as he wrapped the silver chain around her neck. As the metal touched her skin, igniting a scalding heat, she slashed out with her paw and slashed her nails across his face. Blood trickled in their wake.

He reared back and clutched at his face, yelling profanities. The silver chain slipped from her neck. She was free. She darted away from the screaming hunter, only to collide with another. Blondie skidded into her as he was thrown across the floor by David, who had clearly appointed himself Jace's ally.

He looked down at her and grinned. "Sorry," he said, as he grabbed Blondie and slammed his fist into the man's nose.

Frankie didn't waste another second. She could hold her own in a fight, but against several well-trained hunters with silver weapons? That was ridiculous, and she wasn't stupid. She bounded into the hallway, ready to escape the whole thing, but a crushing hand grabbed her tail and yanked her back.

Jersey used the spare moment to slip in front of her. He positioned himself in front of the stairs, blocking her only exit. It was either back into the apartment with all the other hunters or time to teach this piece of shit a little lesson about girl power. She decided on the latter. She ran toward him and slid to a halt in front of his knees, a massive wave of adrenaline making her stronger than ever.

Before he could move, she shifted into human form and punched him hard in the kneecap. He doubled over in pain, clutching hold of his leg. She tried to crawl past him, but he grabbed her shoulder, his multiple silver rings searing her skin. She screamed and pulled away. Her skin tore where the metal had burned her, and pain radiated through her.

THE SIGHT OF blood pouring from Damon's shoulder sent a buzz surging through Jace's veins, and he smiled. He didn't give a flying shit that he'd stabbed the leader of an entire Execution Underground division or that he was getting a little too much satisfaction from the pain of his newest enemy. Beating Damon into a pile of quivering flesh would be a sweet, addicting high.

With a low grunt, the bastard dislodged the blade from his shoulder and dropped it onto the floor. "You're going to pay for that, you worthless mutt."

Damon lunged toward Jace, hitting him right in the belly and knocking him clean off his feet. His breath flew out of him as he hit the ground. Jace felt his jaw pop out of place as Damon's fist collided with his face, his uninjured arm swinging like a massive club as blood from his shoulder soaked Jace's clothes.

Jace maneuvered his legs onto Damon's chest and thrust forward, flipping his fellow hunter to the ground. He straddled Damon's stomach and pounded his fist into the dickhead's nose, treating him to the same blows the bastard had just dished out. Anger pumped through him.

Damon bucked in a fruitless attempt to throw Jace off. His blood pooled on the floor, filling in the cracks between the boards. The more Damon fought, the more blood gushed from his stab wound and Jace could feel him weakening with each hit.

Damon was the best fighter in his division, or so he'd thought. Jace never unleashed his full strength in front of the other hunters for fear of revealing his identity, his unfair advantage—until now. Now he wasn't holding back. The combination of his bloodline, natural strength and the serum all the members of the E.U. received made him a force to be reckoned with.

The bastard squirmed beneath Jace's grip until he'd positioned himself just right, then brought his knee up hard in a low blow to the crotch, a move Damon would never normally make, a sign of how close he knew he was to passing out. Jace groaned but kept on pounding Damon's face. Black and purple bruises were already forming across the hunter's cheeks and around one eye.

"That was a cheap shot, you fucking cocksucker." Jace slammed his knuckles into Damon's jaw and felt the crack of bone beneath his hand. He grabbed Damon by the front of his shirt to hold him down. "You hit like a bitch," he growled.

"Like your bitch?" Damon said through a mouthful of blood.

In one quick twist, Jace snatched his blade from the floor and held the sharp metal against the skin of Damon's throat, then leaned into his face, each word sending his warm breath over his enemy's skin. "If you *ever* call her a bitch again, your smile will run from ear to ear." He lifted the blade and traced it across Damon's mouth up to his cheekbone.

Damon didn't even flinch. Instead, he spat a glob of bloody spit into Jace's face. Jace threw down a punch at Damon's temple so hard he swore he felt the bone soften beneath the hit. He delivered the final blow, knocking the asshole out cold. But that wasn't enough. He wanted to kill the bastard. God, how he wanted to end this.

His fist collided with the mauled flesh of Damon's face again, and he couldn't stop swinging.

A large hand clutched hold of Jace's arm and wrenched him back. "Jace, man. Stop! We've gotta get out of here."

Jace's arm kept swinging with the force of a pendulum. But David hooked him under the arms and hauled him off Damon's limp body.

"Get a grip and let's go. If I'm going to be a fugitive because of you, I'm at least gonna be smart about it." He shoved Jace between the shoulder blades. "Move it. We're wasting time."

Hands shaking from the adrenaline rush, Jace placed one foot in front of the other. He stepped past Ash, who lay like a dead man—though on closer inspection he was still breathing—on the floor, presumably courtesy of David.

A high-pitched and angry scream echoed from the hallway, and Jace snapped to attention. *Francesca.* He bolted into the hall. Trent was standing at the edge of the stairs with five bloody claw marks slashed clear across his face as he blocked Francesca's access to the only exit.

She must have shifted, because she was stark

naked, her hair in total disarray. Blood trickled from her collarbone, where her skin was raw. Trent had used silver on her. Jace snarled.

Francesca growled, an animal sound from her human throat. "Move out of my way, asshole."

Throwing herself against Trent, she knocked him down. Despite how small she was in comparison to him, she held his throat between her thighs and beat his face with her fists. He gasped for air as she cut off his breathing. She snarled and drew her hand back. The air bent and quivered with energy as her hand shifted into a wolf's paw while all the rest of her remained human.

At the sight of her claws, Trent managed to throw her off. She flew back into the wall. Her head hit the plaster with a loud thump, and Jace shot forward, but David beat him to the punch with those long-ass legs of his.

David pulled his .40 from his jacket and aimed it straight for Trent's head. "Get out of here."

Trent didn't move. He stared David directly in the eye.

"I said, get the fuck out." David fired a shot right past Trent's ear. Trent stumbled to his feet and down the stairs as he clutched at the side of his head to cover his throbbing eardrum. David gave a satisfied smile and slipped his gun back inside his jacket.

Francesca groaned, and Jace turned to see her getting to her feet. "Thanks for coming to my rescue,

guys. My head? Oh, it's fine. No concussion at all."
She stared at the floor and rubbed her palm across
her forehead.

Jace scowled. "You didn't give me time to ask."

"If I had, would you?"

Jace stayed silent.

"Well, if he isn't going to ask, then I will. Are
you all right?" David placed a hand on her shoulder.

She shied away from his touch. "Yeah, I'm fine.
Who the hell are you?"

"I'm David."

She nodded. "Francesca."

David stuck out his hand. "Nice to mee—"

"Look," Jace interrupted, "usually I'm all for
warm and fuzzy introductions, but can we please
get the hell out of here before those two assholes
wake up, or Trent decides to be a hero and comes
waltzing back in here?"

David zipped up his leather motorcycle jacket,
no doubt preparing to hop on his Harley Superglide.
"We can't go back to my place, so I'm going to split.
I can't take the chance of hanging around you, J. I've
gotta save my own ass and I've already screwed myself over by fighting on your side. If you need anything, call." He clapped Jace on the back before he
jogged down the stairs.

Jace and Francesca stood alone in the silent hall.
He cleared his throat and padded back toward his
apartment. "I need more weapons."

The door stood open and would clearly never close again, and the crooked six had toppled to the floor in the midst of the chaos. He kicked the rusted numeral across the hardwood and stepped over his fellow hunters. He thought about giving Damon another good blow to the face with the heel of his boot, but he could save that revenge for another time.

He pulled out the chain around his neck and chose the key to his weapons closet. The latch clicked when he turned the handle, and the door swung open. He unloaded the rest of his artillery—every standard handheld on the market, short of an Uzi. He'd had one on order, but the delivery had fallen through at the last minute.

Francesca walked into the bedroom behind him, already wearing a set of clothes from the backpack she'd brought. She leaned up against the wall and sighed. "What now?"

He packed the rest of the weapons into a large black duffel bag and locked up the closet. "If there's been a double killing, I need to check this out." He thought of the face of the man in the photo—Alejandro or whatever the hell his name was. "You can do what you want. I won't keep you any longer. I've got bigger prey to kill." He tried to tell himself that if anything happened to her he wouldn't give a shit, but his gut said otherwise. Damn it, she wasn't his responsibility.

She shook her head. "If you're going to try and

kick me out at this point, you're nuts. How can I go to my pack knowing what I do now and tell them I haven't done anything about it?"

"Why take it on by yourself? Leave the work to someone else."

She placed her hands on her hips. "It's *my* responsibility, and I'm going with you. Besides, you need backup."

He didn't need backup and he'd never had any before, but he wasn't going to even bother pointing that out. He walked out of the bedroom, and she followed behind him.

"Where are we going?" She stepped over Damon's bloody body as if he were a nasty stain on the carpet.

Jace waited until they were out of the apartment and on the stairs. The last thing he needed was for a seemingly unconscious Damon or Ash to hear where they were going. "We'll have to get a motel room. Somewhere they wouldn't expect me to go."

"That sounds like the worst pickup line ever."

He smirked. "If I wanted to pick you up, I wouldn't even have to use a line."

"Are you calling me easy?" She titled her head to the side in annoyance.

"Most women I sleep with are easy. But you, no."

She crossed her arms over her chest. "I wouldn't blame you if you thought that. I did sleep with you the first night I met you. And as much as I'd like to use it as one, being in the midst of my mating cycle isn't an excuse."

"Do you need an excuse to justify what we did? We're consenting adults, so why not have a little fun?" He glanced over his shoulder and saw the caramel skin of her cheeks flush.

FRANKIE TRIED TO concentrate on anything other than the throbbing feeling in the back of her skull as they climbed into Jace's H3 in silence. Pain throbbed throughout her body. She needed to shift. Her human wounds would heal faster if she were in wolf form.

They continued driving even once they'd passed the majority of the cheap motels he'd said they would be looking for and reached the nicer part of the city. Frankie leaned back against the headrest, and her eyes flickered closed. A large hand gripped her shoulder and squeezed hard enough to jerk her awake.

"Don't you dare fall asleep! You hit your head. I don't want you going into a damn coma."

Frankie focused past the blur of exhaustion. She had to try several times to make sure what she was seeing was real. Jace had pulled the car into the parking lot of the Imperial Hotel. The brightness of the lights beamed down on her, and she drank in the opulence like a ravenous animal. Beds. This place would have soft, warm beds.

Jace stopped the car and stepped out. She hopped

out, too, and took her backpack off the floorboard. With this much beauty surrounding her, she looked like a peasant in her scruffy clothes, not to mention her wounds and bruises. Jace opened the hatch and grabbed his duffel before he threw his keys to a nearby valet.

He pointed two fingers from his eyes to the young employee. "I don't care if the back window is already cracked—scratch this baby and you're dead."

The valet nodded, as if he often received death threats from random guests. Maybe there were a lot of uptight car owners in this part of the city.

"Don't worry, sir. I'll take good care of it," the valet said.

Jace gave the guy a pointed look, but he must have been satisfied, since he turned and walked toward the entrance. She hurried after him.

With the marble flooring and the crisp clean atmosphere, the hotel was absolutely stunning. Jace strode right up to the front desk clerk and dropped his duffel bag on the ground, then pulled a thick wad of bills from inside his coat pocket. Frankie choked back a laugh at the contrast between his rough and tough appearance and the postmodern décor. The clerk's eyes widened as she eyed Jace up and down. Her attention jumped between Jace and the bills, then she took more time with his face and his clothes. Frankie wasn't sure whether the visual examination was prompted by Jace's rugged appearance or his divinely handsome face.

He slapped the wad of bills on the countertop. "We need a room. Give me the nicest one you've got."

The clerk blinked several times, interrupted in her examination of Jace. "Excuse me?"

He sighed, then leaned forward on the counter and overly articulated each word. "Give me the best room you have."

The woman just stood there.

Frankie stepped up to the counter and nudged him aside. "I think what he's trying to say is, could you please tell us the best room you have available at this time?" She flashed the girl a sweet smile, careful not to show off her sharp, protruding canines.

The clerk shook her head a little to wake herself up before she turned to her computer. The click of her fingernails against the keyboard combated the canned piano music playing in the background.

Finally the woman cleared her throat. "Besides the penthouse, the top room we have available is the Town—"

"We'll take it."

"All right, the Townsend suite—"

"No, the penthouse."

The clerk's mouth fell open just a little, and Frankie whirled around. "What?"

Jace ignored her and shoved the money across the

counter. "You heard me. The penthouse. I want the key in less than two minutes." He glanced up at the clock. "Starting...now."

The woman grabbed the phone and punched in a string of numbers while mumbling under her breath. Jace flung an ID over the counter—probably a fake one—and continued his countdown.

Frankie's jaw dropped. "What the hell was that all about?"

"If you act like you're important, they'll treat you like you're important." He gave her a pointed look.

Shock flew through her, and she battled her jaw to keep it from dropping. "That's not what I'm talking about. I'm referring to the fact that you just booked the penthouse at the Imperial. I mean...Jace, for lack of a better term, you live in a crash pad of an apartment."

"And?"

"And how are you going to afford this?"

He picked up his duffel bag from the floor and tapped the bills on the counter. "You think I stole this, don't you?" he asked, too soft for the clerk to hear.

She lost the battle with her jaw and gaped at him. "What? I didn't say that."

"You didn't need to say it. But for your information, my employer pays all their employees, all around the globe, *very* well. I don't want for anything. How do you think I bought the H3?" His eyes narrowed as he waited for a response.

"But…"

He sighed. "I live in a shit-hole apartment because I choose to. I'd rather deal with shitty and realistic than fancy and fake anyday."

The clerk cleared her throat to get their attention and held out the key.

Jace took it and looked at the clock. "You were nearly late. Don't let it happen again."

He turned on his heel, shot Frankie a grin and strolled toward the elevator. She hurried after him. Catching the closing elevator doors, he held them until she joined him inside. She hated elevators. The air closed around her and slowed her breathing just the slightest bit.

"If you don't like fancy, then why are we here?" She closed her eyes and leaned onto the inside railing. The elevator hummed as it shot up to the top floor.

Jace reached inside his coat and pulled out a flask. He unscrewed the cap and chugged a swig. "If you'd put a bounty on my head or were looking to kill me, would you start here?"

Frankie thought of the other hunters searching every slummy motel in Rochester for a sign of him. "Point taken."

When the elevator finally reached the penthouse level, the bell dinged as the doors opened into a small lobby. The floor was covered with fluffy white carpet, and she had a feeling that lying on it would be as comfortable as lying in her four-poster bed. A white double door faced the elevator, only the slight tan of the lobby walls adding any color.

Jace walked to the door, his dirt-covered boots leaving dark footprints all over the white carpet. She cringed at the sight. After unlocking the door, he stepped inside as if he'd been there a hundred times.

She followed him, and her breath caught at the sight of the penthouse. "This is absolutely gorgeous."

He dropped his bag of weapons on the floor of the master bedroom. "It's a little too gorgeous to be comfortable, in my opinion. Though I guess if you like gaudy, it's all right."

"Why does anything nice make you so uncomfortable?"

"What do you mean?"

She grinned, ready to throw his words back verbatim. "You said you'd 'rather deal with shitty and realistic than fancy and fake anyday.' I want to know why."

Jace raised a single eyebrow.

She put her hands up. "Your words, not mine. I'm just trying to understand them."

He unzipped the duffel and slipped one of his many handhelds underneath the pillows. "Shitty and realistic is what I'm used to, and I'm comfortable with that."

"You're a creature of habit."

"No, I just don't like change." He tucked another handheld in the nightstand drawer.

"Change can be good." She looked at him.

"Change can screw you six ways 'til Sunday."

She dropped the subject and walked over to the bed. Sitting on the edge, she felt like she was invading someone else's room, someone else's space. She peeled her tennis shoes off her feet and wiggled her toes, then arched her spine. Her neck and back could really use a good straightening.

Jace strolled into the master bathroom and flicked on the light. He shrugged out of his coat and laid it across the counter, then leveled his face inches away from the mirror. He examined his eye, running his fingers over the bruises, which had already begun to heal. She watched as he stood up straight again and pulled his shirt over his head, then threw it on top of the coat.

Thick muscles defined his torso, and his back flexed every time he moved. Her stomach filled with evil, torturous butterflies. Every part of her body that he'd touched burned. A trail of heat washed through her, and she forced herself to look away.

She stared at the fluffy white carpet. A low grunt came from the bathroom, and she couldn't help but look up again. Jace was attempting to pour whiskey down his back and over the scratches lining his shoulder blades from his fight with Damon, Mr. Ice-Blue Eyes.

She walked slowly into the bathroom. As soon as Jace saw her reflection in the mirror, he stopped making a mess with the whiskey

"Here." She took the flask from his hand. "Let me help."

"I can do it," he said, though he dropped his hands to his sides and didn't reach for the flask again.

"No, you can't. You're getting it all over the tile." She unfolded one of the bathroom towels and stepped closer to him. "Can you kneel? I'm not tall enough." Even though she was tall for a woman, standing next to him, she realized she barely reached his shoulders.

He got down on his knees, and she bunched the towel in her hand.

"This will sting." Before he could protest, she poured the whiskey onto his wounds. He hissed as she patted the excess liquid off his skin.

She looked at his reflection in the mirror. A large purplish-yellow ring hung under one eye. His cheeks looked swollen from where he'd been punched in the face, and the cut on his lip was scabbed over with dried blood. But he was still ruggedly handsome and, in many ways, even beautiful. Part of her hated him for that.

"You should put ice on that. I'll get some for you."

He shook his head. "Don't bother. You don't need to take care of me."

"Why not? You took care of me earlier." She re-folded the towel and set it on the counter.

"That was different."

"How was it any different?" she asked as she exited the bathroom.

He followed her into the bedroom but didn't answer.

"Sit on the bed." She pointed to the king-size mattress before hurrying into the kitchen to retrieve some ice. She wrapped it in a towel and walked back out to the bedroom.

Jace's shoulders slumped as he sat down. He placed his hands on his knees and hung his head. Frankie sighed. Just looking at his defeated posture drained all her energy.

She went to his side and knelt in front of him. "Close your eye."

He did as he was told, and she pressed the make-shift compress onto his shiner. He groaned, and his grip on his knees tightened.

"From the way you act, I'd swear you'd never been punched before." She smiled.

"Believe me, I've had my fair share of beatings throughout my lifetime."

She shrugged. "Such is the life of a supernatural."

He opened his one good eye and glared. "I'm not one of you."

"You are—at least partially. You might have been able to fool those goons we took down back there, but you couldn't fool me. I know an Alpha wolf when I see one."

"I'm no wolf, and I'm no Alpha."

She rolled her eyes and nodded to the compress. "Hold this in place while I get some more ice for the rest of your face."

He held the compress as she went back to the kitchen. When she returned, she held an unwrapped cold cube against his lip. Despite the cold ice in her hand, her body filled with heat as she thought of his warm mouth running across her thigh. Her finger slipped, and the pad of her thumb rubbed against the smooth skin of his mouth.

She glanced away and pulled her hand back. Her cheeks flushed red. "Sorry. I—"

He grabbed her wrist until she looked him in the eye. "Don't stop."

Even after he released her, she fought to keep her breathing even. Lowering her gaze, she tried to think of something to break the silent tension. Anything.

He's a hunter. He's a hunter.

She steadied her trembling hand as she tried to soothe his wound again.

"So who were those guys?" she asked, glad to have come up with a logical change in subject. "I know they were hunters, but why were they hunting one of their own?" Then again, he hunted his own kind, too, even though he wouldn't admit it.

"The other members of the Rochester division of the Execution Underground."

Frankie raised a brow. "The Execution what?"

"The Execution Underground. It's an international network of supernatural hunters. The men you saw tonight are the rest of the Rochester, New York, division."

She frowned. "You're telling me there are hunters around the globe out to kill my people?"

"Not just werewolves, other supernaturals, too. But for the most part, if they keep a low profile, they go undetected. We usually don't go searching for them unless they're causing problems or they're inherently evil, like demons."

"You're like the freaking supernatural police."

Jace shook his head, putting down the compress. "More like dirty cops. Not every hunter is a good guy."

She drew a deep breath. "Like Mr. Ice."

"Who?"

"The one you stabbed and beat the crap out of. I heard you call him Damon, but his eyes…they look like ice, they're so cold."

"True." He nodded. "Well, 'Mr. Ice' is the head of our division. He thinks he's tough shit because he slays vamps. You've gotta be more than a good shot to take down a bloodsucker, so he thinks he's got all the right moves. He's not dirty. He's just a miserable person, though none of us know why."

Frankie pitched the half-melted ice cube into the trash can near the dresser. "Why does he want to kill you?"

Jace shrugged. "The killings have been going on sporadically for a few weeks now, and since I haven't bagged the guy yet, Damon's got it in his thick skull that I'm somehow not doing my job. Now that he knows I'm a half-breed and with the whole name-carving shit, he thinks I'm involved. Just gives him all the more reason to get rid of me."

"What sort of grudge does he have against you?"

Jace grinned ruefully. "From day one, I've refused to put up with his bull. That's why he's got it in for me."

She sat down near his feet. "And now that he's decided you're a killer, he pretty much hates you."

"You got it, babe."

"So all we need to do is find the real killer and you can clear your name, right?"

He shook his head. "No can do. I'm branded for life with this wolf stuff. I always knew that asshole would come back and haunt me."

"Asshole?" Frankie stared at him with wide eyes.

"My old man."

"He's dead? I'm sorry to hear that—I guess."

"Hell no. I have no clue where he is, and I haven't since I was sixteen. And if he's dead, I'm sure as hell not sorry. Good riddance." He grabbed a gun and some bullets from his duffel bag.

"Oh." A constricting feeling plagued Frankie's chest as she stared into his face. She could see the pain behind his eyes.

He loaded the shells. "He just up and left one day. Hung us out to dry."

She remembered what it had been like when her parents died, how abandoned she'd felt even though it certainly hadn't been their choice. She imagined that knowing his father had chosen to leave made that pain even worse. "You must have been devastated."

"My mom was. I was sad for her sake, but mostly I was glad he was out of our lives." He locked the gun's barrel into place before he laid the fully loaded weapon at his side.

"You didn't get along?"

Jace laughed. "Sure, we got along—when he wasn't beating me up or smacking my mom around."

Frankie's stomach flipped. "That's horrible. I really don't know what to say, Jace. Have you ever talked about it with anyone?"

He reached into his bag and dug around. "I don't need a shrink."

"I didn't say you did. I meant anyone. A friend. That's the sort of thing that you need to get off your chest."

He shot her a glare. "There's nothing on my chest."

She put her hands up in surrender, unwilling to push the subject. "If you say so." She leaned her weight back on her arms and winced. A sharp pain tore through her collarbone.

"Shit. Trent got you with his silver chain, didn't he?"

Her hand trailed up to the top of her shirt. She pulled down the material to show her maimed collarbone. Since the fight, the blood had clotted into flaky bits, but the few places that were still raw burned at the touch of her blouse.

"Let me get something for you."

She held up her hand to stop him. "No, it's okay. You're worse off than me. Just take care of your eye."

"Do you really think I'm going to sit here and baby myself when you have second-degree burns? I may seem like an ass sometimes, but I'm not *that* much of a jerk." He stood and stalked into the bathroom.

"I don't think you seem like an ass. Or a jerk."

He glanced over his shoulder and eyed her for a long moment. "Thanks." He grabbed his flask off the counter and strolled back into the room, bypassing the bed. He sat down on the floor in front of her, their knees almost touching.

Before she could protest, he wrapped his arms around her and scooped her into his lap. All of her senses snapped to attention and her mind went rigid—but her body had other plans. It melted into him, all her muscles relaxed.

A small smile crept over his face, and she suddenly wanted to hide in any available space. Anywhere, as long as his smoldering stare couldn't run over her body and leave her wishing he would undress her with more than his eyes. She glanced down at her hands.

He hooked his index finger under her chin and tilted her head up. "Hey, what's wrong?"

She swallowed hard. For such a simple question, it felt oddly intimate rolling off his tongue.

"Nothing." She forced herself to be realistic. This was going nowhere. He hated her kind.

"I know from dealing with my mother that 'nothing' always means 'something.' When my dad would come home drunk and rough her up, every time I'd ask her how she was, she'd always say nothing was wrong."

Crossing her arms over her chest, she folded into herself. "I guess I don't want to talk about it."

"That's a better answer, though I wish you would."

"I wish *you'd* talk, too—and don't say that's different. It's not."

A moment of silence passed between them, a suffocating lull.

Frankie sighed. "I'm thinking about what my actions will result in when I return to my pack."

"I'm sure they'll be glad that you're back. By now they're bound to have realized you're missing, and can they really punish you for being taken captive?"

She shook her head. "It's not that simple."

He stared at her, waiting for elaboration.

She let out another long sigh. "I'm in a position of power, an especially high position for a female."

He looked at her expectantly. "What's wrong with that?"

"There's nothing wrong with it. I'm ready to accept my obligations and fulfill my duties to my pack. But it's hard for me to live my life when I'm confined by such strict rules."

"I try not to play by others' rules," he said.

She rolled her eyes. "And we've seen what sort of trouble it gets you in. If I step out of line, I can be severely punished, and because I'm a powerful female, there are loads of males who wouldn't hesitate to kill or defeat me in order to usurp my position. I live with the constant knowledge that someday my pinkie toe may barely cross over some line and I'll end up as someone's bitch. I don't want to be a domesticated girl."

"Sounds like a shitty position to be in."

She thought of all her duties. "In some ways, yes. In others, no. It depends. I know I should do what I want and not allow anyone to dictate to me, but it's hard, in my position. I wish I could be like you."

"Why the hell would you want to be like me?"

"You don't let anyone intimidate you. I don't scare easily, but I'm not immune to fear like you are."

He let out a short huff. "I wasn't always this way."

"Maybe, but you are now."

Jace's jaw clenched as if he were fighting not to grind his teeth. "I swear to myself every day that I'll never give in. I refuse to be like my bastard of a father. But each morning I look in the mirror and I see him staring back at me, and there are so many things that take me back to that place. I let him haunt me, and I can't help it. I still choke at the smell of cigars." He twisted so she could see his forearm. A series of perfectly circular scars marred the inside of his arm. Bile burned at the back of Frankie's throat at the thought of someone hurting a child. "Don't be like me. You can't allow them to get the best of you. Don't let yourself be abused."

"Jace, you can't blame yourself for what happened to you, and you can't be angry over frightening memories. All the pain you felt was real. It would've been too much for anyone to handle, and you were just a kid. That sort of pain leaves scars that go way deeper than the surface. And you don't need to spend so much of your energy fighting not to be like him. You may have a lot of anger, but it's easy to see that you're a good person." She placed a hand on his arm.

He stared blankly at the wall. It took a moment before he responded. "And what does that say about me? I have to fight every day not to be some crazy, abusive drunk, not to treat people like shit and kill the innocent. And half the time I'm barely succeeding. Lord knows I drown myself in liquor, even if my damn supernatural metabolism burns up the alcohol so quickly that I'm rarely drunk. What does that say about my character?"

"That you're a good man. Because, despite any temptation, you keep trying to do the right thing."

He held up the flask. "This is going to hurt a little." He tipped the container over and allowed the whiskey to pour across her burns. The wounds screamed with pain as the alcohol sanitized them.

His hand fell back to his side. "I've never told anyone that before."

She smiled through the pain. "I'm glad you told *me*."

"Do you want me to put a bandage on this?" he said.

"No, if I can shift it will heal quickly. I'll wait until you're asleep. I know you don't like—"

"No, don't bother. I may hunt criminal shifters, but...well, I wouldn't hunt *you*."

Her heart jumped, and she mentally scolded herself as she asked, "What makes me different from any other werewolf?"

"You're useful. I need inside information. If the killer really is a rogue, I'll need to cooperate with your pack, at least temporarily."

"Oh."

She glanced down at her hands and gritted her teeth. Damn, she was an idiot. What sort of answer had she expected?

"I'm going to shift. I'll be right back." She rushed into the bathroom and shut the door behind her, a little harder than she intended.

Pushing her spine against the wood, she slid down to the ceramic tiling. What was wrong with her? What the hell would give her the idea that Jace might actually be interested in her once the power of their hormones was taken out of the equation? And why was she interested in him? She was a werewolf—his worst enemy. The only thing he would remember about their time together was the fact that he'd fucked a wolf. He'd kidnapped her, had her in his control, and that was all that mattered. She was nothing but a piece of leverage that allowed him to say "Take this, fur-faces. I banged one of your bitches." Destined mate, her ass.

Burying her face in her hands, she thought about making a run for it. If she bolted now and caught Jace off guard, she could make it to the stairs. Her body shook from the adrenaline buzzing through her veins. No. She couldn't run. She needed his help to find the rogue.

She let out a long sigh. Damn. Why had she told him about the precariousness of her position? She'd never told anyone that, not even Alejandro. She'd blown her chances on that score, too. She'd never wanted to marry Alejandro, but running away hadn't solved anything. And as a result, here she was, sitting in the bathroom of an overly done-up penthouse pining for a werewolf hunter who couldn't care less.

Useful.

The word echoed in her ears. That was all she was to him. Useful. That was what she got for having sex on an animalistic whim, then letting her dumb-ass brain try to rationalize her actions with delusions of romance and destined mates. Use*less* was more accurate. He undoubtedly only wanted her in order to get to the packmaster. She scoffed. Little did he know…

She pulled her cell phone out of the pocket of her jeans. Flipping it open, she stared at the screen. Alejandro's name flashed next to a missed call message. She pressed a few buttons and the blank slate for a text message popped up. She started typing.

Alejandro, I'm okay. No need 2 worry. Will explain everything l8r. Sorry I missed our

She stopped typing in the middle of her sentence, staring at the words until she finally hit the delete button. The sound of plastic cracking snapped her mind back in place, and she realized she'd thrown the phone at the bathroom wall.

"Damn it."

She crawled toward the broken pieces. It was fixable, but she would need a whole lot of glue and possibly duct tape. But that wasn't the real issue. What mattered was whether she was really going to run from this. From him. She stripped off her clothes and laid them next to the bathtub. The feeling of the cold tile against her naked flesh sent shivers up her spine. Crouching on her knees, she clenched her teeth. She wanted to scream, but the only real release was to shift.

CHAPTER SEVEN

Jace sat on the edge of the bed with his head buried in his hands. What the hell had he gotten himself into? She was a werewolf *and* a captive. How much lower could he stoop? He ran his fingers through his hair and tightened them around his skull. No matter how hard he squeezed, he couldn't hold himself together.

A small crash resonated from the bathroom, like the sound of cracking plastic. Damn. He walked to the door and leaned his ear against the wood. No sound. He knocked and waited for a response. Nothing.

Worried, he knocked harder. "Francesca?"

Muffled by the closed door, nails scratched over the wood in an eerie response.

"All right, I'm coming in." Jace opened the door and immediately stumbled back.

Francesca's clothes lay scattered across the floor, her lacy panties hooked on the rear paw of a large ebony wolf. The eyes staring at him were all too familiar, like molten liquid gold. The wolf cocked its head to the side, and its ears perked up.

No, *Francesca* cocked *her* head to the side. He fought the urge to swear under his breath. She was a werewolf. The wolf *was* Francesca.

"Am I still supposed to call you Francesca when you're…you know?" He rubbed his fingers over his temples and stared at the ceiling. "I can't believe I'm talking to an animal."

The wolf grumbled in response.

He let out a long sigh and pushed his fingers through his hair again. "So am I supposed to call you Francesca? Bark once for no, twice for yes."

The wolf barked twice.

"All right, then, Francesca it is."

She huffed and trotted over to the side of the bed. She leapt onto the mattress with grace, stretched luxuriantly and then curled into a ball. Jace glanced toward the door. If she was planning to sleep, he supposed he could go check out one of the other bedrooms.

Francesca followed his gaze. She rested her head on her paws and whimpered.

"It's okay. I'll use one of the other beds."

She made a noise between a growl and a whimper.

He realized that she didn't want him to go. "I can just take the floor in here, then," he offered.

She whined again.

"Come on. I bet you'd be more comfortable without me anyway." He took a pillow from the bed and dropped it onto the floor. It hit the carpet with an audible poof, and he realized it was probably softer than anything he'd ever slept on in his whole life.

He sat down next to it and leaned back against the wall. Reaching across the floor, he took the flask, then unscrewed the cap and lifted it to his lips, ready to chug down however much whiskey was left. When nothing came out, he threw it on the carpet next to him. Damn. He would need to restock if he was going to make it through bringing a rogue werewolf to justice with a Francesca there to distract him every step of the way.

He glanced up from the stark white carpeting. Golden wolf eyes stared back at him, monitoring his every move.

"Do you distrust me so much that you need to watch me, or am I just that pretty to look at?"

The wolf pawed at its muzzle and buried its head in the comforter. The thought that Francesca was in that wolf—that she *was* that wolf—made the gesture all the more human. He had a feeling she would have been blushing if she could have.

"So, if we're going to stay organized and keep one step ahead of this sicko, we'll need a plan." He glanced at his watch. "The sun should be coming up soon, so we'll get some shut-eye, make our plan when we wake up, and then, when evening rolls around, we'll head out to where the double killings were." He looked her way to make sure she was listening. She watched him with attentive eyes. "We'll have to touch base with David first, to find out where it all went down. The bodies will be long gone, but once we examine what's left of the crime scene, we can take it from there. Hopefully we can still catch a trace of his scent. As long as we can find the bastard, we can take him out. Locating him will be the big problem."

He eyed her again. "Bark once for okay, twice for 'I have a better plan.' I'm sure you have something to say, as usual."

The wolf snarled and barked once.

"Agreement. That's what I like to hear. I'll set the alarm to be sure we don't sleep too late."

He pushed himself off the ground, walked over to the bedside clock and punched several buttons before he figured out how to program the alarm. The sheets rustled as Francesca shifted onto her side.

"How are those wounds looking?"

He sat beside her on the bed. He hesitated before he pushed aside the fur on the wolf's collarbone. The wound was visibly healing before his eyes.

"Looks good. You should be better by tonight."

The wolf laid her head on her paws and closed her eyes. Her fur was a rich, ebony black, as dark as night itself, the same gorgeous color as her long, shining hair—both beautiful and a deadly camouflage to hide her from her enemies. And man, those eyes—wild, untamed and majestic. They held an entrancing quality, one he had never encountered in a normal human being, the eyes of a free animal.

That asshole packmaster of hers was too much of a coward to send out his troops, so she was out there on her own. What type of leader sent a female as his muscle to track a rampaging rogue? Her packmaster deserved to suffer just as the killer's innocent victims had.

Jace pulled his gaze away and flicked off the bedroom light. Like her, he could see perfectly in the dark, thanks to his inner wolf's nocturnal vision, and the weight of her gaze as she watched him hung heavy on his shoulders. He moved back to the pillow. He took a deep breath, and the words slipped out before he could control himself. "For the record, you're a beautiful wolf."

Without looking back at her, he lay down on the floor and rested his head on his pillow. He thanked God she couldn't respond.

THE SCREECHING SOUND of the alarm rang in his ears, and something wet licked at his hand. *Werewolf.* His eyes shot open, and he scrambled to his feet. Adrenaline propelled him until he realized the wolf was Francesca. Right, he'd slept in a room with a werewolf all night—probably not his brightest idea. If she'd wanted to, she could have ripped his throat out.

"What do you think you're doing, waking me up like that?" Jace demanded as he stood and strode over to the alarm, hitting the off button with more force than was necessary.

Francesca's tail bristled, and a shiver ran down her spine. Jace's eyes widened as her fur melted back into her skin. Her muzzle shortened. Her tail folded in on itself, and her ears shrank and rounded out. A moment later he was staring at Francesca, propped on all fours and completely naked.

She threw her long hair over her shoulder and sat up. "I could've barked in your ear or bitten you. If I were you, I wouldn't complain about a little tongue action."

He frowned. "Bite me and you'll find a silver knife against your throat."

She rolled her eyes. "How gentlemanly of you." She stood.

Jace drank in the beautiful curves of her nude figure. Slender, muscular legs, round, smooth hips, a toned stomach, and a set of headlights that could leave a guy blind with lust.

He ripped his gaze away from her and turned around. He felt his body grow hard, and he tried to ignore the strain against his jeans. "I never claimed to be a gentleman."

"Good, because you didn't have me fooled for a second."

He heard her pad lightly toward the other side of the room, where her backpack lay against the wall.

"You can turn around," she said after several moments.

He turned to find her wearing a white tank top and a pair of worn jeans. His gaze slid over her curved frame and his dick jerked. Damn, even when she was clothed—or barely so—he wanted to run his tongue over every inch of her skin. He forced himself to ignore the deep urge tugging at his groin.

As if she read his mind, she glanced down at her clothing. She met his stare again and frowned. "These are my work clothes. I don't dress like this *every* day."

"I didn't say anything." He tried not to dwell on the way her jeans squeezed her perfectly round ass or how her tank top framed the most perfect pair of breasts he'd ever laid eyes on.

She shrugged. "You implied it with your eyes."

Jace pretended he didn't hear her comment and took his leather coat off the dresser. "Grab your things while I call David. I don't know if we'll be coming back here or not." He shrugged on the coat and used the hotel phone to dial David's number.

After a few rings, the call went to David's voice mail. Jace hung up and redialed, and kept redialing until David finally answered.

"Hello?"

"What's with you not picking up your phone?"

"I'm on the lam, J. I'm trying to be cautious."

"Yeah, and I'm hunting for a werewolf, so I'm trying not to waste time."

"Then hurry up and spit it out," David said.

"We need to know where the double killings were."

"We?" David asked. "You know, I really don't like the idea of you—"

"Mind your own business. Either help me or hang up the phone."

"I can't tell you where it's at. It's hard to find. I'll have to show you."

"Meet me at the place in an hour. You know where I mean. Make sure you ditch your phone just in case Shane put a tracker in it."

Jace hung up the phone without another word— David would be there.

AFTER JACE THOROUGHLY chewed out the valet for slamming on the brakes too hard when he pulled the H3 up to the hotel doorway, they drove toward the edge of the city. He ordered Francesca to check the rearview mirror every couple of minutes to ensure they weren't being followed. He'd checked his ride religiously for tracking devices, and while nothing electronic had been attached, there was no arguing with the fact that an H3 stood out.

"I don't see anything," Francesca said. He could tell from her quiet demeanor that her nerves were just as on-edge as his. The last thing they needed was to be tracked down by his fellow hunters again.

When they reached Honeoye Falls, Jace took the back way to the Lucky Bastard. The bar was usually dead early on a Tuesday night, and tonight was no different. With the tiny lot nearly empty, he parked the car and surveyed their surroundings. David's black 2011 Harley Super Glide, one of his many motorcycles, was parked at the side of the lot. Two nondescript cars, which Jace recognized as the bartenders', were parked across the blacktop.

Francesca stared at the sticker on the bar's front door.

Welcome to Honeoye Falls. And scribbled beneath it in thick marker: *Three bars, one graveyard and four hookers.* She let out a small laugh and walked inside.

Four hookers who tried to hit him up for free on a regular basis, the three bars where his dad had drunk himself into fits of uncontrollable rage, and the one graveyard where his mother was buried. Yeah, welcome to Honeoye Falls all right.

With one last look over his shoulder, Jace strolled inside.

The dark cherry wood of the bar shimmered in the dim lighting. Francesca stood next to an old jukebox that only played well-known Garth Brooks and Johnny Cash songs, flipping through the selections with a blank look on her face. David sat at the bar sipping a craft beer as he watched Francesca with a wary eye.

Jace sat down at the bar next to David and watched as the bartender cleaned a tall beer mug a few feet away.

"Hey, John. You want the usual?"

It took Jace a moment to respond to the bartender's question. He spent a lot of time here, even now that he'd moved deeper into the city, but only the owner, Jimmy, knew his real name.

"Yeah, slip me a couple bottles of Bushmills, will you? I need to restock."

"Coming right up."

He watched the bartender walk away before he turned to David again. "So where were these bodies at? I need to map where the attacks took place and check out the scene. There has to be some sort of pattern to what this psycho is doing, and if there isn't, there's a reason it's random."

"I can't concern myself with this for too long, J." David sipped his beer, then set his glass on the bar top, staring blankly at the liquor shelf. "I've got a Chinese baby downtown who's been possessed by that demon that's been giving me shit, and she doesn't have much more time. If I don't rip that thing out of her soon, she'll be dead and the demon will move on to its next host." David turned toward him. "Have you ever seen a possessed baby? It's horrifying. I can't have baby blood on my hands."

"I promise I won't keep you too long, David. Just show us the spot and then you can go save some Chinese babies."

"They're not *all* Chinese. Just the *one* is Chinese. And the nationality doesn't mean jack."

"No argument there."

Francesca walked up to the bar. "As much as I'd love to stay here and listen to Johnny Cash all day, if you guys are done making drunken small talk, I think we have more important business to attend to."

David set down his glass. "It's not that simple."

"What do you mean, 'It's not that simple'?" Francesca crossed her arms over her chest.

"The bodies were found in Manhattan Square Park, on top of that big metal piece of shit. You know, that little structure thing."

"Okay, yeah, I know what you're talking about, but I thought you said it was somewhere hard to find," Jace said.

"I didn't want to say much over the phone. You know how good Shane is with anything electronic. They could've hacked into both our phones. I've got a disposable cell now. I can't give you the number, but I can call you and then throw out the phone, if needed." He stared at his drink for a moment. "The site is easy to find, but there *is* something I want you to see there, and I'll need to show it to you."

The bartender returned and pushed three bottles of Bushmills toward Jace, who slapped some large bills on the counter in return. He turned back to David. "Fine, I needed to restock my liquor, anyway. Finish your drink and then meet us there."

COLD, DREARY AND downright sketchy, Manhattan Square Park was the last place Frankie wanted to spend her night—not that she currently had many other options. She walked next to Jace along the park's dim pathways. Even though her natural high body heat warmed her, she wrapped her arms around her chest and pulled her jacket closer. How many times had her parents told her to stay away from here at night when she was a teen? The thought of being mugged gave her the heebie-jeebies, even though she could easily hold her own in a fight.

She scanned the surrounding darkness, thankful for her heightened night vision. Nothing, as far as she could see. They continued on for several more minutes. Just as her shoulders started to relax, Jace reached for his gun. She heard it, too. Footsteps. He pulled his weapon just as David stepped into the dim glow of the moonlight.

"I don't think it'd be a good idea to blow my head off." David grinned. "You wouldn't get your clues, and the city of Rochester might start to have a demon infestation problem. Follow me."

Without a word, Frankie and Jace trailed behind him until they reached the metal structure. David climbed the aluminum steps two at a time, and they stayed on his heels. When they reached the top, he crouched down and pointed at the ground.

"This is where they were found. Right out here in the open. But as a precaution, I scanned the place. Watch this."

David reached inside his leather and removed a copy of the Old Testament. He flipped to a page written entirely in Hebrew. He dug inside his pocket, then scattered rock salt across the platform as he continued to read. As his voice rose, obviously leading to the climax of his chant, he pulled a lighter from inside his coat. He stood and raised it high above his head before he knelt down again, pressing the flame to the cold metal. A trail of fire ignited, and a large symbol appeared—a perfect circle with two wavy lines perpendicular to each other running through the middle.

"What the hell is that?" Frankie asked. For a brief second an image flashed through her mind: a blonde woman with a long sword battling an enormous man wearing wolf skins. What the hell? She pushed the thought aside, but the image was so vivid and clear. Where was her imagination going?

David stared at the burning flames. "I'm not sure. A circle is one of the universal conduits, like water. It can give you full access to the beyond—usually a one-way ticket to hell." He looked at Jace with a grim anger behind his eyes. "I don't think you're dealing with a regular werewolf. I think you've got a shape-shifting demon on your hands, and one I've never encountered."

"I have to say, I've been called a lot of things, but shape-shifting demon is a first," a deep voice said from behind them.

A chill shot down Frankie's spine. The silhouette of a man hidden within the shadows loomed over them. She dropped into a defensive stance, bared her canines and growled. The small hairs on the backs of her neck and arms stood on end.

"I don't give a shit who or what you are, I hope you're ready to die," Jace growled.

"I had a feeling you'd say something like that."

The man stepped into the light, and Frankie stared at him.

Tall, with broad shoulders, flowing auburn hair, sea-blue eyes and loads of muscle. The heavy scent of his skin hit her full force. Her eyes widened as she sucked in a harsh breath.

A smirk crept across the man's face. "Seems like your bitch has a keen sense of smell." He stepped forward. "My name's Robert, though your papers have been calling me the new-age Jack the Ripper—surprisingly accurate. Tell me, what do you think of my work?"

"I'll tell you what I think. I think you're one sick fuck." Jace raised his gun and pointed it at Robert's head. "One sick fuck who needs to be buried six feet under." Jace fired.

The sicko dodged more quickly than Frankie would have believed possible, and instead of his chest, the bullet pierced his shoulder. He yelped and stumbled back, knocking into the metal railing. Blood poured down his shirt. He clutched his hand to the wound.

David jumped to his feet. He drew his own gun with one hand and his cell phone with the other. As the killer stumbled toward them, David snapped a picture of the symbol with his phone while he kept his weapon trained on the killer.

A satisfied grin crossed Jace's face as Robert fell to his knees, still clutching the bleeding wound. Jace raised his gun and pressed the barrel against Robert's forehead. "You better say a prayer and hope that Satan doesn't make you his bitch every day for the rest of eternity."

"I think you're in for a surprise." Robert pulled a hunting knife from his belt and stabbed Jace in the thigh.

Blood spurted from Jace's leg as he doubled over in pain. The crimson liquid splashed over Robert, turning his twisted features even more demented.

Robert stood, smiled in self-satisfaction and plucked the bullet from his shoulder. The blood trickled to a stop. He held the bullet out in his hand. "You think you can kill me that easily? And you're a hunter?" He dropped the bullet in front of Jace. It hit the metal with a loud clang.

David cocked his old-time revolver and aimed. The sound of the shot rang in Frankie's ears, muffling David's voice when he spoke. "We might not be able to kill you—yet—but we sure as hell can cause you a lot of unnecessary pain."

Frankie ripped her gaze away from the action. David could handle it. Jace was kneeling, spewing curses she had never even heard before. His blood formed a small pool of crimson around him, the heat from the liquid billowing with steam in the freezing cold. She pressed her hands against the wound and applied as much pressure as she could, but his blood continued to flow with frightening speed.

"Shit." She stripped off her coat and rolled it into a long strip. Using all her strength, she forced Jace to straighten his leg. She looped the material underneath his thigh and tied it off above the wound. She hoped that bastard hadn't hit an artery.

She grabbed Jace's face and forced him to look her in the eye. "Don't take the tourniquet off." She turned to leave, to help David in the fight, but Jace grabbed hold of her wrist.

"Don't you dare get hurt. Give him hell." He released her.

David was fighting hand-to-hand with the bastard—or hand-to-gun. He had jammed the butt of the revolver into Robert's jaw. Blood spewed from Robert's mouth and stained his teeth red.

Frankie ran straight for him and thanked God she

had enough focus to transition. She dove for Robert and shifted mid-jump. Her canines collided with his stomach, piercing deep into his flesh. He toppled over from the force of her attack.

Within seconds he had hold of her by the scruff. Lifting her as if she weighed no more than a newborn pup, he threw her away from him. She hit the platform hard and skidded across the smooth metal. Her back legs slid over the edge of the structure. Her stomach dropped and her fur bristled as she clawed at the platform and tried to hold herself in place. She yelped. Just as she was sure she was about to fall to her death, a pair of large hands clutched her paws. Jace hauled her back onto the platform.

"What did I say about not getting hurt?"

She whimpered to say "I'm sorry" and panted to catch her breath.

A loud groan echoed through the night. The sound of David's strained voice mumbling in Hebrew registered in Frankie's overly sensitive ears. A low growl escaped her at the sight of Robert lifting David into the air by his throat. David grasped Robert's hand and clawed at his fingers to no avail. His mumbling grew fainter as his air supply was cut off.

Without thinking, Frankie darted in Robert's direction, teeth bared and ready to strike. The sharp points of her canines latched onto his throat. David fell from his clutches as the three of them toppled over the railing. Frankie closed her eyes. She heard a loud shrieking yelp and faintly wondered if she'd hit the ground yet. She couldn't feel her body. Someone shook her shoulder, and a wave of pain shot through her as her consciousness faded into blackness.

JACE DIDN'T GIVE a shit that his leg was injured or that he was bleeding like a stuck pig. He skyrocketed down the platform steps and sprinted to Francesca's side. At the force of the impact, she'd shifted into human form, and her naked body lay on top of the frozen grass and half-melted snow.

"Francesca? Hey, Princess? Don't you pass out on me. Don't you do it, damn it!" He probed her neck for a pulse and massaged the bones. Pulse steady, and her neck was perfectly intact. But her right arm and shoulder were a whole different story.

Shit. He couldn't move her and risk injuring her further, and he couldn't call the cops. An unconscious naked woman and two men covered in blood, with bullet casings scattered everywhere, wouldn't make for an easy explanation.

He glanced at David, who lay on the ground several feet away. His leg was bent unnaturally, but he had managed not to pass out. Instead he stared up into the night sky with wide, shocked eyes.

"David, are you okay?' The world spun, and Jace steadied himself with his free hand. In one quick rush, the blood drained from his face and a frosty cold nipped beneath his skin.

David glanced in his direction. "Jace? Jace? Oh, fuck."

WHEN JACE FINALLY came to, he was sprawled across an old beat-up sofa, the cushions beneath him crying from his overwhelming weight. He cracked one eye open to find a pair of shiny thin glasses reflecting the light straight into his retina.

"What the hell? Get that light out of my eye."

The glare dimmed, and Jace peered up at a pair of large hazel eyes and a mop of wavy brown hair. Who the…?

"Shane?"

"Oh, good, you recognized me. Hopefully that means we won't have to test for any brain damage due to overwhelming blood loss."

"What?"

"Shane, I think I can take it from here." A large hand brushed the kid aside, and David slid into focus. "Hey, man. You okay? You looked whiter than a ghost the last time your eyes were open."

Jace groaned in response. His whole body felt drained and devoid of any energy.

"You lost a ton of blood, J." David paused. "By the way, you may need to clean out the H3. Just sayin'."

The image of the sadistic killer's face flashed in

Jace's mind, and he suddenly recalled why he felt like complete and utter shit.

"Where's Francesca?" Jace pushed himself up on his elbows.

"I'm right here." Her gorgeous voice sounded in his ears like a sweet melody. "My arm was broken, and I was a little bruised up, but I'm fine now. I heal fast, you know."

"That is *not* fine. I'm going to torture that son of a bitch when I get hold of him."

David pushed lightly against his shoulder, trying to ease him back down. "It's cool, J. Take a breather. We're lucky we got out of there with so little damage—other than my leg, that is."

Jace's eyes widened as he remembered. "How bad is it?"

Shane cleared his throat. "He broke it pretty badly. Then he was forced to walk on it to get you and Francesca into the H3 before I got there. Even with extensive physical therapy, he might still have a permanent limp, and he'll definitely be out of commission for a while."

Jace met David's gaze. David's eyes burned with rage, and Jace knew that if David had the ability, he would kill Robert with his bare hands. If there was one thing David couldn't handle, it was people screwing with his job, and being physically impaired was practically number one on the list of things that would completely mess up David's hunting skills.

"David, man, I'm sorry. I shouldn't have—"

David shook his head and cut off Jace. "Don't even go there, J. I'm a big boy. I can handle myself, and I chose to get involved in this, so just leave it be."

Jace nodded and grumbled as he shoved himself into an upright position. Francesca was sitting in a brown suede La-Z-Boy with a blanket wrapped tight around her body. A sharp pang hit Jace hard in the chest; he'd never been so envious of a blanket. His body stiffened, and a slow ache throbbed in his groin as he pictured Francesca wrapped up in his arms, his hands stroking her smooth skin. He shifted, and a pain in his thigh snapped him back to reality. He was ass-deep in a hunt for a sadistic killer, and the last thing he needed was to be hung up on a beautiful woman, much less one who was a werewolf.

He examined his leg and assessed the wound. It was nicely bandaged up, and he felt the pull of stitches underneath—professional-level work. Shane must have been the one to dress the gash, and Jace shook his head and wondered if a medical degree was another item he could add to the long list of the kid's assets.

"Thanks for fixing me up, Shane."

"You're welcome. All I needed to do was—"

Jace cut the kid off before he launched into another long lecture. "David, you shouldn't have brought him into this." He nodded toward Shane. "What the hell do you think Damon's going to do to him when he finds out that we were at his place?" He glanced at Shane. "This *is* your place, right?"

"Actually, this is my grandmother's apartment. She's out playing bingo tonight. We already took all the necessary precautions to keep Damon and any other members of the Execution Underground from finding us," he said, speaking a mile a minute. "Oh, and I gave you a new phone for contact purposes. No trackers on it, obviously. It's in the console of your H3."

Jace gave him a thumbs-up. "Gotcha. Thanks."

David cleared his throat as he managed to stand with the help of a large wooden crutch. "Jace, we can't beat around the bush here. There is something seriously scary about that fucker."

"Were you able to figure out what type of demon he is?"

David shook his head. "That's just it. When he was strangling me, I recited Psalm 91 three times. Add in a shofar and that's the big fat Jewish mother of all exorcism rituals. He didn't even flinch. He's not a demon, J. And whatever the hell he is, I don't like it."

Francesca snuggled deeper into the blanket, as if to shield herself from the gruesome details. "If he's not a demon, then where did that symbol come from?"

David shrugged. "I honestly have no clue. Maybe he's got one those hell-crawlers working for him. They'd do anything for a little bloodshed."

"I don't think it's a demon. I've seen that symbol before, and I've never crossed paths with a demon in my life. As far as I know anyway," Francesca said.

David's eyes widened. "You know that symbol? He's a werewolf?"

Jace snorted. "I thought so, but now... A were-wolf hopped up on steroids, maybe."

"No, he's not a werewolf. And no, it's not one of *our* symbols." She eyed Jace, forcibly including him with her people. "I can't remember where I've seen it. I just know I have."

"Well, that doesn't give us much to work with."

"Look, I'm sorry I can't remember, but I'll keep thinking on it. But don't act like that's our only hope. We've got information to work with. First off, we know that he *is* able to shift, most likely into wolf form, since that's what his scent smells like, but we can't rule out any other possibilities.

"Secondly, we know he has abilities that a regular werewolf doesn't. Did you see how easily he lifted David and me together? He's got extra strength. Not to mention the healing thing. That guy pulled a bullet out of his own chest, for God's sake. I'm guessing a demon could have similar strength, but since he's immune to David's exorcism, that rules out the possibility that he's a demon. Third, there's the symbol. We just have to figure out what it means."

All three men stared at her in silence.

She sighed. "So, we need to take a different approach. There is no way we can fight this guy with just two men and one female wolf. We're going to need an advantage, something he isn't expecting."

Jace leaned back into the couch again. "And what exactly would that be?"

"You'll need to shift, Jace."

He blinked several times, unsure if he'd fully processed what she said.

"But Jace *can't* shift, can he? He's only half werewolf," David said.

Jace cringed. Hearing the words said out loud, in a room with two other hunters, stung like a bitch. Anything was better than being one of the monsters. Hell, the black plague would have been preferable.

Frankie sat forward. "It's not that he can't shift, he just *hasn't* shifted."

Jace gritted his teeth and swallowed his rage at the whole discussion. "What are you talking about?"

"With some training, you could learn how to shift."

Jace shoved himself off the couch and hobbled from the room, courtesy of his damaged leg. "No, I won't do it," he called back over his shoulder. Anger ripped at his insides.

David caught him by the arm. "J, at least listen to what she has to say."

"David, don't you start this with me. You know—"

"J, we're talking about people's lives here! Would

you stop thinking about yourself for one damn minute and listen to the woman?" David yelled.

Jace pulled his arm away but stepped back into the living room. In all the years he'd known David, the man had never so much as raised his voice to anything other than some sick demon wearing a human's body like a swanky new suit coat.

"Thank you." David turned to Francesca. "Continue."

Francesca nodded. "As I was saying, all you would need is some training."

"And you could train him?" David asked.

She let out a long sigh. "No, I couldn't. He'd need to become a part of a pack in order to shift, at least temporarily. Shifting for the first time isn't easy, and the presence of other wolves lessens the difficulty. Supernatural strength in numbers. There are a lot of things he'd need to learn after being approved by the packmaster and the pack."

Jace scoffed. "There is no way in hell your asshole packmaster would allow a hunter into his pack."

She shoved the blanket away. "It's not the packmaster's approval you'd need to worry about—it's the pack's. If you're willing, I can guarantee that I can get you in far enough to let the pack vote on it."

"How do you know you could get me past the packmaster? All he sent to look for that son of a bitch was you. No offense, Princess, but you're only one person. If he cared so much about catching this killer, why didn't he send more people?"

Her jaw set into a hard line. "Look, even though more people weren't sent, it doesn't mean anything. Just trust me."

"How do you know so much about what he thinks?"

Her hands clenched into fists, and she stood. "Because I *am* the packmaster."

CHAPTER EIGHT

FRANKIE'S HEART WAS pounding so hard she could feel the pulse in her neck. Silence hung in the air as the room filled with palpable tension.

"My name isn't Francesca. Francesca is my mother's name." She cleared her throat and fought down the bile rising in her stomach. "My real name is Frankie. Frankie Amato. I'm the Rochester packmaster."

After several long moments the men's utter shock and confusion passed. Frankie watched in horror as Jace's face tightened with rage. Rage she knew was directed straight at her.

Jace snarled. "Get out."

Her eyes widened. "What?"

"Not you." He turned to David and Shane. "You two, get out."

David stepped toward him. "Jace, keep your cool, man. We—"

Jace growled. "Out."

David and Shane left the apartment. As the door closed behind them, Jace turned toward Frankie.

The already constricted feeling in her chest tightened in a sharp pain. She'd expected nothing less than pure, unadulterated anger from him. But the expression painted across his face contained more pain than anger. His emerald eyes revealed his true feeling: betrayal.

"Did it amuse you that I didn't know your real name? Your real job? When did you plan on telling me the truth, huh? Not before we screwed, obviously? Before or after I trus—" He paused, then cursed. "Damn. What am I talking about? I sound like a woman. You don't owe me anything. Forget about it."

"Jace, I'm sorry I didn't tell you, but you're a hunter. Even though you said you wanted to partner with the pack now, I thought you might kill me if you knew I was the Alpha, the packmaster. It seemed like too sweet a chance for a hunter to pass up. Once you let me go and we started working together, I didn't know how to come out and say it. But why does my role as packmaster have to change anything? Why does it matter?"

He laughed, showcasing his disbelief. "Why does it *matter?* It matters because I've had a hard enough time trusting you throughout this whole ordeal because you're a werewolf. Now I find out you're the pack Alpha and you don't think that changes anything?"

"If you were okay with who you thought I was, why aren't you okay with me being packmaster?"

He spun around so he wasn't looking at her and ran his fingers through his gorgeous auburn hair. What she would give to run her own fingers through it...

"I wasn't okay with it."

"You sure seemed okay with it when you were screwing me." Frankie gritted her teeth. She knew it was a low blow, but she didn't care.

Jace froze. His whole body stiffened before he straightened and squared his shoulders. Before she knew what was happening, he slammed her against the living room wall, grinding his massive cock against her as he wrapped her legs around his hips.

"You're right," he growled into her ear. The heat of his breath sent shivers down her spine. "I am perfectly okay with screwing you."

His soft lips trailed down to her collarbone, and she sucked in a harsh breath. She was already wet for him.

"Jace..." His name came out in a breathy voice she hadn't intended.

His chest pressed into hers, holding her against the wall as his hands trailed down the curves of her body. He rubbed one rough-tipped finger under the edge of her shirt, and she melted. Soft lips and rough, masculine hands.

"Is this what you want?" He slid his hands under her shirt and snaked his palm underneath her bra. He rubbed her nipple between his thumb and forefinger.

She gasped and dug her hands into his hair. Forcing his head toward her, she kissed him hard. Their tongues intertwined in a sensual rhythm. What he could do with that tongue of his… He sucked on her bottom lip, and she felt herself coming unhinged. Her whole body relaxed into his.

He pulled back and broke lip contact. His eyes burned for a moment, then he shook his head as if to clear it. Slowly he released her and stepped away. "If I can't expect the truth from you, don't expect anything from me. Once this is over, I'm done cooperating with your people, and if any of you step out of line, I *will* be there to hunt you down."

He walked out of the apartment. Frankie wrapped her arms around herself and tried to ease the chills rushing through her body. Her stomach twisted into a knot. She slid down the wall until she was sitting on the floor. Pulling her legs to her chest, she rested her head on her knees.

JACE STORMED DOWN the stairs despite the pain in his leg and out into the street. David and Shane were standing outside, talking in low voices. When he burst out the front door, they both glanced in his direction. Shane rushed inside, but David stood his ground. Jace perched on the edge of the stoop, reached inside his coat for a Marlboro and lit up.

The sweet smoke filled his lungs, but nothing could calm him now. He thought back to the other night when he'd found Francesca…Frankie…whatever…in that alleyway, the way she'd reacted to the sight of his gun. As hard as he tried, he couldn't even count how many things had gone wrong since then. Where was his head at?

In between her sweet legs, that was where.

His dick hardened as he remembered how her body felt pressed against his. The taste of her lips. A deep growl rumbled in his chest, and he sucked hard on his cigarette in a vain attempt to drown out the memories. If he was going to get her out of his head, he would need something a lot stronger than a cigarette.

"You need a minute to yourself or can I pick your brain?" David said from behind him.

"Be my guest."

With some careful maneuvering, David lowered himself down to Jace's side and nodded at the cigarette. "That's gonna kill you some day, you know."

Jace dragged in another long smoke-filled breath. "Now you sound like her. Besides, it doesn't affect me as much as it would a human. You know that."

"What's going on with you and her, J? You're usually more focused than this."

Jace shrugged and blew out more smoke. "I don't know."

Sighing, David rested his elbows on his knees. "She's beautiful, and she's gotten under your skin."

Jace ignored him and flicked away his ashes. They sat in silence for several minutes before Jace cleared his throat. "She's a werewolf."

"I know. So?"

"She's Rochester's packmaster, David. I hunt her kind for a living and she's one of the head honchos. How the hell am I supposed to do my job when I'm sleeping with the enemy?"

"Since when have you cared about playing by the rules? At the rate you're going, unless you bring this asshole's head to Damon on a silver platter, you're out, and even then, you better pray on bended knee that he has one forgiving bone in his body. You lied about your bloodline so you could be a hunter. Why start sweating the details now? Do as you please. You have nothing to lose."

"When did you get so lenient about the guidelines, Mr. 'Be at the Meeting on Time and Don't Disrespect Damon'?" Jace mocked.

David crossed his arms over his chest, and a grim look tightened his features. "Since Damon forced me to choose between my job and my friends."

Jace stubbed out his cigarette and clapped David on the shoulder. "Thanks for having my back."

David relaxed a little and leaned back against the door. "You owe me big-time, like 'sacrifice your firstborn child' big-time."

Jace chuckled and offered David the flask from inside his coat.

David refused but tapped his forefinger against the metal. "Take a large shot of that before we keep talking. You aren't buzzed enough to discuss this yet."

Jace didn't need to be told twice. He swallowed three large gulps, nearly draining the flask dry. The warm liquid sloshed down his throat.

"You know that you seriously need to consider taking her offer, right? About learning how to shift?" David said.

Jace shook his head. "I can't, David. You know I can't."

David frowned. "No. I know you don't want to. There's no *can't* about it, J."

Jace shot him a glare and tightened his grip on the flask, wishing there was still whiskey in it. "You should know better than anyone that I can't, David. I refuse to be anything like that dirtbag piece of shit who was my father."

"I hate to say it, Jace, but forget your daddy issues for a minute and screw your head on straight. Shifting doesn't mean you're anything like your lowlife father. You're not a coward. You need to face any personal issues you may have and do this. The longer you wait, the more women that monster will slaughter. And the only way you'll be like your father is if you sit around and do nothing to save them." David slowly rose from the stoop and reached for the door.

Jace sighed. "You sure have a way with words."

David paused. "Being a closet book nerd all those years in high school came with a few perks, aside from keeping me golden in Allsún's eyes. She always loved it when I'd read the books she liked."

A smirk crept across Jace's face. "You were such a pansy back then."

"Bite me."

"Gladly."

David lingered in the doorway, burning holes into Jace's back with his heavy gaze. Jace stared at the concrete in front of him. The image of the dead women's bodies, shredded before they were sexually violated in death, was seared into his memory. Their faces would never leave. They'd had years of life ahead of them, families and loved ones to miss them. And so would any others who that bastard targeted. Yet here he sat, wasting precious time as he sulked about his pathetic issues and tried to preserve his own sanity. And for what? So he could spend the rest of his days living like a drunken bum?

"That was a shitty move, David, playing on a guy's emotions like that. But I'll do it." Then he mumbled a few creative profanities to show what he thought about that decision.

David laughed and stepped inside the building.

"We're leaving soon, before I change my mind," Jace yelled after him. Then he let out a long sigh. The killer knew who he was. How did Robert know him? Why would he want Jace's attention?

Do I know him?

Robert's cold blue eyes lingered in Jace's mind.

A gust of cold wind slapped against Jace's back and sent a shiver down his spine. He forced himself to remember the contorted look of rage on his father's face as he transitioned, stopping somewhere between man and wolf, the ripping sound his claws made as they tore into his mother's clothes. His eyes had been just as cold as Robert's. At only ten years old, Jace had wanted to carve out the man's heart with a dull-bladed knife. The bastard deserved a slow and painful death, and Jace hoped he'd had one. And now he was about to become a monster, just like his old man.

If there was a God, Jace really needed his help.

THE DOOR TO the apartment creaked open, and Frankie shot to her feet, scrubbing the tears away and straightening her clothes. The scrawny guy with the mop of wavy hair stepped into the room, and she sank down to the ground again. What was his name?

"Sorry, if you want me to clear out I will," she said. "I don't want to intrude."

"Oh, no, by all means stay. My grandmother will be out late. She loves her bingo."

She nodded. There was something about him. She couldn't decide whether it was his gold-rimmed glasses, his hollowed-out cheekbones or the fact that underneath all the displays of intellect he was kind of attractive—in a nerdy way. If he took off his glasses and put his hair in a ponytail, he could even be hot.

"I don't think I ever introduced myself. I'm Dr. Shane Gray" He nodded and gave her a nervous smile, one that clearly showed he wasn't used to socializing.

"Frankie. Nice to meet you, Doc." She fiddled with the hem of her shirt. "Thanks for fixing me up. Guess your years of med school worked in my favor."

"Actually, I'm not a physician."

She lifted her eyebrows. "Then how did you—"

"I read...a lot," he said.

"So you're a hunter, too, then?"

He bit his lower lip before he answered, as if he wasn't sure he wanted to share. "In theory, yes. I don't really work out in the field often. My doctorate is in the study of the paranormal and the history of religion, specifically the occult." He paused and glanced at his feet. "I'm more of a consultant than an actual hunter."

"Oh. There's nothing wrong with that." She smiled and tried to be encouraging. A moment of silence passed. She tapped her fingernails against the floor, then looked up at him again. "No hunting at all? None?"

Shane shook his head. Silence fell over them again, but this time he broke the quiet. "He'll change his mind, you know."

"Excuse me?" She tilted her head to the side.

"Jace is stubborn, but he's not a bad person. What happened to those women will motivate him, and if it doesn't, David will. He'll shift."

"And he'll hate me." She sighed, and her whole body deflated. "I didn't want to lie to him, but if he knew, he might have killed me since the opportunity was there. Once he let me go and we started working together, I couldn't admit it. I knew this would happen."

The door opened, and they both fell silent. Frankie sat up straight as Jace stepped into the room. His gaze darted between them.

Shane cleared his throat. "I'll go downstairs and check on David. I might've missed something when I was examining him earlier." He rushed out of the apartment, cleaning his glasses with the edge of his shirt as he went.

The door closed, and Jace leaned his weight against it as soon as he'd locked it.

He pointed over his shoulder with his thumb. "Shane is kind of a nerd," he said. "A lovable nerd."

She nodded. "Yeah, I noticed."

A long moment passed. Frankie stared at her feet, while Jace shoved his hands into the pockets of his jeans. She watched him from the corner of her eye. She tried not to imagine where the zipper led. She blushed.

I shouldn't be thinking about him like that, especially now.

He was the first to break the silence. "I'll do it," he said.

She glanced toward him, hoping he meant what she thought he did. "Do what?"

"You know what I'm talking about. Do I need to spell it out? I'll learn how to shift."

Her shoulders relaxed. "You're serious?"

"No, I'm telling you this just for shits and giggles." He nodded. "Yeah, I'm serious. I can't let any more women die."

She wanted to run to his side, throw her arms around him and thank him, but she didn't think that would go well, so she settled for plain and simple. "Thank you."

He pointed at her. "Listen. I'm not doing it for you, I'm doing it for those girls."

She sighed. "Can't you stop hating me for just one minute?"

He turned away.

When he didn't respond, she stood and marched toward him. "I never wanted to lie, Jace. I'm not a liar."

He faced her again and his jaw clenched into a sharp angle. "No? Because it sure seems to me like you lied."

"You held a gun to my head, Jace, and you expect me to think you wouldn't have killed me if you'd known?" She dropped her hands to her sides. How could he not understand her reasoning?

He growled as if she'd insulted his manhood. "I don't kill women."

"Yeah, well I'm not a normal woman. I'm a were-wolf, and you hunt women like me. Remember?"

He stepped forward, towering over her. If she'd been a weaker woman, she might have been intimi-dated. "I've never hurt a woman." He stepped away from her and moved to the other side of the room. He pulled aside the ugly flowered curtains and stared into the dark street. "I wouldn't have killed you."

Frustration gripped her. How could she make him understand? "How was I supposed to know that?"

He closed the curtain. "You didn't seem to think I'd kill you when you were lying in my bed later that night."

Her breath caught. She bit her lower lip and fought back tears. She wouldn't let him see her cry—not again. "I am *not* a whore."

"I never said you were."

She choked on her own words. "You…you im-plied it."

He shook his head as he walked back toward her. "I'd never say that."

She covered her face with her hand and sighed. "I know it was just an easy lay for you, but for me—"

Her back hit the wall so hard all the air rushed out of her lungs. She gasped as he hoisted her ass up, pulling her legs around his hips. He ground into her until she bucked against him. A wave of heat radiated through her core. Massaging his fingers against her spine, he cradled her. Pleasure coursed through her, and she leaned into him.

Anger radiated from him, yet his touch relaxed her. He tucked his head between her neck and shoulder. Inhaling her scent, he let out a low growl. Slowly he ran the length of his tongue over her earlobe. "You like doing this to me? Making me want you?"

Frankie couldn't form words.

His teeth grazed the tender flesh, and she moaned. He dragged his lips down the skin of her ear, her neck, her shoulder, until he nibbled on her collarbone. His tongue swirled over her skin in sensual movements.

After several moments he pulled away. Before she could comprehend what he was doing, her panties were around her ankles and his thick cock was rubbing across her entrance.

"Do you want me?" He ground himself against her as he asked.

Every logical cell in her body screamed no. But her body said otherwise as she rocked her hips against him.

Apparently that was all the response he needed. He sheathed himself inside her, stretching her wide. She took every inch of him inside her.

She breathed against his ear, tickling him, and his cock jerked. A feeling of hot need filled her, and she pushed her hips harder against his.

"Did you miss this?" He slid out and rubbed his length over her thin pink slit. "I did."

She shivered beneath his touch. A smirk spread across his face. He drove himself inside her again. She cried out as he pounded into her, each thrust sending electricity shooting through her.

As he rode her hard, he palmed her breast outside her shirt, then slipped his hand inside and under her bra. He circled each of her soft nipples in turn, using his thumb and forefinger until they were hard and aching for his touch. Then he trailed his fingers over her skin, down the line of her abdomen until he quickly found her clit. He rolled his fingers over her in sensual circles. The seat of her sex pulsated, and her body shook.

She slickened as he slid in and out of her with increasing ease. Adrenaline raced through her veins as he claimed her. The sounds of his pleasure sent chills down her spine, and she inched closer and closer to climax.

She let out a deep-throated moan.

"Do you like it when I take you deep like that?" He thrust into her again.

His body was heaven—her own little slice of divine bliss. She nearly laughed at her own thoughts as she watched him push inside of her. "Little" had nothing to do with it. Her body ached for him.

When she didn't say anything, he reached up and lightly tugged a strand of her hair. "You didn't answer me."

The small jolt sent waves of sexual desire through her. She wanted him, so badly, so…

"You still didn't answer my question," he whispered next to her ear.

She gasped and nodded. "Yes."

He tugged on her hair again. "Yes, what?"

Her whole body tensed as she neared her peak.

A feral snarl ripped from Jace's throat, and his irises flashed wolf-gold. He bared his canines and growled. "You're going to come for me, and then you're going to tell me just how deep you like it."

Frankie's heart pounded as he rubbed harder and harder against her clit with his fingers, never losing momentum as he thrust deep inside her. "Come for me."

White-hot ecstasy rolled through her as she reached her release at last. She shook against him as wave after wave of pleasure engulfed her body, consuming her until she couldn't take it anymore.

Her entire being threatened to crumble to pieces beneath his skilled hands.

She gasped. "Jace, I can't take any more. I can't…" She tried to tell him that she'd never felt this much pleasure before. That her body was so overwhelmed that she…

He kept shoving into her, pounding into her flesh as he fingered her. Her whole body tensed as she felt herself climbing toward a second climax.

"Jace." She panted. "Wait." Already she was shattering again, and she wanted him to come with her.

A low growl ripped from his throat. "Tell me you didn't want it the first time we were together. Tell me you don't want me now and I'll stop."

She opened her mouth. A small moan escaped her lips.

"Tell me…Frankie."

Words…words…why couldn't she find any right now?

He pushed against her with his chest, and she melted into his touch.

She *did* want him. No matter what he thought of her, she still wanted him.

"Jace, I…" Closing her eyes, she tried to gather her thoughts. She wanted to… "I…I don't want—" She didn't want him to leave. Ever. The words were trapped in her throat by the realization that she wanted this man more than she wanted her next breath. How could she have fallen like this?

The pressure on her body eased as Jace released her. Her feet hit the fluffy carpet, and she slumped against the wall. Despite the central heating, the winter chill penetrated the air—and her. It hit her full force, the moment she'd missed out on slapping her in the face.

"Jace, wait."

"Forget it." He turned his back on her as he straightened his clothes. She didn't need to see his face. The tension in his muscles told her everything.

He cleared his throat. "I'm sorry if that was unwanted. Believe me when I say I won't bother you again." He walked toward the door without looking at her. His hand twisted the doorknob. "Tell David where and when your pack meets."

After a long moment she finally managed to speak. "You're still going to shift?" Damn it. That wasn't what she needed to say. But she couldn't tell him now, could she? Couldn't say she didn't want him to go. He'd pushed her away more times than he'd claimed her.

He paused, his shoulders flexing as he inhaled. "I told you, I can't let more women die."

A sharp pang sliced her heart. "Jace, I don't want—"

He interrupted her midsentence. "You don't need to explain yourself, Frankie. I get it."

She stepped forward and raised her voice, forcing herself to say the words. "But I…I don't—"

He walked out and closed the door behind him. The latch clicked into place and her heart hit the floor.

"I don't want you to go...."

But it was too late.

CHAPTER NINE

JACE AND DAVID stepped into K9's, trailing behind Frankie. The deep red carpet squished underneath Jace's massive leather boots, and the floor vibrated with the beat of the music. The medium-size circular room was filled with private booths surrounded by matching red drapery to obscure the view for more exclusive meetings. A slender woman with manufactured globes attached to her chest danced on a pole in the center. She slapped her thigh and slid her ass up the metal rod as she gyrated to the music. Her bleached-blond hair flipped like she was riding a wild bronco. Jace couldn't have been more turned off.

He scanned the room, his eyes moving from face to face. Goose bumps crawled up his skin, and the hair on the back of his neck stood on end. He didn't need to be a hunter to know that he was in a room full of animals.

He followed Frankie farther into the club, with David hobbling behind them with his crutch. Jace's eyes widened as they moved deeper into the room, taking them closer to the stripper. From near the door, the ceiling looked normal, but standing in the middle of the building, he stared up at tier upon tier of seats, every floor thumping to the same stupid dance music. Didn't anyone listen to AC/DC anymore?

His attention snapped back into the here and now as Frankie came to a sudden halt. A muscled male werewolf was rushing toward her, talking at a hundred miles an hour. A low growl rumbled in Jace's throat. David grabbed him by the back of his shirt and pulled him back until they were out of hearing distance, courtesy of the loud music.

"Stay cool," David mumbled. "Do you want to get us kicked out?"

Jace whipped around and half snarled into David's ear, "That's her boyfriend."

David raised a single brow. "Her *boyfriend?*"

Jace ground his teeth together, fighting back a serious bout of jealously. Why the hell did he care? He shouldn't be so hung up on her.

"Jace—"

David and Jace's conversation skidded to an abrupt halt at the sound of one loud, pissed-off female.

"No!" Frankie yelled. She ripped her wrist away from the newcomer. "You're not my keeper, Alejandro. I'm your *packmaster.* Alpha or not, you don't have any authority." She started to march away from him but stopped mid-step. "Tell the DJ to turn off the music."

The bastard didn't move.

"Now," she growled.

Without another word, she climbed onto the stripper's platform. The stripper sauntered over to her and leaned forward, ready to play up some girl-on-girl action.

Frankie glared at her and crossed her arms over her chest. "Move."

The music stopped, filling the club with an awkward silence. A male voice with a thick Spanish accent boomed through the room.

"At this time, we'd like to request that all non-pack members leave the building. That means *everyone* but the pack members. Thank you."

A collective rustle spread through the club as a few people gravitated toward the exits. Jace's ragged breath slowed to an even pace before David released him. He was thankful his friend was there to keep him in check. They couldn't blow this.

Frankie stood on the platform with her hands on her hips, silently waiting for everyone's attention. Standing there, she looked like an average, even-tempered woman. But Jace had seen the fire blazing behind her eyes firsthand—a fire that would never burn out.

A crowd gathered around them as people filtered down from the upper levels. When everyone fell silent, she held her head high and dropped her arms to her sides. "I'm calling you all in, because I'm asking for pack—"

Just then her bastard boyfriend pushed to the front of the crowd. "Where were you?" he demanded.

Muttering erupted across the club. Frankie's hand clenched into a fist, and she raised her voice over everyone else's. She had a set of pipes.

"Alejandro, Alpha male or not, you will shut your mouth, before I have someone shut it for you."

"But—"

"Yeah, Frankie. Where were you?" someone called as murmurs of dissatisfaction filled the room.

"Quiet." She raised her voice again, and a hush fell over the crowd again. "I was trying to stop the killer."

Her boyfriend let out a deep roar. "You were *what?*" He stomped up onto the platform and started yelling right in her face. "You didn't have pack approval. You could have been killed."

"I don't need pack approval, Alejandro. I'm *packmaster*. I'm exempt by royal bloodline. Now. Sit. Down." She stared him straight in the eye, challenging him for dominance as their animal instincts bubbled to the surface.

He accepted her rule for the moment and finally glanced away. He stepped down from the platform, defeated and, at least in Jace's opinion, humiliated. She'd put the jerk in his place.

"As you all know, we've been searching for weeks

with no results, so I decided to go looking for him on my own, and I've finally tracked his scent."

"Did you kill him?" one of the pack members yelled.

"No." A look of major impatience crossed Frankie's face. Apparently she didn't like interruptions. "And we have a couple of new problems. He's escalating. He's started killing in pairs."

Alejandro stepped forward, chest all puffed out and looking grim-faced, as if he were ready to give someone a good beat-down. "Then we need to catch him, before he catches any more innocent women."

Words of agreement passed through the pack.

"It's not that easy, Alejandro," Frankie said. "He's strong. Stronger than normal, and there's something...wrong with him."

Alejandro let out an angry grumble. "Of course there is something wrong with him—he's a cold-blooded killer."

Frankie ignored him. "He's not a werewolf. At least not a normal one. I've never seen or heard of any werewolf like him."

The room fell so silent that Jace could hear the light breathing of the individuals around him.

"We need someone who knows what they're doing, so I've brought help. Hunters." She gestured to Jace and David. All the eyes in the room turned toward them, and a surge of adrenaline rushed through Jace's veins. Damn, did that put the pressure on or what?

A male werewolf stepped forward, his muscles flexing. "You brought *hunters* into our home?" He growled so low that the hairs on the back of Jace's neck and arms stood on end. "I said from the very beginning that a bitch should never rule our pack." He lunged toward Frankie.

Jace pulled his gun and fired into the air. The wolf stopped in his tracks a good three feet from Frankie. Jace stepped up onto the platform, holding his Mateba like it was an extension of his arm. "Yes, I'm a hunter, and I'm fully armed."

He strode over to the edge of the platform and pointed the barrel straight at the jerk who'd come at Frankie, then asked, his voice laced with rage, "Does anyone have a problem with that?"

No one spoke, and the would-be attacker melted back into the crowd.

"Now, I believe your packmaster was speaking to you. So pay attention."

Jace thumped David on the back as he returned to his spot among the onlookers.

Frankie glanced at Jace almost disbelievingly, then shook her head as her determination and resolve showed in her body language again. She straightened and held her head high.

"As I was saying, this might not be a normal werewolf or even a werewolf at all. We need experts to help us. These hunters are only interested in catching this killer. They're not here to hurt us."

A member of the crowd stepped to the edge of the platform. "What do we need their help for? What damage can they do with their silver weapons that we can't with our canines?"

She gestured toward Jace with her free hand. David stepped aside.

"Jace is a half-breed. He's not allergic to silver, and he has all the strength of any normal werewolf. The killer can also withstand silver, and gunshot wounds barely faze him. Jace is the only one who stands any chance against him."

The boyfriend shook his head. "Then why the hell did you bring him here? If he's the perfect man for the job, why bother to notify your pack, since apparently, you don't need our approval to do anything?"

Frankie let out a feminine, but firm, growl. "You're right. *I* don't need your permission." She pointed a finger at Jace, while she glared at Alejandro. "But *he* does." She dropped her arm back to her side. Her face screamed fury. All the bastard had to do was push her one more time, before the atomic bomb inside her went off—Jace could see it.

"Jace has never shifted. He needs to learn, and I need the pack's approval in order to teach him." She drew a deep breath, and he could sense her gauging their reaction. "It's the only way. We can't do this on our own." The silence that followed after her words faded was deafening.

A small grunt came from the other side of the crowd. A small woman with a long mop of curly auburn hair emerged, shoving through the sea of people. "I vote yes. If Frankie thinks he's our only chance, then I trust her." She smiled, and it practically illuminated her heart-shaped face.

Oh, shit. Jace knew that face. He'd seen it before, though only in pictures. He shot David a sideways glance. David stood paralyzed, his eyes locked on the woman. It had been years since Jace's best friend had seen the woman he loved. Yet there she stood, plain as day. Looking exactly the same as all the pictures David ever showed him.

What the hell? She was a werewolf? Why had David never told him? At least that explained why David had been so understanding about his own mixed blood.

Allsún turned her head, and her eyes widened as they fell on David. Abruptly, she turned and pushed her way back through the crowd. David followed her as fast as he could with his injured leg.

DAVID FOUGHT DOWN the massive lump that had lodged itself in his esophagus. His stomach flipped, and the taste of vomit itched at the back of his throat. Five years. Yet there she was, waltzing into his life again and filling up what he'd grown to think was a permanent hole in his heart.

Anger clenched at his insides as pain shot through his leg. But he didn't care, he pushed through the pain. He had to see her. She was the only one in the world who truly mattered to him.

Someone bumped into his shoulder, slowing him down. Shit. She… Oh, damn. She was bolting for the outside door. He watched as she shoved her way through the crowd and ducked underneath the arms of anyone who got in her way. She slammed the back door open and ran full speed into the alley. Despite his leg, he trailed not far behind her.

The cold night air hit him hard as he stepped outside. Allsún was here. He could smell her sweet vanilla perfume. He limped down the alley and found her sitting, eyes closed, behind a Dumpster. A small calico cat sat curled in her lap.

"Allsún? What are you doing?"

She opened her eyes and peered up into his face. "What does it look like I'm doing? I'm petting my newest cat and getting my ass soaking wet from the snow." She glanced down at the animal again.

Not bothering to take as much care as he should, David sat down in the snow beside her and ignored the sharp pain in his leg. "You shouldn't be here," he said. He reached out and brushed back the curls from her face. His fingers trailed across her cheekbone and down her neck, and she relaxed at his touch. "But I'm glad to see you, gorgeous."

"You never did know when to let sleeping cats lie." She stroked the stray feline sitting in her lap. "You never let things go."

"What are you talking about, Allie?"

She finally looked at him. Gold starbursts encircled her pupils—a stark contrast to the green of her irises. David could spend his whole life gazing at the stars in her eyes.

"Following me here. Tracking me down after all this time." She hoisted the cat onto her chest and stood, turning her back to him. "It's been five years, David."

He rested his head against the concrete wall of the alley. "One thousand, six hundred and ten days."

She paused, then faced him. "What?"

"That's how many days I've had to live without you." He stared down at his Harley-Davidson boots. "More than four years. Almost five, but not yet."

She gaped. "Don't. Just don't. Okay?"

"Don't what?"

She squeezed the cat tighter. It let out a low-pitched grumble of a meow. "Don't pull any of your overdone romantic lines on me. I'm not sixteen anymore," she said. She cradled the cat and walked several feet away from him.

"They're not lines."

"Damn it, David. Why are you here? Why now? Why search me out now?"

He frowned. "I wasn't searching for you." He used his crutch for leverage and pushed himself off the ground, then followed her down the alleyway. "I didn't know you'd be here. I'm just as floored as you are."

"You seriously expect me to believe that?"

"It's the truth, Allsún. I gave up looking for you a long time ago. I thought if you wanted to come back, you would."

"You're right. If I'd wanted to, I would have."

He cringed. Her words stung, and he could tell she knew it. She'd always known how to cut straight to his heart.

"Let me guess, you're here chasing demons?" Her jaw tightened into a hard line, and a sour look crossed her face.

"I'm helping the pack catch the killer who's been ripping women to shreds."

She rolled her eyes. "How very admirable of you."

"I wasn't trying to sound admirable. I'm just telling the truth, Allsún." He followed her farther down the alleyway. The cat's glowing yellow eyes peered over her shoulder, gleaming in the light from the street.

"You can't blame me for thinking that. You always wanted to be the hero."

"You know it wasn't about that." He shook his

head. She *did* know that. She was just hitting him where it hurt again.

"There are a lot of things I don't know about you, David."

His hands clenched into fists at his sides. She could push every emotional button he had within a matter of minutes. He stared at her back. Her long curly hair cascaded over her shoulders in waves. It had only reached her chin the last time he'd seen her.

"The first time I've seen you in nearly five years and you're already bringing that up?" He exhaled the breath he'd been holding and held back all his frustration. "We can't even greet each other without arguing?"

She stroked the cat. The animal purred and pushed its face into her neck. He would have loved to nuzzle his face into that crook, run his lips over her collarbone. Silence lingered in the air, leaving a stale taste in his mouth.

"You were in there as a pack member. What are you doing mixing with the werewolves, Allsún? You're not one of them."

"That's none of your business."

"Fine. You don't want to talk to me, I'll leave." He strode back toward the club, then paused at the door and clutched the handle.

"I'm with them because I needed company," she called.

He turned around. She was standing at the end of the passage and watching him.

"I'm sure you heard my mom died," she said.

He nodded. "I visited her, after you spread her ashes."

Allsún sighed. "After that, I was lonely. I couldn't find any other faeries in the area. Not even other half-bloods. The werewolves were the closest thing I could find. Frankie lets me hang with the pack. She says all supernaturals are distant cousins."

David's lips lifted in a half smile. He'd known Frankie wasn't all that bad. She would be good for Jace. "That was really nice of her."

Allsún nodded. A moment of silence passed again.

David cleared his throat. "I miss your mom."

"Yeah, me too."

He could hear the strain in her voice.

"I hate that she had to see us separated before she died." He glanced at Allsún. She set the cat down on the ground. It weaved in and out of her legs before it scurried away.

She stared at him with her arms crossed over her chest. "Why would you say that?" Her voice was calm and completely flat. Anger radiated off her in waves. Her perfectly rounded hip jutted out to the side, and she tightened her soft lips into a thin line.

His cock hardened and he shifted, hoping she didn't notice his erection. Man, she was sexy when she was angry. He wanted every inch of her. He directed his eyes to the pavement and prayed the feeling would pass. "I said it because that's how I feel."

"Yeah, well, you shouldn't have said it." She shook her head. Her voice climbed as she paced the alley. "You have no right to say that. Not after what you did."

"What *I* did? *You* were the one who left *me*, Allie. Not the other way around. I loved you. I wanted to marry you."

She stomped toward him and stabbed her finger into his face. "Don't you dare act like none of it was your fault. You can't play the victim with me, David. I won't fall for it."

Anger boiled underneath his skin. "You were so scared of hurting anyone that you left us all behind and hurt everyone anyway."

She stepped away from him.

He regretted the words as soon as they'd left his lips. "I didn't mean that the way it sounded. What I meant was—"

"Don't!" Her hand quivered at her side, and he could see her thoughts on her face. He almost wished she would go ahead and smack him. Tears gathered in the corners of her eyes.

"Allsún…"

Without another word she turned, and ran down the alley and out of his life again.

Whoa.

Jace shook his head, trying to forget what just

happened, and focused back on Frankie. He would deal with David's emotional baggage later.

Just as Frankie was about to speak again, someone else parted the crowd. A beefed-up male werewolf who looked like he'd been injecting steroids before he'd been weaned off the bottle stepped onto the platform.

"You can't call for a vote, Frankie." He held his head high and puffed out his chest. Another pack member wanting to look like a badass.

She brushed him off as if he were nothing more than a fly buzzing near her food. "Step down, Marshall."

Marshall shook his head. A cocky grin crossed his face. "That's packmaster to you."

Frankie raised an eyebrow and crossed her arms over her chest. She scoffed. "Excuse me?"

Marshall stepped farther onto the platform, making certain to flex his massive biceps as he went. Jace had to fight not to laugh. The asshole might as well have put a sign on his forehead that said Overcompensating.

"I'm the new packmaster," Marshall said. "When you failed to take a mate, pack law dictated that you were no longer able to be packmaster. The title passed to Alejandro, but he refused to take a mate other than you, so he didn't qualify. I'm next in line after him."

Frankie laughed. "You've got to be kidding me,

Marshall. Get over your little power trip and step aside."

Marshall let out a low growl. "Under pack law, I am the new packmaster, and I won't let any ex-pack leader bitch talk to me that way. And I sure as hell won't let any hunters near my pack."

Frankie snarled and bared her canines. "That's where you're wrong, Marshall. You see, Jace happens to be half-werewolf and he *was* there during the call. I'm not mated to any of our pack members, but I *am* mated to Jace." The crowd fell silent and Jace watched Alejandro's face fill with anger.

Jace froze. He'd slept with her and now he was *mated* to a werewolf? His head spun with anger at himself for not listening to her warnings that night. What the hell had he been thinking? As much as he wanted to be nothing but pissed off, though, a small sense of relief flooded him. No wonder he was so hung up on her.

Frankie continued. "So by pack law, I am still in power and if I say we'll have hunters help us in catching this sadistic son of a bitch, then my word goes."

Marshall cracked his knuckles. "You'll have to fight me for the position, then."

Frankie laughed. "Don't make me embarrass you in front of your fellow pack members."

Without warning, Marshall charged Frankie full speed. But her reaction time was clearly faster than he'd expected. She hit him with a spinning back-kick that collided with his face. He dropped like a sack of chemically enhanced potatoes, clutching his bloodied nose.

Before he could jump to his feet, she grabbed him by the shoulders and kneed him straight under the chin. A loud crack of fracturing bone sounded as he toppled back onto the floor. After delivering one final blow to his solar plexus, Frankie jammed her tennis shoe into his windpipe and stared him down.

The growl that ripped from her throat sent a chill down Jace's spine, and he suddenly knew why she was packmaster.

"Fuck with me again and I will cut off your balls and feed them to you like they're scrambled eggs." She pushed his head to the side with her foot and turned away from him.

Marshall peeled himself off the floor, bloodied and humiliated.

Paying no further attention to the asshole, Frankie cleared her throat and addressed her pack. "As I was saying—"

Marshall ran at her from behind and lunged.

"Frankie!" Jace yelled.

She spun around just in time for Marshall to collide with her midsection. He knocked her back and tried to climb on top of her. Twisting just out of his grasp, she shot to her feet, grabbed hold of his head and chin, then wrenched them to the right. With a deafening crack, she snapped Marshall's neck as if were a chicken bone. He crumpled to the floor, lifeless.

For several moments Frankie stood there, panting as she regained her composure. Then she rolled her shoulders, let out a long breath and turned back to the crowd. Her voice was filled with fury. "If any one of you ever tries to assume my position again, the means by which I kill you won't be so painless." She cleared her throat. "I am now calling for a vote on whether Jace should be allowed to shift."

Jace stared out at the room, memorizing the members of both sides as the tension grew with each passing second. Two groups—those loyal to their packmaster and the dickweeds who wanted to fight.

Alejandro got up in Frankie's face, and it took everything Jace had in him not to rip the bastard to shreds right then and there. "There's no way I'll allow it," Alejandro said.

Frankie shoved him out of her face. "It's not up to you, Alejandro. The whole pack needs to take a vote."

Jace could tell by the way her hands shook that her patience was about to break.

Without another word to Frankie, Alejandro turned to stare down at Jace and glared. "If you're as strong as we are, prove it."

"Jace—" Frankie began.

Ignoring her, he stepped forward and gestured for

her to move aside. "Frankie, don't try and tell me I can't do this. If they want proof, I'll give it to them."

"I wasn't going to say that." She gave him a little smile. "Just don't kill him."

Jace couldn't help but smirk as he stripped off his coat and handed it to her. Rolling up his sleeves, he stepped onto the platform. The little prick dropped into a fighting stance, like he was about to go all ju-jitsu on his ass. It took every ounce of control Jace had to keep a straight face. Within seconds, Alejandro charged. Jace dropped to the floor and swept the other man's feet out from under him. Alejandro toppled to the ground in a pathetic heap.

Jace shot to his feet again. "You were seriously going to try and body-slam me?" He ground his boot into the bastard's spine. "I'm twice your fucking size."

He lifted his foot, ready to deliver another blow. Alejandro grabbed him by the ankle and twisted, pulling Jace down onto the platform, his hand throbbing from trying to break his fall. Jace kicked out hard, and the heel of his boot collided with the moron's nose. Blood gushed from Alejandro's nostrils like a waterfall. Jace glanced at his foot. Damn, he really needed to clean all the dried blood off his boots.

Alejandro pinched the bridge of his nose and tilted his head back in a futile attempt to slow the bleeding. He coughed as the blood seeped into his mouth.

"You know you don't get a break just because I busted your nose, right?" Jace hoisted himself to his feet.

Gripping Alejandro by the front of his shirt, he threw a right hook. His fist collided with Alejandro's cheek, and he felt the familiar crunch of broken bone and damaged cartilage beneath his knuckles. Jace yanked his arm back to deliver another blow.

Sharp animal claws ripped across Jace's face. Dropping Alejandro, he stumbled several steps backward, then touched his cheek, his fingertips finding fresh blood. The bastard had managed to half-shift, his hands covered in fur with the claws of a wolf.

"You can't fight me without your claws, huh?" Jace stepped toward him. "Shift full form for all I care." He plowed forward like the world's fastest bulldozer and aimed straight for Alejandro's center of balance.

Alejandro threw himself forward to meet the attack, shifting in midair. Jace stopped in his tracks to throw his opponent off-stride. The large black wolf growled at him, its teeth bared. Jace readied himself just as the wolf pounced. Jace's sheer size gave him the upper hand. The two of them rolled to the floor with Jace on top. He slammed his fist into Alejandro's furred jaw.

The wolf let out a high-pitched yelp and squirmed beneath him, fighting to be free. His canines dug into Jace's shoulder, ripping through flesh as if it were butter.

Jace let out a cry of pain and pulled back. To hell with letting this dickhead get away with this crap. Blood poured from his shoulder, but he fought through the pain, reached down to his ankle and pulled his blade. Throwing himself on top of the wolf, he pinned the animal to the floor and pushed his blade against Alejandro's fur-covered neck.

"Your pelt will look nice spread out on my apartment floor." He moved to draw the blade across Alejandro's throat.

"Jace, don't!"

Frankie rushed over to him and pulled on his uninjured shoulder. "You've won, Jace. Get off him."

For a long moment he didn't budge, but finally he gave in to her pleas and decided to move on his own. A low groan escaped the asshole's lips as Jace stood and stepped away.

"Greg, take care of Alejandro!" Frankie yelled, as she started to lead Jace away.

"Coward." Alejandro's accusation stopped Jace in his tracks. "Only a coward steals another man's woman."

Jace paused, then turned to face Alejandro. His eyes narrowed to thin slits. "What are you talking about?"

"Alejandro, shut your mouth," Frankie snapped.

"She's mine," Alejandro hissed as if he were a venomous snake, ready to strike.

"That was a direct order!" Frankie screamed at Alejandro. Her cheeks were red with anger.

"She was mine," Alejandro said to Jace, ignoring her. "She was promised to me. She was going to be my mate. My *wife*. If she's yours now, it's only because you were there when anyone would have done. Don't kid yourself that she actually gives a damn about you."

Jace met Frankie's eyes. He didn't need to ask. He knew the truth from the fading light in her chocolate eyes. Shit.

She latched onto his arm. "Jace, it's not like that any—"

He plucked her hand off his bicep and stepped away. "Stop."

"No, Jace, you don't understand. It's a mist—"

"You're right. It *is* a mistake." He turned to Alejandro. "Keep her. I never wanted her to begin with." He stormed out of the club with a heavy weight on his shoulders and an empty numbness in his chest.

DAVID PRESSED HIS palms against the brick wall to support his weight. His warm breath clouded in front of his face as he exhaled raggedly. She'd been right within his reach. Inches from his grasp, but he'd lost her again. The image of her face lingered in his mind. Her green-gold eyes. Her auburn curls and full lips.

The permanent ache in his chest throbbed. All the years that had separated them had disappeared as soon as he saw her face. He let out a low groan. She was always on his mind, and she visited him in his dreams every night. He pushed off from the wall and walked down the alley. Shit, he was pathetic. Hung up on a woman who didn't want him, a woman who'd left him with no explanation and without looking back.

I can't see myself with you forever. Her words echoed in his head.

He punched the metal Dumpster, sending a loud bang rattling through the alley. She wasn't even there, and still his brain had melted to mush because of her.

His hand was throbbing from the blow, and he cradled it against his chest.

ROBERT LINGERED ACROSS the street from K9's, waiting for the opportune moment. All he needed was for someone, anyone, to come out of the club. Someone he could use to lure Frankie to him. He'd stood there, waiting in the cold, for at least half an hour. They would all have to leave eventually, he told himself. Then, as if the gods had granted him a stroke of luck, a small, curly-haired bitch emerged from the alleyway behind the club and ran down the road without looking back.

For a brief moment Robert wondered what she was running from, but then a grin spread across his face. It didn't matter. Now she was running from him.

He followed her without hesitation, easily keeping up with her. After several blocks she slowed to a walk and then stopped to catch her breath.

She bent over and braced her hands on her knees. After a long moment she straightened and sighed. The smoky outline of her breath swirled in the air before it quickly dissipated.

A sudden gust of the northern Canadian wind hit, and she gave a visible shiver. She rubbed at her bare arms and cursed. The streetlights cast dim shadows over the empty streets. She would look so sweet on his torture rack.

She quickly reached into the rear pocket of her jeans, probably in search of her phone. Now was the time. Slowly, he approached her from behind. In seconds her phone crashed to the pavement, a spiderweb of cracks fracturing the screen as he grabbed her from behind.

She screamed and elbowed him in the gut. He grunted but ignored the temporary discomfort. Then she jammed her heel down onto his instep, grabbed his hands and swept her leg behind his. She gave a quick twist, and suddenly he was toppling to the ground as she stumbled out of his grasp. Dirty whore. He was going to enjoy ripping her to shreds. He grabbed her ankle and wrenched her down to the ground beside him.

"Hold still, you little bitch." The heel of her shoe collided with his neck, and she twisted to see him. He saw his golden wolf eyes reflected back in hers.

He smiled. "I enjoy a woman with some fight in her." He allowed her to move beneath him, testing her strength and resilience.

She rolled onto her back, their noses nearly touching, before she spat in his face. He recoiled slightly. She used the opportunity to pull her knees to her chest, lodge a foot against him and push. He slammed his hands into her shoulders, knocking her head into the pavement.

His silver dagger glittered in the orange light of the streetlamps as he held the blade against her windpipe. "Don't worry. I'll wake you before the fun starts." He laughed and swung at her face with his free hand. The light in her eyes faded as blood gushed down her forehead.

CHAPTER TEN

JACE STORMED OUT of K9's and into the street. His heart was pounding like a construction worker's jackhammer, each blow heavy and fast.

Not just a boyfriend. A fiancé. And no one got engaged unless they were in love.

Love. The word slammed around in his head. What the hell was wrong with him? He should have known. He paced, cursing under his breath. She was a female werewolf, and not just any werewolf: the Rochester packmaster. Sure, she'd claimed him in public, but that had only been to hang on to her position, because bottom line? She was *engaged*. Not only had he messed up the first night, he'd fucked her again and been shut down completely afterward. How many times was the universe going to stick it to him?

"You gotta be fucking kidding me!" Jace yelled.

A woman passing by on the other side of the street clutched her purse tighter and sped up her pace.

Jace growled. "I don't need this." He pulled a cigarette from his pocket and lit up. The smoke filled his lungs but didn't calm him down. How could he calm down with all the lying bullshit being flung at him? She was perfectly willing to screw him, even though she couldn't even admit she wanted him, not to mention she was promised to someone else.

Adrenaline pumped through him, and he flexed his free hand into a fist at his side. He'd made a total idiot of himself, thinking for even two seconds that sexing up a werewolf was acceptable. Dumbest idea he'd ever had. What an idiot he'd been to think she had real emotions when she wasn't even human.

He sighed and blew out a puff of smoke. "Of course neither am I."

"You're not what?" a male voice said from behind him.

He turned to find David leaning up against the building.

Jace ran his fingers through his hair. "Nothing."

"Well, something's up with you."

Jace raised a brow. "You're one to talk. You look like shit."

"Thanks for the compliment, sugarplum."

Jace shrugged. "Any time, baby. So what happened to you?"

David shook his head. "You saw. Allsún was here. What about you?"

Jace took another drag on his cigarette. "You go first."

Jace watched as David stuffed his hands in his pockets and stared up into the dark sky. You could never see the stars in Rochester. Every night the lights from the city obscured them. That was one thing Jace missed about Honeoye Falls.

He threw his butt to the ground and stomped it out with the heel of his boot.

"David, how come you never told me Allsún's a werewolf?"

David shook his head. "Because she's not. She was just looking for the company of other supernaturals."

"What do you mean 'the company of other supernaturals'?"

David sighed. "She's half faerie—pixie, specifically."

Jace cleared his throat. "Excuse me?"

"You heard me."

"Pixies? You're in love with a damn pixie?" He lit another cigarette and took a hard drag. "What is the world coming to?"

"Most of them still live on the Isle of Apples. You know, Avalon. It's hidden off the coast of Scotland. So when her mother passed away a few years back— her mom was full-blooded—Allsún didn't have any other faeries around. Your girl let her sort of join the pack, so she would have other supernaturals to be with, even if they're werewolves."

Jace raised his eyebrows. He couldn't believe what he was hearing. "That's wild."

David rolled his eyes. "Tell me about it."

A moment of silence passed before Jace cleared his throat. "She's not my girl, David."

David scoffed. "Oh, shove it, Jace. Just because she's a werewolf, that doesn't mean—"

"She's engaged."

David's eyes widened. "What?"

Jace nodded. "You know that guy Alejandro? The one who gave her a hard time earlier? She was set to be mated to him. It's like their equivalent of marriage. Bastard flat out said she was going to be his wife."

David fiddled with the collar of his shirt, like he couldn't find enough room for his neck. "I'm sorry, J. That's rough."

"Nothing to be sorry for. But I don't know how I'm gonna work with her now." Jace watched his smoke climb toward the sky.

David scanned him up and down as if he'd grown ten extra heads. "What do you mean, you can't work with her?"

Jace paused. He glanced at David but didn't respond. He didn't want to get into this discussion.

"No. No." David shook his head. "You still have the hots for her after all that?"

Silence stretched between them.

"That's rough. But you can handle it, J. You didn't know she had a fiancé or a mate or whatever, but now you do. Just deal with her on a business level only. Hands off. Doesn't matter if you're attracted to her. You can think she's the greatest piece of ass to walk this earth, just keep it in your pants and you'll be fine."

Jace rolled his eyes. "You always did have a way with words."

He was about to go on when the door to K9's burst open and Frankie raced out into the street. She glanced around frantically. Great, just as he was starting to calm down.

She spotted him and ran over. "Jace, you have to let me explain."

"You don't need to explain anything to me, Frankie. Believe me. I get it."

"No, you don't understand. Alejandro and I—"

"Just give it a rest already. You heard me in there. I don't want a relationship with you anyway, so you're all his."

"Jace," David hissed.

Frankie opened her mouth again, but Jace raised a hand. "I'm done with this drama. Unless you have something to tell me that will lead to catching Robert and then me getting the hell out of here, I don't want to hear it."

Even in the dark, he could see her swallow hard. Then she nodded. "The pack was impressed by your…well, your crazy anger in there, so they agreed to let me teach you to shift."

A smile spread across David's face. "That's more like it."

She forced a grin. "Uh, yeah, so we can start training tomorrow. But there's one complication—David can't come with you."

Jace frowned.

"It will be just you and me."

Looking completely unperturbed, David said, "Well, have fun, you two." He clapped Jace on the shoulder. "Call me when you need a drink, J, or when you learn how to shift, whichever comes first." Then he limped down the road to the garage where he'd parked his car, since he wasn't going to be riding his motorcycle for a while with the condition his leg was in.

"Um…so I guess we'll start tomorrow. Sleep would be good first. It won't work if you're tired," she said. "At least 'til you get good at it."

Jace stubbed out his last cigarette. "Yeah, I'll see you tomorrow." He turned away from her, ready to follow David to the car.

"Jace, there's another problem."

He faced her again. "What now?"

"My apartment was ransacked. I was staying at the hotel with you. Remember?"

Apparently the universe wasn't done sticking it to him just yet.

FRANKIE CHOKED ON the stale air in the hotel elevator. Standing next to Jace inside the cramped space made her claustrophobic. The lingering smell of his smoke and whiskey mixed with his own distinctive scent and made breathing even more difficult. Finally the bell dinged and the doors opened. She scrambled out and ran for the penthouse door.

Jace brushed past her, unlocked the door and charged into the room without a word. She slipped in behind him as he strode straight to the bedroom, quickly stripping off his boots and his leather coat. She wandered toward her bag on the far side of the room. Something had to give. She couldn't handle this sort of tension, not the entire time she was trying to train him.

It was her own fault, of course. In less than twenty-four hours he'd found out that she'd both lied to him about her position *and* neglected to tell him she was engaged. Now he needed to know the rest of the truth.

"Look, Jace. Can I just explain?"

He set down his boots on the white carpeting and placed his hands on his hips. "There's nothing to say. Don't waste your breath."

A heavy weight pushed down on her shoulders. She couldn't let him think she was a cheater or that Alejandro mattered to her the way Jace no doubt thought he did. She'd never cheated at anything in her life, and aside from lying about her name, she'd never even lied before. Brutal honesty: that was what she prided herself on. With him so angry, though, how could she get him to listen, much less believe her?

She picked up her backpack and walked into the bathroom. Closing the door behind her, she stripped down and changed into a pair of yoga pants and a fresh white tank top. When she finished changing, she stared in the mirror for a long moment before she twisted on the faucet and splashed cold water over her face.

Enough.

She turned off the sink, threw open the bathroom door and marched back into the bedroom.

"I'm not his wife *or* his fiancée."

Jace glanced in her direction, then away. "Frankie, give it a rest."

"No. You're going to listen to me. I have something to say. I don't care whether or not you want to hear it, or whether or not you care. I need to say it, damn it." She crossed her arms over her chest.

He didn't look at her.

"I've been slated to be Alejandro's mate since the time I hit puberty, but I've never had any feelings for him beyond friendship. I love him, Jace, but I'm not *in* love with him. Our…engagement, if you want to call it that, doesn't—didn't—mean what you think. I know you don't want any sort of relationship with me. I get it. You've made that abundantly clear. But I want you to know that I never intended to cheat on anyone, and if I hurt you, I never meant to, because

I never chose to be with Alejandro. I don't regret being with you, not one bit, because for once in my life I got to choose who I wanted to be with. I just wanted you to know that."

Jace stared at the floor before he stripped off his shirt and lay down on the bed.

A wave of heat rushed through her as she scanned the lines of his body. The muscles in his chest flexed as he breathed, and his biceps tightened as he rest his hands behind his head. She forced herself to look away. He didn't want her.

"Tomorrow you can start teaching me how to shift," he said.

ROBERT SAT AGAINST the wall of the warehouse and watched his victim's eyes flicker open, only for her to shy away from the light. A dim lone bulb hung over her head, casting shadows across the room, figures lurking like demons in the dark. He sat quietly and observed her reactions. She tried to roll her shoulders, to stretch, but she couldn't move. She glanced up. Her wrists were shackled together above her head. Wrenching her arms, she tried to fight against the restraints. Her whole body swayed. She looked at her feet. The toes of her flats barely scuffed the surface of the concrete beneath her. Her lip quivered as if she were about to burst into tears.

Pathetic really. Just heartbreaking enough to be vomit-inducing.

She struggled against the shackles. After several minutes her muscles slackened and she hung from the ceiling, rocking like a pig waiting for slaughter.

Slowly he sauntered to her side, his footsteps echoing through the warehouse. The gleaming silver of his blade flashed in the dim lighting as he pushed the weapon against her windpipe.

"Finally awake."

Blood trickled down her collarbone. The delicious red of a ripe fall apple. He drew the blade away from her throat and stepped in front of her. "I'm glad you decided to grace me with your consciousness. I've been waiting."

"Please, let me go." She closed her eyes and muttered a small prayer. But God wouldn't help her. Not here.

He laughed. "Why would I go through the trouble of keeping you alive if I was just going to let you go?" He stepped into her, his body flush against hers. "You're not getting off so easy. I need you to bring Frankie to me. One of her fellow pack members in danger. She won't be able to resist."

Her eyes widened. "You don't understand. She won't come for me. She—"

"Shut up." He clutched a single hand around her throat.

She obliged and closed her mouth. When he was certain he felt her fear pulsing beneath his hand, he released her throat and stepped away from her.

"What do you want with her?" she said.

Robert laughed. "Do you even need to ask?" He picked up a nearby wrench.

"Honestly, I really do. I—"

He threw the tool at her full force. She screamed, though the metal hit the ground a foot away and barely skidded into her foot. He frowned. He'd always been shitty at throwing anything other than daggers, and it was starting to piss him off. He cracked his knuckles.

"Don't play dumb with me, bitch." He let out a feral growl. "I know your packmaster has been fucking around with Jace."

She inhaled a sharp breath. "The hunter," she said.

Robert sneered. "Yes, the hunter." He paused, and ran his eyes up and down her body, then moved toward her again. Pressing himself against her, he buried his nose in the crook of her neck. The sweet smell disgusted him, but there was another scent, as well. "I smell a human…." He nearly touched his nose to hers as he leaned in and said, "I can tell."

She let out a sob.

"Would you stop making that awful, ugly face?" He stepped away from her and walked across the room to sit on an empty wooden crate. "I've always hated you women and your overly dramatic feelings."

"You're just another disgusting misogynist."

Robert grinned and examined her as if she'd become suddenly interesting. "You're right. I *do* hate women."

She huffed. "What? Mommy never loved you when you were a baby?"

The twisted smile on his face faded into a scowl. "My mother was a werewolf whore, just like you. My mother used to take men into her room every night. She told me to ignore the noises, that they were just playing games." He pushed around a small pile of dirt with the toe of his shoe. "I believed her—for a while."

"You're pathetic, and your mommy issues are no excuse for killing and torturing women."

He looked up from the floor and stared at her. "You're right. None of that is my mother's fault. I absolve her of all blame for my crimes." He stood and marched toward her. "I do what I do because I enjoy it, all of my own accord." He pulled out his knife again.

She cringed. All the muscles in her body tightened, preparing for the pain.

"I won't bleed you dry just yet."

She sucked in a deep breath.

"I'll wait for when Frankie and Jace get here. But listen to me when I say no one…calls…me… pathetic." He slashed his knife through the air and across her right cheekbone. A surge of power and energy shot through him, and he relished every drop of it.

Blood ran down her face as she screamed. The liquid trickled over her neck and onto her green shirt, staining the fabric a putrid brown. He stood back and marveled at the sight.

As casually as if he'd been talking to the cashier at a grocery store, he smiled. "I'll be back soon. Enjoy."

A LARGE HAND clamped down on Thomas's shoulder. The voice of the shadowed man echoed as he said, "You will not be limited by mortal bounds." His voice filled the small clearing where they stood, the forest painted in blue hues as if the brush were made of the sky.

Thomas's eyes widened. A light sparked in his irises, and a smirk spread across his face. "You mean I'll be immortal?"

The shadowed man stepped in front of him. "Don't overestimate your abilities. No one is immortal but the gods. You will age, but at a slow pace, and no minor wound will harm you, but make no mistake, your time will come. Like your father, someday you must pass down your power. You will choose when that time is. A respectful son shall wait until the time is right, just as you must wait now."

"Like a respectful son..." Thomas looked up into the face of the shadowed man, who towered over him in his enormity. "What do I do now?" he asked.

"Go. Return to your rightful place at your father's side. He will tell you when his time is up. Until then,

learn what wisdom you can from him. Great power lies ahead of you."

The shadowed man lifted his hand, and with the wave of his wrist the blue forest melted.

When the blue world had faded from his view, Thomas scanned his surroundings. He stood in the middle of a small backyard behind a small redbrick home. Inside, framed in a window, a middle-aged man stood at a kitchen sink, his hands buried in suds.

"Wait and learn his *wisdom?" Thomas shook his head before he strode toward the house. He wrenched open the patio door and stepped inside, his boots tracking dirt onto the once-white linoleum. "Hey, Dad. I'm home."*

Thomas's father glanced up from the dishes and smiled. "You're later than I expected, Tom." He set the plate he'd finished washing onto a towel along with the other cleaned dishes—three stacks of plates, several bowls, a single glass and some well-used silverware. He turned to the casserole dish in his hand and scrubbed at the leftover macaroni. "What were you up to? Your mom put some dinner for you in the fridge. The macaroni is in the yellow Tupperware container, and there's some steak on a plate in there. It's covered with tinfoil."

Thomas walked to the fridge, keeping his eyes trained on his father. "I was just...uh...running late at work, Dad. We had an extra shipment come in." He pulled the refrigerator door open and removed the covered steak. After unwrapping the aluminum foil, he shoved the plate into the microwave and hit start.

He scanned the room. His gaze paused on the block holding the steak knives. "Can you hand me a knife, Dad?"

"Sure." His father reached over the counter, selecting one of the steak knives from the wooden block. Still facing the sink, he held the knife out behind him, and Thomas took it from his hand.

He clutched it in his palm as he stared at his father. The blade gleamed in the light. "Hey, Dad, I have something interesting to tell you...." He stepped forward.

"Yeah?" His father looked up from the dishes and saw, reflected in the window, his son standing over him. His eyes widened. "Tom, what are you—"

Tom met his gaze as he stabbed the knife into his father's spine. "I just wanted to tell you, I'm sorry."

JACE'S EYES SHOT open as he woke from a deep sleep. He blinked several times and felt his heart pounding in his throat. Holy shit. Dreaming of his father killing his grandfather—a man Jace had never even met? Damn, he had too active an imagination. Besides, his mother had said his grandfather had died of old age before she and his father, Tom, had ever even met.

He didn't need to be thinking about this shit.

His nightmares were freaky enough without delving into family drama. And damn, if that shit was true…no wonder he was as fucked up as he was.

He rolled over onto his back and glanced at Frankie. She lay sleeping beside him, hair sprawled over the pillowcase, fast asleep. He wanted to touch her. As much as he was angry with her, resented her for making him feel so much when she yielded so little, he couldn't find the strength to detach himself completely, though he wished he could. She'd insisted she was a free woman and that she'd wanted to be with him. But he couldn't afford to believe her. And yet… He could have moved into another room in the suite or ordered her to sleep elsewhere. But as he'd chugged Bushmills from the flask he'd refilled and she'd sipped from a second bottle, they'd settled together on the bed, neither talking nor touching. Sleep had finally claimed her, and he'd been content to watch her rest, to hear her breathe. Yeah. Maybe it was in his genes. A level of debauchery and selfishness that went bone deep.

Dear Lord, he had to try to shift tomorrow, and so far in his life he hadn't so much as shifted even a single limb. He let out a long sigh and shook his head. If the nightmares in the early morning hours were any sign of what the day would be like, he was going to need a lot more whiskey.

CHAPTER ELEVEN

JACE'S SKIN CRAWLED when he walked into K9's the next day. In all his years of hunting, he'd never been as nervous as he was standing on the platform, a perfect training ground, with Frankie.

Him shifting? He cringed.

"Okay, let's get this over with," he said.

Frankie rolled her eyes. "It's not that easy, Jace. You're not going to learn it in a few hours."

"It seems simple enough for all of you. You do it within a matter of seconds," he said.

She sighed and shook her head. "We're full-blooded. It'll be harder for you. And even we had to learn how."

His face fell into a frown. "How long does it usually take to learn?"

She let out a long sigh, as if all her hopes were deflating like an old balloon. "Weeks. But we can't afford that. You only have a few days."

"You've gotta be shittin' me. I may be good, but I'm not *that* good."

She placed her hands on her hips, and a look that

was pure attitude crossed her face. "Unless you want more women to die, you'll shift and you'll do it soon. We're going to be working all our waking hours until you get this mastered."

He rolled his eyes. "If you say so, teach."

"Don't be a smart-ass. Are you ready?"

He shrugged. "Let's go."

"To start with, I want you to try and shift on your own. You won't be able to, but do what feels natural. What would you start with?"

"Well, I'd start with taking off my clothes. I don't want to rip my expensive threads." He poked his finger through a hole in his coat.

"Okay, Casanova. Strip down, then."

Jace shrugged off his coat and pulled his shirt over his head, then tossed them to the side.

FRANKIE'S EYES WIDENED. The memory of Jace's arms flexing as he drove himself into her invaded her mind. Heat shot to her core. She shouldn't be thinking like this. But the way his stomach tightened when he thrust into her… The thought lingered. She smiled and bit her lower lip, then snapped herself back to reality. "Now what would you do?" she finally managed to say.

"Get down on my hands and knees?"

She waved him forward. "Don't ask me. Go ahead."

"I can't believe I'm doing this." Jace knelt on the

platform and lowered his weight onto his hands, then got off his knees and balanced on his toes. "All right," he said. "This is all you're getting out of me. You've got about three more seconds of this before I stand up again."

She shook her head and sighed. "That's all I needed to know. You can get up now."

He stood and faced her. Her eyes drank in the lines of his body and the hard muscles disappearing under his jeans. She clenched her jaw and tried to focus.

"Okay. From that, I can tell that you're what we'd call a crouched shifter. Basically, there are three methods of shifting. The first is to stand as tall as possible, usually with the spine arched back, and allow the energy to flow through you from the bottom up." She straightened her back and imitated the pose.

"The second is to crouch down, like you did. You can drop into a deep knee-bend and arch your spine, or you can get all the way down on the ground. Crouching is common because it allows you to focus all your energy in one condensed space, and since you're in a similar position to your animal form, it's easier to transition. Then there are shifters who can switch in either stance, dual-shifters, but that takes a lot of practice. Only our best warriors can do that. So since you're a crouched shifter, you'll want to drop down rather than straightening when you're trying to transition."

Jace nodded. "Crouched shifter. Got it."

"Okay. Now crouch down again. Whichever lowered stance feels comfortable."

Jace bent his knees and arched forward like a large animal waiting to pounce.

"Channel your energy wherever it's strongest. Focus on pushing all your energy there."

He raised a single brow. "What energy?"

"What do you mean, 'what energy'?"

"I don't know what you're talking about. I don't feel any energy."

She sighed and walked to his side. "Straighten up again."

He rolled his shoulders back to stand at his full height, towering over her. The closeness of his body to hers sent a fresh wave of heat straight through her. "It's the energy inside you. The kind you feel when the moon is full. That sort of stirring. Right here in your chest." She placed her palm over his solar plexus. She looked up, and their eyes locked. She had to fight to get the words out. "It's right here. It pulls at your whole being, like something connected to your soul." She glanced at the floor. "Do you feel it?"

Jace placed his hand over her hers. "Only when you touch me."

She met his eyes again, and her breath caught. They stood in total stillness.

He stroked his thumb over the top of her hand. "I'm sorry your parents forced you into a relationship you didn't want," he said, barely above a whisper.

She swallowed, trying to find the ability to speak. "Thank you. I'm sorry, too."

He kept staring, and Frankie wasn't quite sure how to handle it. She inched closer. He cleared his throat and stepped back. Her hand fell from his chest to hang limp at her side. Yeah, she was an idiot. Always rushing in, when he only rebuffed her at every opportunity. *Learn to take a hint, Frankie.*

Jace cleared his throat again. "I can feel it when the moon is full. But I can't feel it now. So since I can't really feel it, how am I supposed to gather it?"

"You're going to have to learn how to feel it." Her palm tingled from where she'd touched his skin. Her arms didn't feel right hanging at her sides, so she crossed them over her chest. She wanted to wrap them around him. Instead, she tightened them around her body, trying to hold herself together. "You've probably suppressed it so long that you can't feel it anymore. Can you think back to the last time it was there?"

"When I hunt."

"What do you mean?" she said.

He stared at the wall as if he didn't want to look her in the face. "When I'm out hunting...well, you know." He glanced at her to gauge her reaction.

"Werewolves? Our people?"

Jace frowned. "When I'm hunting, I can feel something stir inside me. Almost like an animal living under my skin. A beast."

"That's an interesting way to describe it. I've never heard anyone say that."

"Well, that's how it feels to me."

"Is there any way we can simulate the feeling you get when you hunt?"

He squared his jaw and rubbed his temples in slow circles. "Not unless you bring Alejandro back in here and let me tear into him."

"Aren't you funny," she said coldly. "What's your problem with him, Jace?"

"I have a problem with any moron who thinks he's a badass and God's gift to women."

"Sounds like someone else I know."

Jace's mouth drew into a tight line, but it soon curled into a smirk. "The difference is, I actually *am* God's gift to women."

Frankie rolled her eyes.

A moment of silence passed between them as he scanned the length of her body and her skin seemed to catch fire. He could caress her with one look.

"Come here," he said.

Without thinking about what she was doing, Frankie shuffled forward a few inches, then stared into his eyes and froze.

He strolled across the platform and pulled her

against his body. He laced his fingers through her hair, and a blush heated her cheeks.

"If you stand close to me, I might be able to shift."

His grip on her tightened, and she could feel his erection push against the soft skin of her stomach. He leaned his face into hers, and she fought hard not to gasp as his lips lingered dangerously close to her ear. His warm breath danced over her skin.

"Just stay with me."

A LOUD BANG echoed through the air as Robert entered and slammed the door open. The sound of his own footsteps pounded in his ears, and he watched as his victim cringed. Anger coursed through him. He was sick of this. Where the fuck were they?

He growled at the pathetic girl. "Why the hell haven't Frankie and Jace come running to rescue you yet?" Surely they knew she was missing, had found her ransacked apartment by now, hadn't they? That had been a lucky break, finding her wallet in her backpack.

She remained silent, eyes cast down.

A grin spread across his face. He clenched his jaw and cracked his neck. He would refrain from killing her—for now. He would wait until the right moment. He wouldn't lose control. "No matter. They'll get here eventually. I'll make sure of it."

She tightened her lips, obviously fighting to keep her mouth shut.

"What's wrong? Cat got the werewolf's tongue?"

She stared at him, not saying anything.

He frowned. The whole situation grated on his nerves. "I'm finding very little enjoyment in this."

"Then let me go."

He laughed. This particular piece of female trash was even more ignorant than he expected. "Why would I do that, when I can just spice up the current situation?"

Her eyes widened as he unsheathed a new blade from his belt. It sparkled in the dim lighting.

"Silver." He nearly purred as he ran a single finger over the hilt.

"Did you know that one of the most sensitive parts of the body," he said, "is the collarbone?" He pointed the blade at her. "Answer me," he growled.

"N-no. I didn't know that."

"Well, you're in for a treat, because you're about to find out firsthand." He smiled.

In seconds blood gushed from a gash on her collarbone, dangerously close to her major arteries. The iron stench of her blood filled the air as she screamed, and Robert relished the fragrance. He knew that with each shriek the pain in her neck increased, and his smile widened as she switched between screaming agony and silent suffering. Finally she fell silent and gasped in ragged, painful breaths.

"As you can see, I was correct about the collarbone," he said. A grin spread across his face. "Feels good, doesn't it? Makes you feel alive." He paused and scanned the length of her body. His eyes traced over the blood, distracting him momentarily. He pulled himself back. There was more blood to be had.

"Did you know the clitoris has three times the amount of nerve endings as the entire head of a man's penis?"

She let out a strained whimper.

"Answer me," he said.

Tears poured down her face as she shook her head.

"You didn't? Well, aren't you lucky you have such a knowledgeable teacher? Be a good student and pay attention." He placed the tip of the knife on the button of her jeans. "I have no interest in mutilating your feminine parts. I'll need those for later." His cock jerked at the thought of taking her cold, lifeless corpse.

"Please let me go," she begged. "I've never done anything to you. Please."

"I'm afraid that's not possible."

"Let me go, you sick bastard!"

"Mind your manners," he growled, and pressed the flat of the blade to the skin of her forearm. When she didn't react, he pulled the weapon back, looked at it curiously, then laid it on her skin again. His eyes narrowed into thin slits. "What's this? A werewolf not affected by silver?"

Her head hung from her neck like a broken limb.

He placed the dull surface of the knife under her chin and lifted her head, forcing her to meet his eyes.

"What are you?"

"I'm nothing. I'm just human." She held eye contact.

He slapped her across the face. Her head jerked to the side, and he admired the red mark that marred her cheek. "You can't be a human. The werewolves wouldn't have anything to do with you." He scanned her up and down as if she were some newly discovered species. "You're not a regular werewolf, and you aren't a Berserker...."

"A what?"

He ignored her and continued. "So what are you?"

She didn't respond.

"I asked you a question."

She bit her lower lip and shook her head no.

"Have it your way." He sheathed the blade again. He crossed the room and retrieved a coil of rope, then removed a key from his pocket. She struggled against her shackles. Without a word, he grabbed hold of her feet and wrapped the rope around her ankles, binding her legs together. Then he unlocked the shackles.

She toppled to the ground in a pathetic heap. He grabbed both her wrists in one hand and bound those, as well.

He stared at the pinkish-colored rash ringing them, where the iron had begun to...eat away at her skin? "What's this?" he said, lifting her wrists into the light of the single bulb overhead. He clutched her by the upper arms and shook her hard. She flopped in his grasp like dead weight. He threw her back onto the floor. Her back hit the concrete hard, and her curls spilled into her face.

"What are those?" He shoved her head to one side, smashing her cheek into the floor. His fingertips ran over the top edge of her ear. "Pointed ears."

She panted like a distressed dog until he released her. She writhed until she slowly inched away from him.

"A faerie." A devilish grin spread across his face as he made a tsking noise with his tongue. A more interesting victim than he'd thought. A rush of glee overcame him. "This is going to be interesting."

CHAPTER TWELVE

AFTER THIRTY-SIX HOURS of hanging around outside K9's in the hopes of running into Allsún, David changed his tactics. Sure, he'd also been waiting to see if Jace would finally manage to shift, but every waking spare moment had been spent thinking about her.

Now David stood outside the steps to the Temple Building apartments and sighed. He'd taken a major risk coming here. Allsún wouldn't exactly welcome him with open arms. Wheedling her home address out of Frankie had been for Execution Underground purposes, or at least that was what he'd told her—and himself. But he knew his motives had been purely personal. After five years of missing her, he just couldn't let her go again so easily.

He lingered outside her building, thinking this was probably one of his dumbest ideas yet.

He climbed slowly up the steps, glad his new walking cast meant he didn't need crutches anymore. His finger hovered over the call buzzer. A tight feeling squeezed his lungs. He wasn't sure he could handle it if—or when, most likely—she told him to get lost. With a deep breath, he sucked up his feelings and pushed the button.

He waited for her voice to come over the intercom. Nothing. He pushed the button again. Still nothing. He pressed the buzzer several more times, but there was no response. She had to be there, because he'd been watching so long that he would have seen her if she'd gone out. Could she see him from her apartment and just wasn't answering? Looking up, he examined the windows. Not a single set of blinds or curtains open. He checked his watch. Almost midnight. She must have left and he'd just missed her. Defeated, he turned to leave just as the front door creaked open.

A man poked his head out. "Can I help you?"

David assessed him. He looked like he belonged on a magazine cover, the kind of guy who couldn't walk past a mirror without admiring his own reflection.

"Yeah, I'm looking for Allsún O'Hare. She might go by Allie."

The man nodded. "Oh, yeah. Cute little thing, mop of curly hair? Apartment 209."

A slight surge of protectiveness pulsed through David. If he hadn't been sure this guy swung the other way, he might have been pissed. "That's her."

The man looked thoughtful. "You know, come to think of it, I haven't seen her since yesterday, actually. I'm the super here, by the way. Victor." He stuck out his hand.

David shook his hand but didn't introduce himself. "Nice to meet you. Look, is there any way I could get up to her apartment? Just in case she's there and the buzzer is broken."

"The buzzer's not broken. I heard you because I have a master receiver and it buzzed in my room. Usually I don't allow nonresidents to come in without being buzzed up." He eyed David up and down, and grinned. "But since I haven't seen her, I think it would be good to check on her. Come on up."

David ignored the super's flirtatious look and followed him up the stairs. After two flights, they stopped outside door 209.

Victor knocked on the door. "Allsún, it's Victor. There's someone here to see you." He paused. Nothing but silence answered back. "Allsún, are you all right? Are you in there?" He knocked again.

"Can we go inside?" David asked.

Victor shrugged. "I guess." He reached to his belt and removed a large set of keys, then sorted through them until he found one marked 209. He slowly opened the door and stuck his head inside. "Oh, my gosh. Oh, my gosh."

He stumbled back. David's heart stopped beating. He threw open the door and burst inside, gun drawn. "Holy hell."

The apartment had been ransacked. The desk had

been overturned, scattering office supplies across the floor, and books had been thrown in every direction when the bookcase had been knocked over. Someone had ripped the sheets to shreds. The words *Come and get her, Frankie* were painted in crimson across the wall. The smell of blood permeated the studio apartment. David let out a strained cry and tore out of the room and past the rattled super as quickly as he could with his injured leg.

"Where are you going? I need to call the cops!" Victor yelled after him.

David ignored him and did his best to hurry down the stairs and out to the street, where he threw himself into his Escalade and sped away. Damn, he needed his motorcycle back.

FRANKIE LET OUT a long sigh. Thirty-six hours. Thirty-six long, drawn-out hours, and Jace still wasn't any closer to shifting than when he'd first started. They'd spent night and day standing in the middle of K9's, trying every possible approach she could come up with, but with no success. Thirty-six never-ending hours, and still nothing.

"This is bullshit," Jace growled.

She crossed her arms over her chest. "The more frustrated you get, the less this is going to work." As much as she wanted him to lose his anger and cut the attitude, she couldn't blame him. Even *she* was starting to get tired of the ordeal, and she wasn't even the one trying to shift.

"It's not working to begin with. How can it possibly be any worse?"

She fought back a scream. If she had to hear one more complaint, she was going to rip her hair out by the roots, followed by Jace's.

Marching straight up to him, she placed her hands on her hips. No way was she listening to any more whining. "Jace McCannon, you listen to me—now. It normally takes weeks to learn this, but you only have a matter of days, and we've already used up over twenty-four hours. I suggest you suck up your frustrations and shift." She felt her teeth grind together as she battled back her impatience.

He frowned. "You really know how to put a guy in his place, don't you?"

She poked him hard in the chest. "I'm packmaster, and you're a temporary member of this pack. It's my job to kick you into shape. Now shift."

Jace let out a low growl. "Fine." He dropped into his lowered stance.

She stepped back to the edge of the platform. He needed to do this. They couldn't waste any more time. "Use your anger and frustration, Jace, but exercise control. You're in charge of your emotions. Push your anger inside you. Push it to the place you feel stirring when the moon is full. Concentrate."

Jace's muscles strained, his irises taking on the

intense fire they possessed every time he urged his body to change. She circled behind him, watching his every move. She had to make sure he was focused.

He growled. "Why can't I do this?"

"You're not focusing." She walked in front of him. "Jace, you need to focus."

He clenched his fists and glared at her.

She sighed. "Think about the victims. If you don't shift soon, more innocent women will die."

He crouched farther down. "I will *not* have their blood on my hands."

She watched as all the muscles in his body strained. His loud cry reverberated off the walls. Beads of sweat ran down his face, and she could see the anger flowing through him from his head all the way to his…fingertips?

He let out an exasperated grunt. Her eyes widened.

"Jace!" she yelled. His hands were beginning to transition. "Don't stop."

Ignoring her, he straightened to his full height and snapped, "More people will die, all because I can't fucking shift."

"Jace, look at your hands." Frankie grabbed hold of one wrist and shoved it toward his face.

The air around his fingers and palm vibrated as if it were bending to his will. A slight layer of hair sprouted over his knuckles, before it quickly disappeared.

He met Frankie's eyes. "Holy shit. Well, that's progress, at least."

She smiled, and her grin stretched from ear to ear. Relief filled her. A few more tries and he might be able to do it. But she had to pace him. If he wore himself out, it would never happen, and his frustration was already about to skyrocket.

She cleared her throat. "You can do this. But for now, take a break."

Jace's hands fell to his sides. "Thank God." He walked to the edge of the platform and grabbed a bottle of water. He turned away and chugged the bottle. When he was finished, she watched as he recapped it, then patted his pockets. "Damn it. I left my smokes in my coat. Gotta run to the car." He set the bottle down and jogged out of the room.

Once he left, she allowed her mind a moment of peace. It had been too long since she'd danced. One hour of the familiar salsa movements and she would feel refreshed. Without thought, she moved her hips in a sensual rhythm, dancing with the confidence that no one was watching her while she daydreamed.

She spun around in a controlled twirl, then stopped mid-spin. Jace was standing on the other side of the platform, his gaze locked onto her. Her eyes widened, and heat burned across her face as she blushed. "Sorry. It's been a while since I've gotten to dance, so I couldn't help myself."

He shook his head. "Don't apologize. I was enjoying watching you."

The blush on her cheeks deepened, and the heat spread to the lower parts of her body, radiating all the way to her core. She stared down at the platform. With one look, he could make all her resolve melt. She bit her lower lip and tried push away the thought of him sheathing himself inside her. If only she could be with him one more time. But one more time would never be enough. She would always want more.

She fought not to cringe as she thought of their sex-capade in Shane's apartment. Damn it. She should have found a way to tell him that she'd choked on her words. She'd wanted to tell him not to leave, that she wanted him, but she'd screwed up royally in so many ways. He resented her for numerous reasons now: lying to him, the debacle at Shane's apartment, not to mention the situation with Alejandro. It was no wonder he'd been so cold, so angry, with her. As frustrating as he could be, how could she not forgive his stupid behavior when her own actions were the cause?

She scrambled to change subjects. "I usually have a partner to dance with." She sighed. "Alejan—" She started to say Alejandro's name but caught herself. "Salsa just isn't as much fun without a partner."

A smug smile spread across his face. "Okay, you've convinced me. I'll dance with you."

Her head shot up, and she met his eyes. "You're kidding, right?"

"I can take a hint when I hear one. You want to dance with me," he said, and winked.

She placed her hands on her hips. "Quit teasing me. I wasn't asking you to dance, and you know it."

He nodded. "Yeah, I know. But why not give it a try anyway?"

She eyed him up and down with a skeptical expression. "You really want to?"

He shrugged and stepped toward her. "Why the hell not? It beats standing here trying to shift and looking like a moron while I'm doing it."

She paused for a moment. He was right. Why not?

Because it would make her want him again. Because her body would kick into overdrive despite the protests from her brain. Because he would undoubtedly push her away afterward. On the other hand, dancing would help take his mind off his frustration, and that might help him learn to shift more quickly. Before she could change her mind, she walked over and stopped in front of him, staring up into his face.

"Give me your hands," she said.

He placed his palms in hers, and his touch sent a familiar electric shock pulsing through her body. Every nerve inside her stood on edge. Without prompting, he pulled her close until she was flush against his body. His warmth flooded over her skin, and it took every ounce of self-control she had not to kiss him right there, to ask him to make love to her in the middle of the club. She hated the way her body responded to him so readily.

Focus, Frankie. Stop staring and focus.

"The man normally leads in salsa, but for now, just let me lead you." She glanced at him again. It was so hard to look away when she was so close. A deep longing burned in her chest as he returned her gaze.

"Step back. Now forward. Now back, and extend your left foot."

With extreme gentleness, he cradled her in his arms. He was a natural lead, and not even Alejandro's trained touch could rival how sweetly he held her. His movements were surprisingly polished and smooth. Nothing like the gruff man she knew him to be every time he opened his mouth. He was tender with her now, as he'd been in those rare moments when they were intimate or at those chance times when she'd caught him staring at her.

She bit her lower lip. Dredging up those horrible moments in Shane's apartment would do her no good. Still, for a brief second she opened her mouth, willing to let her words flow freely, but she quickly snapped her jaw shut. As much as she wanted to tell him the truth, there was no point. Knowing her luck, it would only make things worse.

His hand slid onto her lower back with care, pulling her from her thoughts.

Shit. She didn't want him to let go. There was no

doubt about it—her body wanted him, needed him as badly as she needed air, water, food. And some part of her heart did, too.

But he didn't want her.

He doesn't want me.

She looked away and repeated the mantra in her head. He'd flat out told her he didn't want her, but apparently her libido and, especially, her heart needed more convincing. She would look like a damn fool if she said anything to try to change his mind.

A small grin spread across his lips. "You know… I hate to admit it, but this isn't so bad."

She looked up to find him staring down at her, and it seemed as if a fire ignited behind his eyes.

"Especially not when it's with you."

His steps slowed, and for several long moments they lingered a hairsbreadth away from moving closer. His intense emerald gaze locked on hers. Handling their situation just wasn't possible. She couldn't let this continue.

She pulled away from him. "We should get back to shifting."

She turned away and folded her arms over her chest, as she tried to hold herself together. If she didn't stop now, she wouldn't be able to control herself; she would want him too much to resist. Having him so close but being unable to have him was pure torture. She wasn't sure how much longer she could take it.

"I've NEVER TORTURED a member of the Fae before, though I'm very excited to play with these iron weapons. It's fun to experiment." Robert examined the hot iron poker. "I think this needs more heat, don't you agree?" He placed the poker tip back into the inferno he'd built. "I'll get this all warmed up for you."

The glowing orange metal pulsated in the dim light of the warehouse. The pathetic woman closed her eyelids.

"Open your eyes," he demanded.

He towered over her as she lay chained to the warehouse floor. The iron shackles around her wrists and ankles slowly peeled away her skin as she shied away from their scalding touch. Oh, how sweet this torture session had been. One of his best yet.

"Now tell me, what is a faerie doing with a pack of werewolves?"

She bit her lower lip.

"I said, what are you doing with the werewolves?"

When she still didn't respond, he carefully nestled the poker against the sensitive skin of her stomach. She writhed as the iron burned another bloody hole into her flesh. The sounds of her screams echoed off the warehouse walls. He savored the sight of the hot iron eating away at her body, the skin peeling back in wavy curls.

He let out a low, feral growl. "Answer my question."

Gasping for air, she stammered to reply. "I'm

just an affiliate. I'm the only faerie in the area, so Frankie let me join the pack to be around other supernaturals."

A devilish grin spread across his face as he twirled the poker in his hands. "That's better."

She gritted her teeth and stared at the weapon, shivering. Her terror got him off. He let the blazing iron linger over her, promising repeated pain if she didn't cooperate.

He reexamined the tip of the poker. A small piece of burned flesh remained. Perfect. This was coming along nicely. He stoked the fire. "So you know Frankie personally, yet she hasn't come after you?"

Despite the shackles holding her in place, her hands clenched into fists. He grinned. He would make sure every ounce of fight she had in her was gone before he was through with her.

"Over twenty-four hours, yet she still isn't here. You must not be very important to her."

"You're lucky Frankie *isn't* here. She'd rip you to pieces."

He smiled. "I beg to differ. The last time the bitch and I met, I gave her a lovely beating."

"You're a sick freak."

He ignored her comment as he fiddled with the poker, admiring the glowing end as if it were a rare piece of art. "I guess she hasn't gotten my message. Perhaps I'll have to go with a more direct route. If

Frankie won't come for you, I may have to bring her here myself."

Robert set down the poker and walked toward the exit.

"What do you want with her anyway?" she yelled.

As he reached the door, he turned and grinned. "Isn't it obvious? I'm not after your packmaster." He pushed open the exit door. "I want the hunter who's protecting her."

DAVID CHARGED THROUGH the doors of K9's, ignoring the pain in his leg as his heart pounded in his chest. Despite the cold, sweat poured down his back from the heat of his rage.

Frankie was standing on the platform in the middle of the room, Jace crouching beside her like he was some sort of animal.

"What the hell did you do?" David demanded as he reached the edge of the stage.

Jace looked toward him. "David, what's up? Are—"

David turned on Frankie as he fought for control. "What did you do? Where is she?"

Jace stood and grabbed David's shoulder. "Whoa, David. Back off. Where's who?"

David snarled, a noise that seemed far too animal to belong to him. "Maybe you'd know if you answered your phone. Allsún's missing, and it's your fucking fault." He jabbed a finger at Frankie.

Her eyes widened. "Allsún O'Hare?"

David glared. The anger coursing through him was white-hot. He would murder that bastard Robert. He would tear him limb from limb. He would gouge out Robert's eyes with his thumbs for even looking at her.

"What happened?" Frankie's jaw fell open.

"That's what I want to know." David stepped toward her. "Why was there a message to you on the wall of her demolished apartment—written in blood?"

All the color drained from Frankie's face until her skin looked ashen. "I don't know where she is, David. I had nothing to do with this."

"I swear, if I find out you caused this, I'll force you to shift and then skin you for your—"

"David!" Jace grabbed him by the front of his jacket. "Frankie's been with me the whole time. She didn't do this. It's Robert, and you know it. It's Robert, man. It's not Frankie's fault."

David panted hard, each breath so heavy it strained the leather of his jacket.

"We'll get her back, David," Jace promised.

"I'll call Alejandro. I'll have him gather the pack. We need to select who'll go after her—our best fighters. And we'll need to find out where she's been taken," Frankie said. She met David's eyes. "We *will* find her, David. Faerie or not, she's been one of us for a long time."

"I will *not* wait around while you decide who is going to save her," David growled, turning his anger on Jace. He stared down into his fellow hunter's face. "If it wasn't for you and your damn werewolf shit, I could go save her myself. But now look at me!" he yelled. "Between my fucking leg and the fact that Damon's marked us both as traitors, I can't even fucking save the woman I love, all because I had to try and help your sorry ass."

If Jace were angry, he didn't show it. He stepped back, though he clearly wasn't intimidated. "I know. I shouldn't have drawn anyone else into this, and I never should have let you fight my battles for me. It's my fault your leg is fucked to hell and back, and I'd take it back if I could, but I can't. I promise you I will save her, David. I swear it." He met David's gaze head on.

David snarled. "That's not good enough. We have to do something *now*. Whether you like it or not, I will *not* sit around while he has her."

He turned his back on Jace and began to walk away.

"David, if you go after her now, you'll get her killed," Jace said.

David stopped in his tracks but didn't look over his shoulder. He heard Jace step toward him.

"If you go in there injured like you are, you're both going to be killed, and how will that solve anything?"

David's whole body trembled as he fought down the rage growing inside his chest.

Jace placed a hand on his shoulder and squeezed. "I swear to you on my life, I'll get her back. But you know we can't go out unprepared."

David's hands clenched into fists. Jace was right, and he knew it, but his anger refused to subside. He should have been able to save her. He should have been able to track that fucker down right now, and murder him slowly and painfully. A loud, angry scream sounded in the air, and it took David several seconds to realize it was his own.

CHAPTER THIRTEEN

FRANKIE PACED AROUND the platform with her cell phone at her ear. The ringing seemed to echo on a never-ending loop. Finally an automated female voice instructed her to leave a message at the beep.

She growled into the receiver. "Pick up your phone, Alejandro." She hoped he heard her on his answering machine.

A small beep sounded. "Hello?"

"Allsún O'Hare's been kidnapped."

Alejandro cursed under his breath. "Do you want me to assemble everyone?"

"Yes. You know the drill." Without another word, she hung up the phone, then turned back toward David and Jace. "They'll be here within forty-five minutes."

Her heart dropped into the pit of her stomach as she watched David clutch his head and squeeze. She swallowed past the lump in her throat. "I'm sorry, David. Jace is right. We'll get her back. I swear."

He circled the platform, swearing and cursing under his breath like a madman. So this was the man Allsún loved. Not long after she'd first encountered the petite, half-blooded faerie and agreed to let her into the Rochester pack as an associate, Allsún had confided in her about how she was running from a relationship, a healthy, good relationship that she was convinced she would destroy.

Frankie thought of Allsún's face: the sweet smile that rarely left her lips and her pixie attitude. Allsún was a fighter, but when Frankie imagined her in Robert's clutches, she nearly vomited all over the floor.

The time that passed before the pack assembled stretched on for what seemed like days. With each passing second, the dread in Frankie's chest built and her sympathy for David deepened.

At one point she leaned up to Jace's ear to whisper, "Jace, is he going to be okay?"

They turned together to watch David continuing to pace the room, despite his injured leg, as if he could wear a hole in the ground that would lead him to Allsún.

Jace shrugged. "He's in love with her. Always has been. He'll do anything to save her." He looked Frankie in the eyes. "He won't be okay until she's safe again."

When all of the pack members finally arrived, Frankie stood in the middle of the platform with her head held high but her morale quickly sinking. She should have expected Robert to come after the people who mattered to her and kept a closer eye on

her pack members. She should have made sure that
even the strongest females were escorted by men or
moved in groups. She'd shirked her duties as packmaster, and now Allsún was paying the price.

Once the pack quieted down, she launched head-
first into the problem.

"Allsún O'Hare has been kidnapped."

A roar of angry conversation erupted among the
crowd. She held up her hand to try to silence them.

"We need to move in and locate her, and we need
to do it fast. From what we know, she's been missing
since the night of the pack meeting." She paused to
gauge everyone's reaction. The faces staring back
at her were a mixed bag of emotions, but there was
one common denominator: they were all eager to
retrieve Allsún.

"I know it's custom to vote on which warrior will
save her, but I think this case calls for special cir-
cumstances." She fought hard not to show any sign of
weakness. "As we discussed before, Jace is the only
one of us who has any possibility of destroying this
bastard, because this killer isn't just a normal werewolf, he's something else. We've already approved
Jace to hunt him down, so now let's approve him to
save Allsún in the process."

Small murmurs cropped up around the room,
mostly among her warriors, the highest-ranking
males. After briefly conferring with several of them,
Alejandro stepped up to the stage.

"If you expect us to let a non-pack member do our job, then he needs to prove himself. He needs to show us that he's stronger than all our warriors."

A loud growl sounded as David climbed laboriously onto the platform. "That's a waste of time. We should be out looking for her right now. A whole search party could be out there if we weren't too busy standing here scratching our heads like a bunch of dumb-asses."

Alejandro frowned. "It's pack policy. Only one male and one female will go, so we don't risk multiple members for the sake of one. Frankie is the strongest female here, no one doubts that, so it's a given that she should go, but Jace is not a member of this pack. He's a temporary ornament."

David's mouth tightened into a thin line and a look of anger crossed his face. His temper visibly shot up. Frankie interrupted before he said something that turned the pack against him.

"Let's also remember that Allsún is an associate member of the pack. That means only some of the pack rules apply to her."

Alejandro shook his head. "True, but this rule stands firm whether she's a full pack member or not—one male, one female, to retrieve her."

Frankie's hands balled into fists at her sides. "Alejandro, you're combating my every move just because I—"

"I'll do it," Jace said.

Everyone looked at him.

"I'll pass your little challenge and beat all your asses to a bloody pulp if that's what it takes to save Allsún."

Alejandro met Jace in the middle of the platform, and the two men stood face-to-face.

"You'll fight my warriors and you'll fight me, and you'll prove you're as strong as we are?" He leaned in so close to Jace's face that their noses nearly touched. "You'll prove you can shift *and* fight?"

Jace matched Alejandro's glare. "You bet."

From the confident tone in Jace's voice and the way he stared Alejandro directly in the eye, if Frankie hadn't known better, she would have thought he had shifted a thousand times before. He didn't even blink as he stared Alejandro down.

But she knew the truth. Jace had scraped the surface of shifting with the slight transformation of his hand, but he was nowhere near ready to shift into complete wolf form. And even without being aware of the specifics, Alejandro had to know that Jace couldn't yet match the skills of a seasoned warrior when it came to transforming. He'd set up Jace for a battle he couldn't possibly win.

She grabbed Alejandro by the elbow and tugged him away.

"We need to talk *now,*" she whispered to him. Then she released him and stepped back to address the crowd. "I want eyes and ears on the street, everyone trying to figure out where this bastard has gone to ground with Allsún. Use every available resource." Stepping off the stage, she gestured for Alejandro to follow her as the crowd began to disperse. It took every ounce of restraint in her to ignore David's furious screams of dissent.

AFTER BRIEFLY ATTEMPTING to calm David down and realizing it was a battle he couldn't win, Jace followed Frankie and Alejandro the Prick out of the main room of the club. The two strode down a nearby hallway until they reached an office at the end, the sounds of David's curses still carrying from the main room. The man wouldn't rest until they'd found Allsún, and Jace couldn't blame him for being furious at the delay, but he couldn't focus on David's rage right now. Not when he needed to beat Alejandro in order to save David's woman.

Frankie threw open the door to the office and marched inside, with Alejandro close on her heels. When the door shut, Jace jogged the length of the hallway and pinned his ear against the wood. He needed any advantage he could get, and listening in on the conversation would provide more information than he would be getting out there with David.

Frankie's voice carried through the closed door. "What's your problem, Alejandro? Ever since I got back, you've been trying to block my every move.

You're my head warrior. How do you think that makes me look to the rest of the pack?"

"No worse than you made yourself look."

Jace's jaw clenched. He already he wanted to march in there and teach Alejandro how to respect his leader.

He felt pressure on the door and realized that one of them was leaning against the wood.

"What the hell does that mean?" The pitch of Frankie's voice escalated. She was pissed. Royally pissed. Jace smiled. He hoped Princess hit the asshole where it hurt.

Alejandro scoffed. "What? Do you think no one noticed that you disappeared just in time to miss our mating ceremony?"

Jace heard a low growl, and he wasn't sure whether it was Frankie or Alejandro—or maybe both.

"He took me captive, Alejandro."

"Yes, but for how long? How long before you switched allegiances? Because you brought him into our home as if he were one of us."

Frankie let out a loud huff, and he could hear her walking away from the door. "He *is* one of us, and you know it."

Alejandro banged his fist on what was probably a desk. "He *hunts* our kind, Frankie. He's not one of us."

Jace pressed his ear closer to the wood, listening

hard. Who ever told that bastard he could talk to a woman that way—and his leader, for God's sake?

Frankie's voice escalated to the point of yelling. "He's our only hope of finding and beating this sadistic son of a bitch. You weren't there. I've seen what this sicko can do, and Jace is the only one of us who even stands a chance against the guy. We need him." Her breathing was audible by then. Alejandro was pushing every button Princess had, and like a bomb, she was about to detonate.

"*We* need him? Or *you* need him?"

"What's that supposed to mean?" Her tone was filled with venom.

"You were with him the night of your mating cycle, Frankie. The night you were supposed to be married to me, and he held you captive. Do you mean to tell me that he resisted the Call and that you didn't sleep with him before you returned? Or were you lying when you told Marshall that you and Jace had mated?"

A long moment of silence passed before Frankie answered. "That's none of your damn business," she said in a tone that would have frozen lava in its tracks.

Alejandro raised his voice to match Frankie's in volume. "Like hell it's none of my business. You stand me up at the altar and then bring a hunter home with you to join the pack, and you think it's none of my business? You've been my arranged mate since we were children."

"Exactly, Alejandro," Frankie said. "*Arranged.* Do you understand that word? Arranged, meaning it was set up. I never wanted to be with you. I never *chose* to be with you."

"So because you neglected your duties as packmaster and chose not to mate with the designated warrior, the highest-ranking warrior, I must pay the consequences? *I* must find a different mate than the one I've been waiting on before I even became a warrior? Is that what you're saying?"

Frankie's words were garbled, as if she were holding back tears. "What do you want from me, Alejandro? I can't give you what you want. You're my friend—a very dear friend, despite the fact that you've been acting like a complete asshole lately—and you know I love you." She paused. "But I'm not *in* love with you."

A long silence passed, and even through the door, Jace felt the heavy tension in the air. For a moment he wasn't sure who he pitied more.

"I will act as your mate, even though I'm already bound to Jace—if that's what you want from me," Frankie said.

Jace stopped breathing, waiting for her next words.

"But you deserve a better mate than that, and I think you know it."

Jace exhaled the breath he hadn't planned on holding.

"I don't want any other woman, but I won't force you to be with me. I'd rather be alone. But what about you? If not me, who will your mate be? It can't be the hunter, even if he is bonded to you now. As soon as this is over, he'll resume his job, Frankie."

After a long silence she finally answered, her voice barely above a whisper. "He was there during the Call. I don't know if it…worked or not. I think the mating was one-sided."

Jace's stomach flipped. She didn't want him?

A mix of anger and frustration filled him. He'd managed to get himself hung up on a female werewolf. A sharp pain hit his heart like a Mack truck, and he thought of the warm feeling that shot through his veins whenever he saw Princess.

It took every ounce of control he had not to punch his fist through the wall. Mother Nature had tricked his darker side into a mating ritual he'd never wanted, and all he got was a damn T-shirt that read *Mated Moron*. A woman he couldn't stop thinking about who didn't want him for a mate—he *was* screwed.

He forced his anger inside and tuned back in to the conversation.

"Please, tell me you'll be reasonable and call off this challenge, then," Frankie said.

"No. He needs to prove himself worthy. If he proves himself, he's fit to be your mate and he can be the one to go after Allsún. Though either way, you know he won't stay once this is over."

She groaned in frustration. "But you set him up. You know there's no way he'll be able to shift quickly enough to win."

"Let your mate fight his own battles. He accepted the challenge."

Jace could practically see the smug look on Alejandro's damn face.

He heard Frankie stride to the door and grip the knob, and he quickly moved down the hallway to escape notice, but not before he heard her stick it to Alejandro.

"I hope you know that when you can't kill Robert, the blood of all the women he killed and all the women he *will* kill will be on your hands. You need Jace. You're just not man enough to admit it."

JACE WALKED INTO the shambles of his apartment. The door lay splintered in large pieces from the hallway all the way to the kitchen, left over from the fight. The screws from the hinges had scattered across the floor, and dried blood dirtied the floors. The place looked like shit. Not that he'd expected anything different. The super was too lazy to get off his couch unless someone dragged him off. In this building, if you wanted something done you had to do it yourself.

Jace stalked through the apartment. He checked the closets, the shower and underneath the bed.

Damon, Ash and Trent were long gone. Good riddance…at least when it came to Damon. Ash and Trent were—or had been—his comrades, maybe even his friends.

After wandering into the kitchen, he slumped against the bottom cabinets by the sink. He reached into the brown paper bag, courtesy of the Lucky Bastard, and removed his last bottle of Bushmills. He held it up to the light as he examined its contents. Just great. Already down to the halfway point. He unscrewed the cap and started gulping the liquor. A warm, tingling coated his throat as the alcohol slid down.

The new cell phone Shane had given him vibrated in his pocket. He set down his bottle on the hardwood with a loud thunk before he pulled the electronic piece of shit out of his pocket.

"Hello?"

A desperate voice sounded from the other side of the line. "Jace, we have a problem."

Jace lowered the phone from his ear and glanced at the screen. "Shane?"

"Yeah, it's me."

"You sound awful." The kid sounded like someone had drained him of all his energy.

A moment of silence passed, and then Shane let out a long sigh. "I've barely slept in days. I've been too busy deterring them."

Jace pushed the Bushmills aside. Now Shane had his attention. "Deterring who?"

"Damon and the rest of the Execution Underground."

"You've gotta be kidding me. Why the hell haven't you said something before now?"

"David told me not to tell you. He said you wouldn't want me involved but that you needed me. He wanted you to concentrate on learning how to shift and taking down the killer, so he said to keep my mouth shut and make sure they didn't get to you."

Jace cursed under his breath. "Why are you telling me this now, Shane?"

"Don't go back to the hotel." There was a hint of pleading in the kid's voice.

"Why the hell not?"

Shane paused for a moment, as if he wasn't certain he wanted to say the words out loud. "They've found it."

Jace sat forward, his whole body suddenly alert. "What? How did they—"

"I know you're at your apartment getting drunk right now, but you need to get out of there, too. I doubt they'll go back there again, but you don't want to take a chance. Meanwhile they're ransacking your hotel room as we speak," Shane said.

"Shit."

"Find somewhere to hide out, a location they won't think to check for you."

Jace wracked his brain for somewhere to crash. Damn. Only one place came to mind. "All right. Thanks for the information. I'll find somewhere. Call me if there's any news." He went to hang up the phone, but paused. He lifted the cell to his ear again. "Oh, and, Shane, how the hell did you know I was in my apartment drinking?"

"I put in a camera. Damon wanted it so I could tell them if you came back—like that was ever going to happen."

Jace scanned the room for a camera but didn't see anything. "Yeah, okay. Thanks again." He pressed the off button and pocketed the phone. He grabbed his bottle off the floor and stood, then walked down the stairs and headed straight for the H3. He revved the engine and death-gripped the steering wheel as he peeled out onto the street. He lodged the Bushmills bottle conveniently between the driver's seat and the console. He had a feeling he was going to need it later.

Damn it. All this was his fault. He banged his fist against the steering wheel. The conflict with the Execution Underground, his inability to shift, the fight he'd agreed to with Alejandro, and now he was permanently stuck with a mate who didn't want him. He thought of his name being carved into those poor victims' forearms. Robert had killed those girls to get his attention.

Why was that bastard after him? Jace tried to

think of whether he'd ever met or even seen Robert, some reason why the man was out for his blood.

Nothing.

Damn. All this shit traced back to him somehow, he just had to figure out how.

He pulled over to the side of the road and parked. As far as he could see, he had two options. One: spend the whole night trying to shift and fail. Or two: drown himself in Bushmills and hope shit turned out in his favor.

"Oh, fuck it." He hit the bottle and hoped for the best.

FRANKIE WAS WRENCHED awake from her deep sleep by a loud banging sound reverberating through her apartment and rattling her skull. The door. Someone was pounding on her door. Pushing off the sheets, she stumbled out of bed and across the wooden floor. She grabbed a black silk robe off her closet knob and slipped it on, covering her blue satin nightie. She clutched the material and looked through the peephole. A large dark figure was standing on the other side of the door.

"Hey, Princess. Open up," the man said.

"Jace?" She hadn't expected to see him until the fight, especially once Shane had told her not to go to the hotel. She'd thought staying at her own place again would give her a temporary break from the constant heartache when he was near. She inched open the door, making sure the safety latch was in place.

He staggered forward, his full weight slamming into the door frame.

"Holy crap. Jace, are you okay?"

She undid the chain and threw open the door. Jace stumbled through, a nearly empty bottle of Bushmills in his hand. His green eyes were bloodshot, with dark bags underneath. He looked as if he'd been up all night.

"I never should have picked you up in that damn alley." He slurred his words together until they became an unintelligible mumble. He made the shape of a gun with his thumb and forefinger. "Boom. Done for. Would've been easy."

"Jace, are you drunk?"

"But no, I had to be a fucking moron."

"That's what you're being right now." Anger coursed through her veins.

"And look what happened. Look what happened." He laughed bitterly and stumbled.

Frankie slipped underneath his arm in a futile attempt to support him. He was easily twice her size, and she groaned beneath his weight. "Okay, buddy. Let's get you sobered up. Thank God for supernatural metabolism. At least you'll burn it off quick." She dragged him into the bathroom and toward the shower.

"And why are you doing this, huh? Because you're a good fucking person, that's why."

Trying to ignore his drunken words, she pushed him into the shower and helped lower him to the floor. "Take off your clothes," she said.

He did as he was told. He fumbled with his coat and shirt until he managed to remove them.

She threw them onto the floor outside the shower, along with her robe. Then she reached carefully for the faucet, trying not to get her nightie wet. Cold water spewed from the shower head and hit Jace's half-naked body.

He cursed and wiped the water from his eyes. "I don't deserve you," he mumbled.

"What did you say?" Her breath caught. She knew what he'd said, but she couldn't comprehend it.

He blinked several times as the cold water slapped him in the face. "I said I don't deserve you."

Her throat tightened.

"Taking you captive was the biggest mistake I've ever made, but I wouldn't change it even if I could," he went on. "I never wanted to have feelings for you." He met her eyes with a look that was half joy, half agony. "But I do."

Before Frankie knew what she was doing, she was kneeling in the shower, the cold water pouring over her body as Jace cradled her face in his hands. A fire ignited in her veins, and she pressed closer to him.

He kissed her so deeply, her world spun. His fingers tangled in her hair as his warm tongue moved against hers. The bittersweet taste of whiskey and his natural flavor filled her mouth in an intoxicating blend. His hands trailed from her hair down her spine. His palms settled on her lower back, and he slowly pulled at the soaked fabric of her nightgown.

She gasped against his lips. Palming her ass, he slipped his fingers under the edge of her panties. A wave of heat spread between her legs, and she trailed kisses across his cheek. She sucked on his earlobe, her teeth gently grazing the skin. A low growl escaped his throat, and a fresh wave of heat flooded between her thighs as Jace rubbed his palm against her most sensitive flesh.

He kissed her collarbone. "I have to be inside you," he said. "Now."

Lifting her with him as he stood, Jace pressed her against the wall.

"I've wanted to take you every second since we were last together." He kissed her hard and sucked on her bottom lip.

She moaned and wrapped her arms around his neck.

He pulled away. A slow smile spread across his face while he fingered the edge of her nightgown. "I'm going to rip this."

She barely had time to grin back at him before he kept his promise and her nightgown fell to the tile in wet shreds. As he held her in place, he claimed her breast with his mouth. He ran his tongue over her breast, and she melted into him.

Her nipples hardened, and she pushed her chest against him. He flicked his tongue over her nipples, then slowed to swirl over them. Her breath caught. Hoisting her into position, he held her steady as she unbuckled his belt. She stripped his jeans out of the way, and they hit the floor as he positioned himself outside her entrance, agonizingly close to claiming her.

"All I want is to pleasure you," he groaned. "I'll make you mine right now, if that's what you want. But only if you want me."

There was something vulnerable in his voice, almost a plea, and she knew he was remembering the time at Shane's when she'd pushed him away. It had been a misunderstanding, a miscommunication, but he didn't know that. And rather than take her now while she was wet and ready and already wrapped around him, he still stopped to ask. Was it any wonder she'd fallen so hard for this man?

"Frankie?"

She wanted to tell him she was already his, tell him that he had been at the center of her thoughts since his body lay flush against hers in the alley, but all she could do was nod.

He sheathed himself inside her in one stroke, and she cried out. He rocked—slow thrusts that left her begging for more. He was a gift from the heavens.

Running her hands over his shoulders, she quivered, barely holding herself together.

Warmth pulsed through her body. He slowed down, then worked his way from slow movements into a steady pace that caressed her deeply, thoroughly. She buried her hands in his wet hair.

"I want to make love to you," he whispered, abruptly stopping. He looked around the shower, frowning. "Can I take you to the bedroom?"

She kissed him hard, and apparently that was the only response he needed. He lifted her against his chest and carried her from the shower. Pulling a single towel off the rack, he stumbled out of the bathroom as he held her in his arms, exploring her tongue with his own. When he reached the edge of her bed, he lowered her until she stood in front of him. His eyes roamed over the curves of her body, and though she knew she should have been cold, her skin burned hot from his gaze.

He ran the towel over her shoulders in slow circular motions. He was gentle and strong as he dried her off. She sighed as he reached her breasts, kneading them through the fabric. He knelt and kissed his way down her body to her navel, until his cheek rested just above her mons. He caressed the insides of her thighs before he ran his tongue over her pink slit. He kissed her there, exploring and exposing her every weakness, lavishing her with attention over and over again. When her legs could no longer support her, he followed her onto the bed, smiling as if he'd been the one to receive all the pleasure.

She reached for him, urging him to join their bodies together.

He hesitated for a moment, then settled atop her and buried his face against her neck.

"Jace," she panted as he thrust into her.

He drew back, and their eyes locked.

Frankie watched as his irises slowly transitioned from emerald to liquid gold—the gold of a wolf's eyes. Her heart jumped, and an invisible pull tugged at every inch of her being. She knew she was being ridiculous, but she couldn't help thinking that he'd been her destined mate from the moment she'd first seen him.

"I love you, Jace." The words slipped out before she could stop herself.

A blazing fire lit his eyes. He pounded into her at a fevered pace. In a blast of sweet warmth, he found his release, sending her over the edge until she found her own. She moaned as she rode him through her climax. Without a word, he covered her mouth with his lips and kissed her hard.

CHAPTER FOURTEEN

JACE'S STOMACH FLIPPED. Bile burned at the back of his throat, but it wasn't from the alcohol. He pulled away from their kiss and buried his head in the crook of Frankie's neck. His heart pounded, each beat hard and sharp, like the blow of an ice pick.

Love? She loved him?

He opened his mouth several times in an attempt to say he felt the same way, but the words refused to emerge.

Trying to push the thought from his mind, he focused on making love to her. He couldn't wait to slip inside her and find sweet release again.

Making love? Did he love her?

He gritted his teeth. Shit. He couldn't escape the truth.

She wrapped her legs around him and squirmed until they rolled across the bed and she ended up on top. Straddling his hips, she pushed her chest against his and pecked kisses across his face, first his mouth and nose, then his cheeks and forehead—sweet, playful kisses that sent chills down his spine and a steady ache through his heart.

Was this it? He cared for Frankie, but was this what it was like to love someone? His only point of reference was his mother, but the experience didn't transfer. How could he know, if he'd never been in love before?

Sure, he'd had loads of women, enough to give a few rock stars a run for their money, but he'd never been close to any of them, never felt the need for ongoing companionship. The only companions he ever had in his pathetic life were his Mateba, his Marlboros and the bottle. What a fucking fabulous existence.

Frankie pulled away from their embrace. Her gorgeous ebony hair fell into her face and danced around her shoulders. He licked his lips. Damn, he was hooked. She was the most beautiful woman he'd ever laid eyes on, and there she was, watching him with that dark, doe-eyed stare.

But she was a werewolf—the embodiment of everything he'd hated about his childhood, everything he hated about himself.

"Jace, what's wrong?"

He swallowed down the lump lodged in his esophagus. How could he tell her that he wasn't sure if he loved her? He wracked his brain for the first thing that came to mind, the only other problem scratching inside his skull. "What if I fuck up tomorrow? I can't afford to lose the fight, but I can't shift worth shit and we both know it. One paw. What good is that?"

She gave a short laugh. "My, what a way with words you have. You've got a mouth worse than a whole crew of sailors."

"Unless my mouth is dirty enough that I can bite Alejandro and give him an infectious disease that kills within minutes, it will get me absolutely no-where." A smile crept across his face. "Except maybe between your legs, of course."

She laughed and shoved at his shoulders. "How can you expect me to think you're seriously worried when you come up with things like that?"

"Whoever said smart-asses can't be worried?" He reached out and ran his hand over the feminine curve of her hips. At the feel of his touch, she let out a long sigh.

When he finished feeling her silky skin beneath his fingertips, he rested his hands on her spine. She leaned down next to his face and licked her way across his mouth, laughingly avoiding his attempts to turn her teasing into a kiss.

His dick jerked, and he groaned at the electricity pulsing through his body. He rolled her over so that he lay on top again, and she squealed in excitement. Damn, this was more intimate than he'd planned for. He leaned in to kiss her, but she placed her hand on his cheek and stopped him.

"Don't worry about tomorrow. Even at your

worst—" she eyed him up and down "—even when you're intoxicated and horny, and feeling as if you're entitled to show up on the doorstep of any helpless female you choose…in my opinion—" she ran her hands down his chest "—you're still the strongest man I know."

Without warning, he kissed her, invading her with his tongue and claiming her. It was as if someone flicked on a switch in his brain. Despite his worries about the next day, all he could think about was her. He wanted all of her, every inch. Fighting his frustrations, he prayed to God he didn't screw up and hurt her.

If he hadn't already been drowning his sorrows, her kiss would have been enough to leave him drunk.

JACE WALKED INTO K9's with his head pounding and a constricting pressure in his chest. His stomach rolled as he stared at the already assembled crowd.

Damn, he hated hangovers.

Frankie stayed by his side as they approached the platform, while David followed just behind. The chatter of eager voices echoed through the room. A large, bulky man lingered beside the platform. He crossed his arms over his chest, and his bald head gleamed in the light. His piercing gray gaze fell on Jace.

Frankie nodded to him.

Without any response, the man climbed onto the stage.

Frankie leaned over and spoke into Jace's ear. "That's Alexei," she whispered. "He's Russian. He's a shifter—a snow leopard."

Jace eyed the man. "What's he doing here?"

She followed Jace's stare and watched Alexei hush the crowd. "He's impartial. He's not a member of our pack, so he's judging the fight."

Jace stripped off his coat and handed it to David. "If he's not a member of the pack, how do you know him?"

Frankie shrugged. "My salsa class. He's one of my best students."

David almost laughed. It was the first smile Jace had seen him crack since Allsún went missing. "You've gotta be kidding me. That big muscled badass is a dancer? I didn't realize that Alejandro wasn't the only male shifter with a feminine side." David slapped Jace on the back. "Just remember that when you're kicking Alejandro's ass, J." He placed a hand on Jace's shoulder and squeezed. "You better win this, or I'll kill you."

Jace gave him a single nod.

"Ladies and gentlemen," Alexei yelled in his thick Russian accent. "We gather tonight to settle a dispute between your warriors—" cheers sounded from the crowd "—and a werewolf hunter."

The cheers turned to boos.

"I ask now that one warrior step forward."

Alejandro stepped onto the platform, his eyes trained on Jace and blazing with an angry fire. He was buck naked and already prepared to shift.

"And now, the hunter."

Jace inhaled a deep breath. He pulled off his shirt and tossed it to Frankie before he climbed onto the platform.

When he reached the stage, the air filled with palpable tension. The weight of at least two hundred and fifty eyes fell on his shoulders.

Alexei stepped in between them. "Are you prepared to fight to the death?"

Jace's body went rigid. "What?"

"No!" Frankie yelled. She leapt onto the platform. "No."

"Stay back," Alexei growled.

She stared him straight in the eye and returned the aggression. "Stop this. *Now.*"

Alexei shook his head. "The ritual has already begun. I cannot stop it."

Frankie stepped forward until she was nearly nose-to-nose with the large man. "I'm the leader of this pack, and I say this ends *now.*"

"I can't end it, Frankie." He met her eyes. "Your hunter agreed to this."

"He didn't agree on a match to the death."

"He did, packmaster." Alejandro straightened from his fighting stance. "Pack rules state that any sanctioned fight between a pack member and a non-member will be to the death."

"That was a dirty trick." The anger that rolled off Frankie aroused all of Jace's primal instincts. The hair on the back of his neck stood on end, and he couldn't believe that goose bumps prickled across his arms. Damn. Princess had *cojones*.

"The Alejandro I *used to be* friends with wouldn't do that. My head warrior wouldn't be so despicable." Frankie marched right up to Alejandro and stabbed him in the chest with her finger. "I hope he kills you, Alejandro Miguel Diaz," she said coldly, "because you're already dead to me."

She turned and walked off the platform, disappearing into the crowd.

The whispers erupted again, until Alexei spoke. "Prepare yourselves," he said.

Alejandro dropped back into a fighting stance, and Jace did the same.

Alexei backed up to the edge of the platform. He crossed his arms over his chest once again and nodded. "Begin."

Alejandro charged at Jace full speed, hitting him under his arms in an attempt to tackle him. Jace used Alejandro's own weight against him and sent him stumbling across the stage.

When he regained his balance, Alejandro turned and threw his first punch. Jace dodged, but another punch came toward his face immediately. He blocked Alejandro's arm and tried to sweep him to the ground, but Alejandro wasn't having it. He bent under Jace's weight and dragged Jace down with him.

They rolled on the floor, until Alejandro pinned Jace to the ground. He punched again, this time aiming for Jace's jaw. Jace twisted his head in time for Alejandro to slam his fist into the platform. The warrior let out a loud yelp.

Grabbing hold of Alejandro's injured wrist, Jace grasped his fingers and twisted them in the opposite direction. The bastard crumpled and fell, completely under Jace's control. Jace slipped out from underneath him and pinned the werewolf to the ground.

Alejandro bucked against him, trying to throw him off. "Aren't you man enough to fight?" he said as he strained against Jace. "Or can you only block my moves?"

Jace ground his weight against his opponent, needing to keep Alejandro pinned down, and let out a low feral growl. "Don't push me, asshole."

"Or what? You'll finally hit me?"

Jace slammed his palm into the bastard's throat, then held tight, slowly crushing his windpipe. He could feel Alejandro's veins pulse beneath this hand as the man gasped for air. "Don't make me do this. Agree to let me go after Allsún and I won't kill you."

Alejandro's face reddened as he fought for air, but he gritted his teeth and shook his head.

"Have it your way, then." Jace's hold tightened.

"Don't! Please!" a woman yelled from the crowd.

Jace looked up, but the voice wasn't Frankie's. A petite blonde was running toward the edge of the stage, and that moment of distraction was all it took. Jace glanced back down at Alejandro, only to rear back. Fur had sprouted across Alejandro's skin, and his face had lengthened into the snout of a wolf.

Jace scrambled off Alejandro just in time for the wolf to flash his fangs.

Shit.

The wolf rose onto its feet and crouched, ready to spring. Jace backed to the edge of the platform.

"Jace, concentrate." Frankie's voice rang in his ears, and a surge of adrenaline shot through him.

The wolf snarled as it bounded toward him. Jace focused on the anger rising up inside him. Alejandro hit him square in the chest and knocked him to the ground. They rolled around on the platform in a snarling heap. Alejandro scratched his paws across Jace's face. A sting of pain shot through Jace's cheek, and a warm trickle cued him in: Alejandro had been the first to draw blood.

As far as Jace was concerned, it was practically an invitation. He punched the wolf in the jaw. Yelping, the werewolf reared back. A snarl ripped from its throat. Jace howled in pain as the animal sank its canines into the flesh of his shoulder. Blood poured down Jace's chest.

The wolf released his shoulder and prepared to strike again, like a venomous snake. Jace shoved against Alejandro's neck and focused all his energy into shifting as he stared into the wolf's golden eyes. He felt the beast stir inside him, and a grin spread across his face.

Jace grabbed the wolf by the scruff of his neck and threw him off. Alejandro skidded across the stage; his back legs fell off the platform, and he desperately clawed his way back up. But Jace was already on his feet. He crouched into a low stance and focused on the feeling inside him. He felt the beast stir again, and he latched onto the feeling in a desperate attempt to draw it out.

Alejandro ran toward him, fangs bared and covered in blood.

All the muscles in Jace's body strained. He clenched his fists. He could feel it. It was working. He let out a ragged yell. A surge of power pulsed through him as Alejandro dove for him.

The energy pulsed through Jace's veins. Then everything faded to black.

FRANKIE STUMBLED BACK as a pulse of blue light and energy hit her full force. Screams and yelps echoed through her ears. She nearly hit the floor but managed to keep her balance. She couldn't tear her eyes from the platform. Her breath caught, and before she knew what she was doing, she was shoving her way through the crowd and running toward the stage.

Jace. She had to get to Jace.

David was at her heels. As the energy dissipated, a number of members of the pack howled and shifted into wolf form. But Frankie could only focus on Jace.

She threw herself down at his side and wrapped her arms around him, but he didn't move. He was kneeling in the middle of the platform, as still as a statue. She distantly heard herself screaming his name.

Lines of blue light gleamed on his body, as if he were covered in glowing tribal tattoos. His eyes had transitioned from their normal emerald green to the gold of a wolf's eyes. He stared toward the sky, unblinking.

She shook him as hard as she could. "Jace, wake up. Jace!"

"Frankie, get off him." David grabbed her arm and pulled.

Another pulse of energy flooded the room, emanating directly from Jace. It hit Frankie hard. Her head fell back, and pain boiled beneath her skin. The familiar feeling of her bones cracking and rearranging overtook her, and she felt herself involuntarily begin to shift. Within seconds she lay on the ground, transformed completely.

Hunkering to the floor, she whimpered. Her eyes darted around the room to the other pack members.

The only human left was David, who couldn't shift. Howls and the sound of keening rang out as they all waited for the next aftershock. She covered her head with her paws to block the sound from her ears.

Another wave of energy shot from Jace's body. He jerked forward and rose onto his knees. Even in wolf form, Frankie stopped breathing.

A replica of the symbol they'd seen in Manhattan Square Park glowed between Jace's shoulder blades. Frankie howled as recognition washed over her.

She knew that mark. She had blocked the memory for the last three years, but now, God help her, she remembered.

JACE'S EYELIDS FLICKERED open onto a haze of shining blue. Slowly he pushed himself off the ground, drinking in his surroundings. It was as if the world had been engulfed in a cerulean haze. He stared and could faintly decipher the outlines around him.

A forest. He was in the middle of a damn forest.

He wracked his brain to remember how he'd gotten there but came up with nothing. What had happened? And why was everything like an amorphous blue shadow?

He listened for some sign of life, but heard nothing except silence.

Where the hell was he?

He stood and scanned the area. A flash of what looked like an animal's tail rounded a nearby tree.

Inching forward, he moved toward the elm and stared into the blue forest. A large wolf was peering around a bush, its eyes beckoning him forward. Like everything else, it looked like nothing but a shadow, an outline of what a real wolf would have been.

Shit. This was all wrong. Either he was dead or dreaming, or he'd swallowed one hell of a dose of LSD.

The animal turned and ducked behind the bush again. An invisible string tugged at Jace's chest, and though his mind briefly protested, he soon found himself trailing behind the wolf. Weaving in and out of the twilight trees, he followed it through the forest.

After what felt like an eternity, the wolf disappeared. Jace stepped forward into the edge of a clearing. He tried to call out, but he couldn't hear his own voice.

No need to use words here. Thoughts are far more valuable on this plane. The voice sounded as if it were coming from inside Jace's head. He spun around. A man stood engulfed in the shadows. He stepped out from the trees and stared Jace in the eyes.

Jace moved his lips, but the words refused to come. *What are you?*

A smile curved the shadow man's lips. *A Skinwalker—a Berserker—as are you.*

The words sounded oddly familiar, but Jace couldn't place where he'd heard them. *A Skinwalker?*

The shadow man stepped forward, and Jace stepped back. *You have no reason to fear me, though your thoughts are right. I* am *more powerful than you.*

Jace dropped into a fighting stance. *What do you want with me?*

The shadow man continued to move forward. *My job is to direct you to the right path. I'm your spirit guide.*

If this had been real life, Jace's jaw would have dropped. Instead, he just stared at the man in front of him. *Spirit guide? You've gotta be fucking with me. What sort of drugs did I take?*

The man frowned, the first human expression Jace had seen him make. *I assure you that I am not "fucking" with you.*

Jace straightened to his full height again. *Then who and what are you?*

The Norse called me Heimdallr, guardian of Bi-fröst—the gateway to what you call heaven—and I'm exactly what you are.

What the hell was going on? Jace closed his eyes, hoping he would wake up. When he reopened them, he found himself still stuck in the blue haze. *I'm not following your thoughts here. What is this place?*

The man beckoned him closer. *Come. Follow me.* The shadow man turned and disappeared into the trees. The same pull Jace had felt with the wolf tugged at his chest again, and he walked forward involuntarily.

The shadow man moved through the forest with ease, as if he knew every tree, every branch. *I'm your spirit guide, Jace—the spirit of the wolf.*

Jace regained control of himself and stopped walking. *Wait, so you* are *the wolf?*

The shadow man turned around and met Jace's gaze. The wolf's eyes stared back at him. *Yes. The wolf and I are one.* Then the man turned into the forest again and wandered deeper into its depths.

Jace never took his eyes off the man in front of him. *Why am I here? What is this place?*

You're in the spirit realm. We are past Midgard, or what you know as Earth. We are near Bifröst, the bridge between your world and the realm of the gods, the holy Asgard, where I make my home.

Jace wanted to curse, but still no words would come out of his mouth. *So I'm dead?*

The shadow man ran his hand down a nearby tree, almost caressing the redwood bark. *No, you still reside among the living, though few are capable of entering our world. You are one of the elite.*

Jace could have scoffed. Elite? *I've never been elite at anything, except maybe killing werewolves.*

The man spun to face him and stepped forward. As tall as Jace was, his spirit guide towered over him. *You are elite in your birthright, not in your profes-*

sion. Killing werewolves is a travesty. You've dishonored your bloodline for many years.

Goose bumps prickled over Jace's skin, but he ignored them. *If you think I have an elite bloodline, you obviously never met my father.*

The shadow man stepped over the shadow of a fallen tree and continued. *Your father chose a dark path and used his gift for his own twisted enjoyment. He was not worthy of the Berserker name.*

The questions flooding into Jace's mind were overwhelming. His thoughts raced. The trees and brush of the forest thinned as they continued forward. Another clearing lay ahead.

When they stepped through the curtain of the trees, Jace's eyes widened. Before him stood seven stone statues, each one three times his height. Each depicted a Viking-like warrior dressed in animal skins. The warrior in the center stood tallest—a spear in his hand, and the pelt of a wolf covering his body and head.

The Berserkers, the shadow man said.

Jace couldn't tear his eyes from the stones. These statues were ancient. *What is a Berserker?*

The shadow man moved closer to the stone replicas. *We are Norse gods—Skinwalkers.*

We? Jace pointed to himself. *No, you're wrong. I'm no god.*

The shadow man stared up at the face of the wolf-skin warrior statue. *You are a Skinwalker by birth-right, a Berserker by fate. A remarkable creation.*

Jace couldn't wrap his head around any of this. *What do you mean? There's nothing remarkable about me. I'm a half-breed werewolf. I'm not good enough for either side.* He remembered what had led up to this. The brawl with his fellow hunters, the fight with Alejandro. *Now both sides are against me.*

Walking toward him, the shadow man examined him carefully. *You are no ordinary werewolf. You are a Skinwalker. You have the ability to shift like the werewolves you hunt, but you are set apart from them. They are wolves at heart, but you are a man, a man with the power of a wolf.* He gestured to the statues, before he continued.

We Skinwalkers can shape-shift, but we're not limited in our choices as the werewolves are. When you come into your full power, you will be capable of channeling the power of any spirit animal you choose. He pointed to the statues again, each man covered in a different animal: the pelts of a wolf, a bear, and a wild dog; the mane of a horse, the skin of a serpent, the feathers of an eagle and finally, the tusks of a boar.

Jace shook his head. This was so messed up. *But why do I have the characteristics of a werewolf?*

You can shift into a wolf because that is where your lineage lies. Your family's spirit guide has al-ways been the spirit of the wolf. The creature swept his arm out toward the wolf-man, the head warrior. *It's time you learned.*

Strolling between the statues, the man ran his shadow fingers over the stone surfaces. *In the time of the Vikings, the Berserkers were an elite group of Norse warriors who devoted themselves to nature. It was their belief that by wearing the pelt of an animal, they could harness the power of the beast they imitated.*

As generations passed, their belief became a reality. They became Skinwalkers. The male descendants of the original bloodlines were capable of shifting form to match their family's heritage, to match their spirit guide. For you, that is the wolf.

Jace glanced at the statue of…his ancestor?

The shadow man continued. *But an even more select group rose above the other Skinwalkers. They became the true descendants of the Berserker warriors, not simply by blood but by merit. You are a Skinwalker, Jace, and it is your fate to become a true Berserker, a god of the ancient Norse people. Someday you will assume your rightful place in Valhalla, the heaven of the fallen warriors.*

Jace wasn't sure how to react. The foundations of everything he knew began to shake and crumble. His full power? He thought of Robert, of the women the bastard had murdered. He had to find a way to beat him. *What do I have to do?*

The shadow man's expression turned even more

serious, almost sad. *In exchange for power, a sacrifice must be made.*

Jace glanced down at himself. A large hole formed where the shadow of his body had once been. His panic rose, but he had to beat Robert. *What kind of sacrifice?* he thought.

You must kill one of the male members of your family. His blood must be shed as a sacrifice to the spirit animals before you can gain your full power.

The shadow man faded into the cerulean shadows, which melted together, blurring until the man's image disappeared into the twilight. But his voice echoed inside Jace's head. *This is your fate, Jace Mc-Cannon. Embrace your abilities and you will conquer your enemies.*

FRANKIE'S HEART POUNDED in her chest, and all her fur stood on end. This couldn't be happening. It couldn't.

A loud howl of pain tore from her throat.

David's gaze snapped toward her. "Frankie, are you okay? Frankie?"

His words barely registered in her mind.

Focusing on the symbol glowing between Jace's shoulder blades, she found herself back *there* again.

The smell of blood permeated the house, and the stench hit Frankie's nose with the force of a freight train. She ran up the stairs and bolted into her parents' bedroom.

There was blood everywhere. So much blood.

The red liquid had splattered across the walls. Frankie dropped to her knees and screamed. Her mother and father lay across their mattress, their bodies limp and tangled in the bedsheets, which were stained garnet from their blood. Their throats... Someone had slit their throats.

Faintly, she heard the sounds of sirens in the distance. Hot tears poured down her face, but her vision didn't blur. Rocking back and forth on her knees, she wrapped her arms around her body and tried to hold herself together. The only sound she heard was her screams, and even when she closed her eyes, the only thing she saw was their dead bodies.

All she could see was the way her mother's arm dangled off the side of the bed, her eyes wide open and her other arm reaching for Frankie's father. Her father hadn't seen it coming. He lay propped on his side, his face staring at the ceiling as if he'd only seen his attacker seconds before his death.

A loud sob tore from her throat as she found herself hoping they'd died quickly, without feeling the pain.

Frankie was too engulfed in her shock and mourning that night to take in the whole scene. She'd been paralyzed with grief. Her parents, their blood and their bodies were all she could remember, and she cursed herself every day for it, for not being able to recall more details for the authorities.

But how many times had she seen the police photos? The pictures of the blood smeared on the walls by human hands. No, not human, someone subhuman and sadistic.

Her eyes refocused, and she stared at the symbol on the skin of the man she loved. The same symbol painted on the wall by her parents' killer.

JACE WAS WRENCHED back into reality with a gasp. He toppled forward, his torso hitting the platform. A pair of large hands gripped his shoulders and lifted him back to his knees.

"Jace, are you okay? Jace?"

Jace's eyes darted around the room. There were wolves everywhere.

David leaned into Jace's line of vision and stared him straight in the face. "J, wake up. Jace, listen to me. Damn it." He mumbled Yiddish curses as he repeatedly shook Jace to rouse him.

Jace clamped his hands onto David's shoulders, still dazed. "Stop shaking me, David."

David stopped, but he kept his hold tight. "Jace, are you okay?" he repeated.

Jace tried to steady himself, using David for balance. Swaying, he leaned on his friend. "What happened?"

"I don't know, J. Alejandro was running for you, and the air started vibrating around you. I thought you were going to shift, but then you fell to your knees. It was like a pulse of energy shot out of you, and it kept coming in shock waves. It stopped Alejandro in his tracks and forced all the pack members to shift into wolf form, even Frankie.

Frankie? Where was she?

"Where is she?"

Jace shot to his feet. The world spun, and David caught him. He slung Jace's arm around his shoulders and acted as his support. As Jace searched the crowd, David lowered him onto the platform again. Jace didn't see her anywhere.

"She's okay, J. I was right there next to her. She's probably just helping someone in the pack."

The air filled with groaning as the members of the pack transitioned into their human form. Shredded clothes covered the floor, destroyed during the transformation.

David grabbed Jace's face with both his hands and forced him to meet his eyes. "Jace, look at me. We need to get you out of here."

David's words melted together as the blood drained from Jace's face and he passed out again.

CHAPTER FIFTEEN

IT TOOK EVERY ounce of strength Jace had in order to crack open his eyes and stare at the ceiling above him. Someone had taken every drop of energy in his body and sucked it out. What the hell had happened to him? He fought to keep his eyes open while he searched his brain.

The blue haze. The wolf. The shadow man. The Berserkers.

Holy shit. He tried to get up but quickly fell back onto the couch where he'd been lying. Damn it. He pushed against the cushions with his elbows. He had to get up.

Where was he? His eyes darted around the room. David's apartment?

Someone touched his shoulder and urged him to stay down. Shane's face swam into view, looming over him. "Don't try getting up. You need to save your strength if you're going to channel your Skinwalker abilities again."

Jace gaped. "How in the hell do you know about—"

"I did some research based on what David told

me about what happened to you and the symbol up on your back," Shane interrupted. "We know what you are, and we know that when you tried to shift, you entered the spirit world instead."

The room spun. Jace covered his face with his hands and tried to steady his breathing. Out of this world. The whole situation was out of this world.

David's voice carried from the other side of the room. "Hang on, J, and I'll help you sit up."

Jace frowned and started trying to get up again.

David limped to Jace's side and supported him. "Don't push it. You need to conserve your energy. You have to enter the spirit world again."

Jace shoved against him. "The hell I do."

David gripped him by the shoulders and held him firmly in place. "Jace, you have to. It's our only chance to beat Robert. To save Allsún." He dug his fingers into Jace's shoulder blades, his frustration clear on his face. He over-enunciated each word. "I will *not* let you fuck this up. If you don't do *everything* in your power to find Allsún, I will personally take a hatchet to your head."

If it were anyone else saying those words, Jace would have punched him to a bloody pulp. Well, if he could have moved without feeling like he was about to topple over, anyway. He examined David's face, and he knew that underneath the anger, his friend was dying to get back the woman he loved. Damn it. He couldn't mess this up. "How will going back to the spirit world help me beat Robert?"

Shane raised his hand as if he were answering a question one of his professors had posed. "I did some research once David described what happened to you, and I found all this information about Norse mythology and Berserkers. Most people believe the Berserkers were an elite class of warriors, but the older beliefs are more relevant here. According to this…" He picked up a large book off the floor.

The aged gold lettering glimmered in the light, spelling something out in a language Jace didn't recognize. Shane flipped through the pages. "Here it is. According to the writer, a Skinwalker must go on a journey with his spirit guide before he can reach his full potential. Then a select few of those Skinwalkers can become Berserker warriors. Is that what happened to you?"

Jace's jaw clenched. He nodded.

Shane began to pace the room, the large book cradled in his arms. "The only problem is, it doesn't describe how you become a Berserker and gain the powers of the gods. That's why you need to go back to the spirit world. You have to find out."

Jace straightened and brushed David away. "I already know what has to be done."

Shane stopped pacing and stared at him with eager eyes, and David leaned forward eagerly.

Jace cleared his throat. "There needs to be a blood

sacrifice of another Skinwalker. I need to kill a male member of my family."

A brief moment of silence passed while Shane and David glanced at each other.

Shane let out a long breath. "Shit. We can't possibly ask you to kill a member of your family."

David scoffed. He pointed a large finger straight at Shane. "Oh, yes we can." Turning toward Jace, his eyes filled with determination; he was ready for a fight. "J, you need to track down that deadbeat father of yours and pay him back for all those years of abuse."

Jace stood slowly and walked across the room. Aside from Frankie, who knew only the bare bones, David was the only one who was aware of his history with his old man. Jace swallowed his anger. "David, I don't know where he is. I don't even know if he's alive. I haven't seen him since I was a kid."

Shane slammed the book down on the table. "I'll get right on that." He hurried from the room, presumably heading off to find his ever-present laptop.

Silence hung in the air. Jace leaned against the wall, too weak to hold himself up, while David buried his face in his hands.

"I can't lose her again, J, especially not like this," David finally said. "I would fight for her myself, if I could. But injured like this…all I'd do is get both of us killed because of my damn pride." He glanced up at Jace, a look of pure desperation on his face. "You can do this, can't you?"

"Kill my father?" Jace stared at the wall. The memories of his father beating his mother until she lay sobbing on the kitchen floor invaded his mind.

His father turned his head, directing his anger toward Jace, his eyes glowing gold.

"If I knew where he was, I would've done it already." Jace shook his head. This whole situation was so messed up. "Where's Frankie? Is she okay?"

"She was fine the last time I saw her. A little shaken up from the whole ordeal, but okay. I think she's holed up in her apartment. She bolted as soon as you started to come to."

Pain squeezed Jace's chest. She hadn't even bothered to come see him? To make sure he was all right?

I love you, Jace.

Her words had played in his head on a constant loop ever since she'd said them. But now, with her in hiding instead of by his side, doubt crept in.

A deep feeling tugged at Jace's gut, and he knew he needed to be by her side. Something was wrong. She loved him—didn't she? Shouldn't she be here with him? A low growl escaped his throat. What was wrong with him? Why did he care so much?

"I need to see her," he said.

David straightened. "Jace, you can't. You need to stay focused right now."

Without, hesitating, Jace said, "She's joining me

in tracking this sicko. I need to see her. We need to go after him *now*." He needed to tell her the truth. He'd never said the words back, and he should have.

He shoved himself away from the wall, using all the energy his body had left to get himself out of there. Groaning, he stood up straight and stumbled toward the door.

"J!" David followed behind him as fast as he could. "J, you don't want to go over there, man. Listen to me."

Jace left and headed straight for his woman's apartment.

FRANKIE SAT WITH her legs crossed on the edge of her bed. She stared down at the picture in her hands, the faces of her parents blacked out and ruined, and sighed.

Jace is a Skinwalker. A Berserker.

A shiver ran down her spine as she thought of the symbol glowing between Jace's shoulder blades. As hard as she tried, she couldn't reconcile the two images, the two feelings couldn't coexist in her mind. Jace was rough, his temper astronomical and his drinking…insane, but was he really capable of cold-blooded murder? The image of his gun trained on her the first night they met flashed in her mind. Even though he hunted her kind, he hadn't killed her. So he couldn't be completely evil…right?

She cursed under her breath. Even if Jace was re-lated to her parents' killer in some way, she needed his help to rescue Allsún. Damn it. She couldn't fail her friend, but how could she ally herself with a Skinwalker?

The man she loved and the killer she hated more than anything, members of the same species. She shook her head. Her mother always told her life wasn't fair, but she'd never said that it could be downright cruel. Frankie had learned that for herself—the hard way.

Running her thumb over the photograph, she tried to remember what her mother's hair felt like, the feel of her father's touch, but she couldn't. Only three years since they'd passed, and already her memories of them were fading. She didn't know which was worse: the pain of remembering their deaths or the realization that the man she loved might somehow be involved.

She set down the picture. The look of confusion in Jace's eyes when he'd come out of his trance hadn't been enough to convince her of his innocence. She'd bolted as fast as she could from the club back to her apartment. Since then, her thoughts had been racing nonstop, and she'd been unable to collect them so she could make any sense of how she felt.

The man I love.

She cursed herself. She was an idiot, a total fool. How had she missed the connection? His name carved in the girls' forearms, her apartment being targeted just after she met him, the killer knowing his name, and now the symbol. And what did she get as a result? A man who didn't love her, the possible murderer of both her family and her people. He hunted her kind. How could she ever love such a man? And yet she did.

A loud knock interrupted her jumbled thoughts. With mechanical movements, she wandered to the door and stared through the peephole. Her heart jumped in her chest.

Jace.

Shit. What was he doing here? Why couldn't he leave her alone? Obviously she didn't want to see him or she would have been by his side. She cursed herself.

You told him you loved him last night. How could he possibly know that's changed?

Another knock, harder this time, and the door rattled in its frame. "Frankie, I know you're in there. We need to talk." His voice came loud and clear through the wood, his tone tinged with frustration.

You said, "I love you," but he never said it back. He never said it. What does he care if that's how you feel?

"Frankie, please open the door." His voice softened, as if his energy had suddenly run out.

She inhaled deeply, slid off the chain lock and opened the door.

Jace was standing in the hallway, leaning against

her door frame. Dark circles rimmed his eyes, and he looked drained of all energy, but damn him, he was still gorgeous—still perfect in every way. And how could she possibly think that, knowing he might be connected to her parents' murder?

She turned away and retreated into the apartment.

Following her, Jace stepped inside and shut the door. "We need to talk," he said.

She crossed her arms over her chest and stared at the wall. "You already said that when you were out in the hall. But I don't feel like there's anything to talk about." *Unless we count the crazy coincidences or the mounting pile of problems with our names on it.*

"Did I do something? You're angry." He placed his hand on her shoulder and tried to make her face him.

She pulled away and walked deeper into the apartment. She couldn't look at him.

He followed behind her, close on her heels. "You didn't check if I was hurt. I became practically possessed in front of your entire pack, and David said you just ran off afterward."

Frankie scoffed. He was good, acting like he had absolutely no clue. Complete bullshit, and she knew it. "You've made it clear you can get along just fine without me. You don't need help."

Jace stepped closer, so close that she could feel the heat of him against her back. He snaked his hand around her waist and gently pulled her against him.

"I *can* get along without you, but did I ever say I *wanted* to?"

She pushed his arm off her. What kind of sick person was he, touching her when he knew how she felt? He was the ultimate temptation. Every inch of her wanted to believe him. "Don't act like that. Not now."

"Don't act like what?"

She spun around to face him. "Don't act like you care, because you don't."

He gaped at her. His expression changed from confusion to frustration. "*I don't care?* How have I not shown that I care? I don't know what else you can ask of me. I've suspended all my beliefs for you."

Frankie frowned. "Suspended all your beliefs? What the hell is that supposed to mean?"

He stepped toward her, his volume rising to match her own. "It means that even though I'm a hunter, I've worked with you. I've learned to shift. I even made love to you."

She laughed. Made love? He had to be kidding. "Is that what you're calling it now? Making love? Seemed at the time like you thought of it as just a quick fuck."

He let out a low growl. "I *never* said that."

"You didn't have to." She shoved against his chest, but he didn't budge.

He grabbed hold of her wrists, hard enough to hold her still but gentle enough that he didn't hurt her. She didn't know why he was keeping on with his ridiculous act. "Can you please tell me what I've done, so I can make it right?" Sadness filled his eyes. "What about last night?"

She looked away as she fought to escape his grasp. "How about when you lied to me?"

"Huh? Lied to you? When did I—"

She ripped her hands away from him and stumbled back. "You told me you were half-werewolf, but you're way more than that. You're a Skinwalker. Did you think it was amusing to pretend you were a werewolf so you could take advantage of me during my mating cycle?" Her stomach lurched. Damn, it made her sick just to look at him.

"What?" he roared. "You think I would have slept with you if I hadn't been compelled to do it?"

Frankie's breath caught, and her stomach felt as if he'd just kicked her in it. Her head spun. A sharp pain stabbed her chest, and the weight of his words hit her like a massive, destructive tidal wave. She backed away from him. Tears rolled down her face, staining her cheeks.

Jace's eyes widened, as if he'd just realized what he'd said. "Shit. I didn't mean that. Not like that. Frankie, I—"

Her hands clenched into fists. "Save it for someone who cares, Jace." Her brain tore in two—she wasn't sure whether she wanted to punch him or sob into his shoulder.

He shook his head. "I didn't know I was a Skin-walker. I thought I was half-werewolf."

She turned and pounded her fist into the wall, leaving a dent in the plaster. She rested her head against it. "I don't know why I didn't recognize it. Shit, I'm so stupid. But the details all blended together. I never should have trusted you. I never should've slept with you," she rambled on.

"Don't act like you regret it. I was there, Frankie. You care for me, and don't you dare deny it."

She refused to meet his eyes. "You're delusional if you think I could ever care for you."

He stepped toward her again. "Where is this coming from? Last night you told me you loved me. Now you won't even look at me."

"I didn't mean it!" she yelled. Her chest heaved as her anger came to a head. At that moment, she really did hate him. "When I said I loved you, I was just caught up in the moment. I *don't* love you. Now get the hell away from me."

JACE WOULD GLADLY have taken multiple bullets straight to the heart than hear Frankie's words. Numb. That was how he felt. His entire body was numb. But the pain… The pain would come later. He knew that for a fact.

He stared at her for several seconds before he finally processed her words. His emotions hit harder than a freight train running at maximum speed. It felt as if someone had drained all the blood from his body. His stomach sank. His eyes burned, but he didn't cry, though if ever there had been a moment when he would have shed tears, this was it. "You don't mean that."

"I *do* mean it." She gulped as if she were trying to find the strength to speak. "I can never love you, Jace. You betrayed me."

His jaw dropped. "Betrayed you? How did I ever betray you?" He stepped toward her.

She shoved him hard until he stumbled back. She was ready for a fight. "Don't act like you don't know. You're a Skinwalker *and* a werewolf hunter."

"You say it like I had a choice in the matter."

"A Skinwalker killed my parents! And based on that symbol, Robert's a Skinwalker, too. He's been murdering women and raping them afterward. Your name was carved onto two of the bodies. And you expect me to think all that is coincidence? That you're not involved somehow? I don't know what you've been up to, but you can't possibly expect me to believe you're on my side. You've murdered my kind for years, possibly even my parents, and now you might have been a part of murdering those women, too."

Heat rushed to Jace's face, and before he knew what he was doing, his fist collided with the wall. Fighting back his anger, it took everything he had not to yell, not to tell her how ridiculous she was being.

"You really think I'm a murderer? That I'm capable of that kind of sick, perverted evil?"

She stared at the floor.

"Look at me."

She didn't.

He slammed his fist into the wall again. "Damn it, Frankie, look at me. I deserve that much."

Lifting her head, she met his gaze, tears still pouring down her perfect face.

He reached out and cupped her chin in his hand. "If you mean it, tell me you don't want me here. Tell me to leave and I will."

Her lower lip quivered. She stared at him for several long moments before she brushed his hand away. "I can't trust you. I—I don't want you here, Jace."

His stomach rolled. "Fine."

He walked to the door and paused as he grabbed hold of the knob. "I'll find Allsún on my own." Without another word, he left, leaving the door open. He charged down the stairs and rushed out to the cold city streets.

Betrayal? Fucking betrayal? If there were two things in life he prided himself on, they were being honest and being loyal. He could be one nasty bastard sometimes, but he would at least give himself that much credit.

He continued down the block to his car, his leather coat wrapped tight around him and his hand itching to grab hold of his flask. His thoughts raced.

She doesn't love me.

A sharp pain stabbed his heart. He wasn't sure what to think.

Do I want her to love me?

He shoved the thought aside. He was pathetic. The fact that he'd imagined for even two seconds that he could find happiness in his life was fucking laughable. He was a damn fool. Everything he'd thought he'd known that morning had been thrown out the window, into the street and ran over by a hundred fully loaded semis.

He wasn't a werewolf at all. His whole career of hunting werewolves, the creatures that reminded him so much of his no-good, deadbeat father, was a lie. A Skinwalker? A Berserker? What did that even mean in any real sense? And now Frankie didn't even love him.

Hopes and dreams crushed flat, every one of them.

He turned and stared back at her apartment complex. Damn it. He was kidding himself if he thought he could walk out on her. He stared unseeingly out the windshield. What the hell did he have to lose? She already hated him. And really, he couldn't blame her.

FRANKIE SLAMMED THE door behind Jace, and the resounding bang shuddered through her small apartment. She stood, panting in fury, eyes fixed on the doorway where he'd been standing only moments before. The sting of betrayal stabbed at her heart, and her blood boiled so hot she felt steam could fly out her ears. Damn him for leading her on. Damn him for sleeping with her when he didn't care. Damn him for making her fall in...

Love.

Her emotions ran the gamut as her anger simmered down to a wrenching sadness.

She leaned back against the door frame and slid down it until she reached the floor. Letting out a loud sob, she buried her face in her hands. How could he? She would never understand how someone she loved could be so manipulative. So cruel. She could feel her heart breaking.

He lied to me.

The thought of the pained look in his eyes when he stormed out clouded her thoughts. She couldn't get it out of her head. Damn, he was good. Even when she knew the truth, knew he *had* to be involved in some way, all he had to do was look at her with those gorgeous emerald eyes and she wanted to cave in to him instantly, wanted to believe everything he said.

A large fist pounded against the door, and a jolt ran down her spine.

Jace.

Her stomach dropped, and she tried to stop herself from hyperventilating. She needed to stand up for herself.

Like hell I'm going to let him get away with treating me like dirt. I'm better than this.

Pushing herself off the ground, she stood.

"You know what, Jace, you just need to—" She wrenched open the door and stumbled back.

Before she knew what was happening, Robert came at her full force. He pinned her against the wall and held his knife against her throat. The blade cut into her skin, and a thin line of blood trickled down her collarbone.

Robert sneered. "Nice to see you again, packmaster." He spat the last word and looked down at her as if she was nothing more than a pathetic dog.

Frankie pressed herself as tight against the wall as possible and fought to slow her breathing. Calm. She needed to be calm. "What are you doing here?" She barely managed to choke out the words.

"Retrieving you. You see, I kidnapped one of your little pack members. But apparently she wasn't important enough for you to come save her." He grinned. "Turns out that she isn't a werewolf at all. First time I've ever tortured a faerie. But I have to say, so far I'm finding it quite amusing. Who knew iron was such a useful weapon?"

"You bastard," Frankie growled.

He leaned more weight on the blade and the cut deepened just enough to exponentially enhance her pain. "Enough with the insults, my dear. Dirty mouths aren't appealing on women, even canine whores." He dragged the tip of the knife down her collarbone, stopping inches away from her breasts.

She hissed from the sting. Blood gushed from the tear in her skin, and pain seared through her.

"I'd absolutely love to take my blade to that beautiful chest of yours." He trailed the flat part of the blade over her right breast. "But we'll save that for later."

She glared at him, though she couldn't fight the shivers running down her spine. "You're a sick freak."

With his blade safely away from her throat, she kneed him hard in the groin. He crumpled over exactly as she'd expected. She brought her elbow up and slammed it down into his spine. He toppled to the floor, but he managed to grab her ankle in the process.

He was strong, and when he pulled on her leg she slammed to the floor. She scrambled to her feet, but not before Robert regained his footing, too. He grabbed her shoulder, his knife at the ready. Spinning out of his grasp, she unleashed a roundhouse kick that hit him square in the face.

With a loud curse, he stumbled back, clutching his bloodied nose. Before he could retaliate, she punched him straight in the solar plexus. Gasping for air, he fell to his knees. Now was her chance. She bolted for the door, but before she'd run even five feet, Robert stabbed the blade of his knife through her blue jeans and into her calf.

She screamed in agony. Pain shot up her leg and radiated through her entire body, but she didn't stop. She stumbled toward her door, moving as fast as she could. Blood gushed from her wound, leaving a crimson trail. She reached for the knob of the open door, and she used it to steady herself.

Without warning Robert tackled her from behind. He caught her off balance and slammed her into the wall.

"Back off, you filthy piece of shit." She clawed at his face with her fingernails, scratching anything she could reach.

He clutched both hands around her throat. Lifting her off the ground, he choked her as he pinned her against the wall. "I said, no. More. Insults."

Frankie clawed at his hands, trying to escape. She kicked her feet in hopes of hitting him in the groin, but it was no use. Black spots clouded her vision as she felt herself start to slip into darkness. The last thing she saw was Robert's twisted grin.

"Sleep now, little packmaster. You can rest until the fun starts."

Jogging the half block back to the building, Jace reviewed everything he could possibly say to convince Frankie of his innocence. Somehow, nothing he came up with seemed like enough. When he reached the building, he bounded up the steps, wrenched the door open and headed straight for the stairs.

He stopped in his tracks.

Crouching to the floor, he rubbed his finger across a small red speckle. He lifted his hand to his nose and sniffed. The smell of iron filled his nostrils.

Blood.

Jace sprinted up the stairs to the second floor. Frankie's door hung open. His stomach flipped. "Shit." He ran into the apartment at full speed but quickly skidded to a halt.

Blood. Frankie's blood.

There was a large pool on the floor, with small droplets leading out of the apartment. Robert had her. He knew it without question. All his fault. If he hadn't left her…

A loud roar ripped from Jace's throat as anger flooded every inch of his body. He barely took the time to scan the writing that dripped in fresh blood across the walls before he stormed out of the apartment. He was going to tear that fucker to pieces.

Come to the abandoned warehouse in Honeoye. Better hurry, my dear Jace, before I kill them both.

CHAPTER SIXTEEN

FRANKIE'S EYES SLOWLY flickered open. Her head pounded, pain thumping in her temple like a steadily beating drum. Her whole body ached, and her collarbone throbbed with pain every time she breathed. Damn him for using a silver knife. Pushing herself off the ground, she blinked several times until her eyes adjusted to the dim lighting. She scanned her surroundings and gritted her teeth.

A cage. He'd placed her in a freaking cage.

She grabbed one of the bars and shook it with all the strength she could muster. The iron creaked as it threatened to give beneath her strength, but it would take hours to bend it enough so she could escape. Something told her she didn't have that kind of time.

"We're in a warehouse. Don't bother yelling or trying to get out. It's impossible."

Frankie turned around. Allsún lay sprawled across the bottom of the cage, her arms and limbs spread wide as if she were the female equivalent of da Vinci's famous Vitruvian Man. She didn't move.

"Allsún, are you okay?" Frankie crawled toward her. When she reached Allsún's side, she cursed.

Iron. The cage was made of iron—even the floor.

"Holy shit, Allsún. I'm going to move you, okay? I'm going to move you so your skin isn't touching the metal." Frankie placed a hand on Allsún's arm.

The small faerie cringed. "Be careful, Frankie. My…my skin is stuck to the iron. If you move me, it will peel off."

"Shit." Frankie hit one of the metal bars of the cage in frustration. "I'm going to have to move you somehow. If you stay like this, the iron's just going to keep eating away at your skin." Frankie eyed the length of Allsún's body. She didn't know where to begin.

Legs. She would start with her legs. The only skin showing there was a slight flash of her ankle just above her shoe, the only part of her leg not protected by her jeans.

Shifting toward Allsún's feet, she stared down at her injured friend. "I'm going to move your legs so that your shoes are touching the iron, instead of your skin. Okay?"

Allsún whimpered, unable even to nod.

Frankie cupped her hands underneath Allsún's kneecaps. Should she pull her legs off the floor quickly, like a Band-Aid, to lessen the pain or move slowly in hopes of salvaging some of the skin? Frankie closed her eyes and quickly lifted Allsún's legs.

A blood-curdling scream pierced the air. Frankie's

eyes snapped open. Her stomach flipped. She held back vomit at the sight of chunks of Allsún's skin stuck to the iron. The smell of burning flesh permeated the air. Frankie gagged.

She propped Allsún's legs up with her knees bent and placed her shoes in contact with the iron. Her torso remained flat against the bottom of the cage.

Damn. The difficult part was next. Her arms and her head.

Frankie carefully slipped her hands underneath Allsún's shoulders. Her blouse had managed to protect most of the skin there.

I'm doing this to help her, not to hurt her. She repeated the mantra in her head for reassurance.

"No. No. Frankie, please," Allsún cried.

A large lump lodged in Frankie's throat. "Allsún, I'm so sorry. I know this is going to hurt, but I have to get your skin off this iron. If your head stays where it is, the metal will eat completely through your skin until it reaches your skull. I can't let that happen."

Inhaling a steadying breath, Frankie hoisted Allsún's body off the metal floor. The sound was disgusting, like peeling an old bumper sticker from a used car. Allsún's screams vibrated through Frankie's head as if someone had shoved a tuning fork inside her ear.

In one quick swoop, she had Allsún off the floor and sitting in her lap. The other woman weighed practically nothing, but her blood poured onto

Frankie, staining her white tank top a deep crimson. Allsún screamed and writhed in Frankie's arms.

"Shh. Shh. Allsún, it's okay. It's okay." She gripped her friend tightly around the middle to hold her still. She couldn't let her touch the iron again. "We'll be out of here soon. I promise."

"You shouldn't make promises you can't keep." The voice came from the other side of the room.

Frankie looked up as Allsún's screams started to fade to groans and her bleeding slowed. Leaning against one of the warehouse walls, Robert stared at her with unrelenting, cold eyes.

Frankie scoffed. "A cage, huh?"

A smirk crept across his face. "You like it? I thought it was very fitting."

She snorted as if she'd never heard of anything more ridiculous—anything to piss him off. Anger made people sloppy, and sloppiness meant a better chance for them to escape. "You're really subtle with your insults, aren't you?"

He frowned. "Laugh if you want, but you're the one locked up like the bitch that you are. You're nothing more than live bait."

Frankie stroked Allsún's hair, trying to calm her panic. "What do you mean? You have me trapped. What else do you need now? Why don't you just kill us already?"

"My, my, don't we have a large ego." He moved

away from the wall and stalked toward the cage. "Don't flatter yourself, packmaster. You've never been my target. It's your hunter I want."

Her stomach dropped. "What do you want with Jace?"

He grinned as if he were a cat who'd just swallowed a large canary. "To kill him, of course."

It took everything Frankie had to hold back her anger and remain still for Allsún's sake. "What about ransacking my apartment, kidnapping me? What does that have to do with Jace?"

He chuckled and kneeled next to the cage. If he moved any closer to the bars, she thought, she could speed-shift and slip her muzzle through the opening. She would have liked nothing more than to rip his face off with her teeth.

"You must be even less intelligent than you appear. Let me spell it out for you." He pointed to himself, then her. "*I* kidnap *you,* which leads Jace straight to me. He won't be able to resist saving you."

"And Allsún? What about her? She's not involved in any of this."

Allsún stirred. When she spoke, her voice was hoarse from screaming. "To lure *you* here," she said in a near whisper. "Only it didn't work."

"The troll's smarter than she appears."

"I'm not a troll," Allsún said. "I'm Fae." She winced as she said it, but her voice remained strong.

Robert ignored her comment and stood again. "When you didn't come for her, I took a more…direct approach. There's no question. He'll be here."

Frankie swallowed down the bile burning the back of her throat. Jace wasn't involved. He hadn't betrayed her. Her heart thumped in her chest, its pace quickly increasing until she was near panic. She'd hurt him. She'd told him that she didn't love him, called him a liar, and all the time he'd been telling the truth.

But he was still a Skinwalker.

Frankie's head spun. Had he really not known? Had he really thought he was part werewolf? Could anyone have faked the inability to shift as well as he had? Why had she not believed him?

Silently, she cursed herself for acting on stupid impressions, on following a gut fear rather than facing the fact that even though the man she loved shared something in common with her parents' murderer, it meant nothing.

Frankie growled. "Jace is going to tear you to shreds."

Robert laughed as if she'd told his favorite joke, the kind that never gets old. "Don't fool yourself, packmaster. Do you think Jace can match my strength? My speed? My abilities?"

Frankie didn't say a word. She clamped her mouth shut, but a smug grin spread across her lips.

A fire lit behind Robert's eyes as his anger melted his icy shield. He marched to the cage and kicked one of the bars. "Tell me what you know."

She stared him in the face, challenging him to give it his best shot.

When she didn't respond, he snatched a key from his back pocket and unlocked the door to the cage, his knife pointed straight at her. "Get out."

She didn't move.

Robert let out a deep-throated growl. "Get out. *Now*. Before I get my gun and plant a silver bullet in the middle of your forehead."

Frankie shook her head. "You can't kill me. You need me as bait to get Jace here."

He chuckled. "That's where you're wrong. You see, as soon as Jace finds the little note I left him, written in some of the delicious blood from that neck of yours, he'll come here ready for a fight. Your death will only cause him more pain. Why wouldn't I want that?" He brandished the knife. "The only reason I haven't killed you yet is so I can kill you and fuck you right in front of him." He smiled, and it was a look of pure evil.

A chill ran down Frankie's spine. Every animal instinct in her body screamed for her to run, but she couldn't. She had to listen to him, if not for the sake of her own survival, then for Allsún's.

"Let my friend out of the cage, too. I'll get out if she comes with me."

Robert eyed her for a moment, sizing her up as a potential opponent. "One at a time. Her first." He nodded to Allsún.

Allsún groaned, her body lying limp in Frankie's lap. Frankie gripped her shoulders and gave them a light squeeze. "Allsún. Allsún, you have to get up. We have to get out of here."

Allsún let out another moan and rolled her head to the side. Her eyes flickered open, and she stared at Frankie. "I can't."

"You have to. The longer you're near this iron, the weaker you'll get." Frankie placed a hand on her friend's cheek. "You can do this."

"This is all very touching, but I suggest you hurry the fuck up." Robert's voice rose as his impatience grew.

"Allsún, get up. You can do it. Do it for David."

Allsún inhaled sharply. Her whole body language changed, as if she'd found a new resolve. Frankie helped lift her onto her feet. Stumbling, back bent so she didn't hit her head, Allsún escaped the iron enclosure.

Robert grabbed her by the arm and drew her into his body. He held the knife to her throat, then nodded at Frankie. "Stay," he commanded, as if she were a dog. He kicked the cage door closed, and the lock snapped shut automatically.

"Hey!" Frankie screamed. She crawled on all fours toward the door, then moved to stand. If she could charge at the lock with all the fury she could muster, maybe she could break it open.

Robert held the knife tighter to Allsún's throat, but all his focus was on Frankie. "Don't get up."

She put her hands up in surrender and sank back down to the floor. "I thought you wanted me to come out?"

"I've changed my mind." Robert's eyes remained on Frankie even when he leaned his mouth down to Allsún's ear. "You first." He backed away, dragging Allsún with him.

"What are you going to do to her?" Frankie yelled. She slammed her fists against the bars. The pounding rattled the inside of her skull.

Robert maneuvered Allsún several feet away, where a pair of shackles hung from the end of a chain that had been haphazardly attached to the ceiling.

"Let her go!" Frankie shouted. She barely recognized the voice as her own from the panic in her tone.

"Lift your arms," Robert said, positioning Allsún under the contraption. She lifted her arms like the perfect victim, threatened enough by Robert's knife to listen, but not scared to the point of immobility.

He clamped the wide cuffs around her wrists, and she cringed at their touch.

More iron, Frankie realized.

Shaking the bars of the cage, she tried to think of anything she could do to help her friend. As near as she could tell, she was out of options. It took everything she had in her, but she caved in. She begged. "Don't hurt her. Please, don't hurt her. She's not a part of this. Let her go and kill me instead. Please."

Robert laughed as he examined the blade of his knife. "Who said I was going to kill her?" He glanced over his shoulder at Frankie, his eyes unpredictable and mad. "We're going to have some fun first. I've had lots of practice on wolves—your parents being among the first."

Frankie gasped. This man—this monster—had killed her parents. "You killed my parents?"

"Yes. I killed them. How could I resist killing a packmaster and his wife? I was hoping for a challenge, a step up from the weak rogues I'd been killing. Unfortunately, they proved to be worthless opponents. I've had women, wolves…but faeries are a new favorite of mine." He slapped Allsún. "Isn't that right, my little troll?"

Frankie watched, completely horrified, as Robert stabbed his blade into the soft flesh of Allsún's stomach.

THE TIRES OF Jace's H3 squealed as he sped up to the curb outside his apartment. He barely took the time to throw the car into Park before he bolted from the vehicle. He rushed up the stairs and burst into the apartment, panting and out of breath, but full of adrenaline.

David stood. "J? Man, what are you—"

"Robert has Frankie and Allsún. Old warehouse in Honeoye."

David swore.

"We need to go *now*." Jace grabbed David's jacket off a nearby coat rack and threw it at him. "Shane, get your coat on."

Shane's eyes widened. "What good will I be? I can't—"

Jace let out a low growl. "Get your coat on and get in the damn Hummer. Pronto."

Two minutes later Jace was speeding full-throttle toward Honeoye.

Frankie.

She was his sole focus, the only thing he had to live for. He imagined her face in agony as Robert drew his knife across her skin. The image sent his blood boiling. That sick fuck would pay. He would die the slowest, most painful death Jace could think of.

My fault. All my fault.

The words echoed in his head. Frankie. Allsún. The countless bodies piling up in filthy alleyways. All his fault. He choked down a battle cry that would have shattered the windows.

Shane cleared his throat and leaned in between the two front seats, his face hovering between Jace and David. "We need a plan."

Jace growled. "I'll tell you the damn plan. We kill

that motherfucker and then carve his eyes out with a dull blade." Jace's grip tightened on the steering wheel. "No one touches my woman."

His woman.

Was she his woman?

He thought of the first time they'd made love, the way he had slammed into her and she had taken every inch of him and reveled in it. The way being inside her had felt like coming home. The way her lips had sweetly caressed his.

Damn right she was his woman. Because even when she was ripping out his heart and stomping on it, calling him a liar, he was still fucking in love with her. A weight lifted off his chest. Yeah, he could admit it. He loved her. He didn't give a flying shit if she were a werewolf, if she were packmaster, if she'd lied about her name and who knew what else, even if she hated him. He loved her, and he would be damned if he was going to let anyone hurt her.

"If either of you want this to be successful, we *need* a plan," Shane said, raising his voice, louder than Jace had ever heard it.

"What's the point in making a plan?" David said. He twisted around to look at Shane. "We're going to be massacred. Robert has been a Skinwalker longer. He knows his abilities and how to control them. He has the upper hand, and there's no way Jace can ever one up him, because with his father dead he'll never be able to access his Berserker powers."

"Dead?" Jace asked, stunned. "What the hell are you—"

"Uh, yeah," Shane said from the backseat. "I did some online research after you ran out like the hounds of hell were after you, and...I'm sorry, Jace, but David's right. He's dead."

Jace felt as if the world had been placed on pause. There was no room for anything in his mind except for the news David had delivered and Shane had confirmed. He continued speeding toward the warehouse, but his vigor and anger flickered for a moment before reigniting. His father was dead? The old bastard was finally dead? He wasn't quite sure how to feel. Sadness—that was what he should have felt, if he'd had a normal childhood. Instead, all he could feel underneath his drive to kill Robert was a sense of relief.

And then the rest of David's words finally penetrated his brain.

He shook his head to clear it. "Wait. Is that true? That no matter what I do, I'll never be able to use any of the Berserker powers?"

Shane sighed. "Unless you can go back and talk to your spirit guide again and he has something else to suggest, yeah, it's true. You're the last of your bloodline. There's no one else left for you to kill even if you wanted to. And even with your Skinwalker abilities, Robert still has the advantage, because he's been using his gifts so much longer. You can't even shift at will."

The tension filling the car was staggering. Jace felt suffocated. Several minutes of silence passed before he finally let out a long sigh. This was it, then. He was almost certainly going to die. But that was okay. He would do anything, give anything— even his life—if he could just save Frankie. Finally he spoke.

"Here's the plan. We do whatever it takes to get Frankie and Allsún out of there. Shane, your job is to drive them to safety. I'll give you the keys to the H3. David, it's your job to get them out, then go with them and Shane and make sure they're safe. Don't even consider coming back to help me. There are demons in this city you need to take care of. The Execution Underground can't lose you, and once I'm out of the picture, Damon will see that. I'll take care of Robert. No matter what it takes."

David shook his head. "Are you sure, J? Can you do this?"

Jace nodded. "I have to. All I can do now is pray it's my lucky friggin' night and I don't go down with him."

ALLSÚN'S SCREAMS ECHOED off the warehouse walls and rang in Frankie's ears. Adrenaline shot through her, and she fought to hold in her anger—she couldn't allow herself to shift unintentionally—but the rage filling her was on the point of exploding.

"Let her go, you sick bastard!" She shook the cage bars so hard the damn thing nearly tipped over.

Blood poured down the front of Allsún's torso, staining her shirt and jeans. All the color had drained from her face, and Frankie could tell she was fighting not to pass out.

Robert laughed as he glanced at Frankie. "Don't worry. I'm not killing her." He brandished the knife again and stabbed the tip into Allsún's arm.

She shrieked and writhed from the pain.

"See that right there." He pointed to the wound, raising his voice to be heard over Allsún's screams. "It's a shallow wound. Deep enough to cause pain, but nothing that will cause her any permanent damage."

He plunged the knife into Allsún's thigh, inches away from her femoral artery. "Actually, you should be thankful I haven't taken her life already. I find myself growing bored."

Seeing him torment Allsún conjured thoughts of her parents. Had Robert tortured them the same way? Her body trembled with fury. She couldn't let herself think about it.

"You are a sick, pathetic excuse for a human being," Frankie spat.

Robert paused with the knife in the air and turned

toward her. Blood dripped from the blade onto his hand as he began to laugh. His laughter filled the warehouse—the cackling of a madman.

"A pathetic excuse for a human?" He walked toward the cage. "That's where you're wrong, you filthy mutt. You see, I'm not human. Not in the slightest." He knelt in front of the cage and pointed his blade toward her face. He lowered his voice to a near whisper. "I'm more powerful than any man will ever be."

He stood and backed away from her, but his eyes never left hers. "And now, courtesy of your little outburst, I've become very angry, and believe me, you *really* won't like it when I'm angry. Because when my anger builds up, I need to relieve it, so if you'll excuse me, the faerie and I have some much-needed business to attend to."

He turned away, and Frankie heard him unbuckle his belt before he unzipped his pants.

Allsún screamed and struggled against the chains holding her. "No, please. Frankie, help!"

Frankie pulled against the bars so hard the metal bent several inches and the cage actually toppled over. "Don't you fucking dare!"

Robert chuckled. He pushed his body flush against Allsún's, and she cringed at his touch. "Don't worry. I won't rape her." He ground the bulge in his pants against her small hips. Allsún whimpered, and he placed the knife against her throat. "At least, not while she's alive."

Shots echoed through the warehouse as Jace fired three rounds from his Mateba straight into Robert's back. The bastard staggered, falling forward and sending Allsún, who was shackled and hanging from a chain, swinging in the air.

Jace's eyes darted around the room. Frankie was struggling with the metal bars of a large cage that had tipped onto its side, her attention trained on him.

Tears poured down her face and blood covered her chest. "Jace!" she yelled.

Jace placed a single finger over his mouth to silence her and pointed to the rear exit door where David was even then slipping inside the building. As Jace watched, David limped toward the cage, making sure Robert didn't spot him.

Slowly Robert rose to his feet, still much too close to Allsún. The bullets pushed their way out of his back as the skin stitched itself back together, visible through his torn shirt. He turned to face Jace, the desire of a murderer burning in his eyes.

"Haven't you learned? Your silly little bullets can't kill me, Jace." Robert smirked.

Jace held his gun steady, pointed straight at Robert's head. "Maybe. But they can sure as hell cause you a lot of pain."

Robert stepped forward, arms wide in a welcoming gesture. "Why bother fighting, Jace? Give yourself up now and I'll let them both go. Untouched."

Jace shook his head. "You really think I'm that stupid?"

A wide grin spread across Robert's face. "That's debatable. But considering your bloodline, for my own sake, I hope your lineage alone makes your intelligence above par."

"What the hell are you talking about?" Jace focused his eyes on Robert, trying hard not to glance in Frankie's direction as David quietly picked the lock on the cage. If only Robert would move toward him, David could get to Allsún, too.

Robert stepped toward Allsún and ran his hand down the length of her thigh. She writhed in a fruitless attempt to avoid his touch. "You still haven't figured it out yet, have you?" he said, then turned to leer at Allsún.

While Robert wasn't looking, Jace inched forward. One step. Two.

Turning to face Jace again, Robert wiped the blood off his knife with the edge of his shirt. He eyed Jace up and down. "You never once questioned why? Why your name was carved into the arms of my masterpieces? Why that werewolf bitch was attacked just after you fucked her like the whore she is?"

Jace let out a low growl. "I don't try to understand

the logic of psychopaths. If you wanted to kill me, you should have just done it that night at the park. Enough with the theatrical games."

Robert frowned. "Killing you then would have been too easy and entirely lacking in emotional satisfaction. I wanted you to know exactly why I chose you as my sacrifice. We have so much more in common than you realize."

"I am absolutely nothing like you." Jace's jaw clenched into a tight line, and he ground his teeth together. If he didn't fight back his rage, he would charge Robert right then, and that would be a mistake. He needed to wait for the opportune moment.

"We're both a rare breed. Skinwalkers destined to follow the Berserker bloodline." Robert laughed mockingly. "To think that you were convinced you were half-werewolf. Self-righteously killing for years to atone for your absent-daddy issues. No reason to cry in fear now, Jace. He's long dead."

Jace stepped forward. He couldn't let this creep get into his head, under his skin. But how…?

"How do you know about my father?"

Robert shook his head and clicked his tongue as if he were disappointed in a small child. "I thought you would have been smarter than this, Jace McCannon."

Anger pulsed through Jace's veins. "You heard me, asshole. How do you know about my father?"

A twisted look twinkled behind Robert's eyes. Jace had seen that look before. His breath caught.

Robert grinned in triumph. "Because Thomas McCannon was *my* father, too."

CHAPTER SEVENTEEN

JACE STOOD FROZEN in a vacuum of his own thoughts as he processed the words Robert had just spoken. His stomach churned.

Robert was his brother?

No, there was no way. He didn't have any brothers. He had been his parents' only child.

Jace shook his head. "You're bluffing—another one of your sick mind games. Are you so desperate that you have to fuck with my head? Be a man and just fight me already."

Robert wagged his index finger at Jace. "Now, now, don't throw a hissy fit because you're no longer the only child, big brother."

A snarl tore from Jace's throat before he could stop himself.

Robert took a step toward him. "Don't try to kid yourself, Jace. You know it's true. I know you can see the resemblance."

Jace stepped back. "I don't give a shit whether we look similar or not, you're not my damn brother. It's not possible." Jace couldn't hear this. He couldn't. Not another damn word of it.

Robert made a tsking noise, then sighed. "Explain to me how it's not possible, brother. How many times did our father stumble home drunk after he'd spent the night fucking countless whores? Tell me. Tell me how many times he tossed your mother aside to sheath himself inside some nameless slu—"

"Shut up!" Jace roared. Was it really true? And if it was, how the hell had Shane missed that bit of information? He fired another round into Robert's torso.

Robert's body jerked with the hit, but he didn't fall. Laughing hysterically, he stared Jace down with the same fucked-up look Tom had always given him. "When our father finally left you, he shacked up with my whore of a mother. But unlike you, dad took me under his wing. He told me all about you. How you were weak, not man enough to follow in his footsteps. But I was stronger. So much stronger."

He gestured to his chest and pulled his shirt open to show the bullet emerging from his body and the skin healing over, as if to demonstrate his superiority. "He taught me how to kill, how to live. I knew I was a Skinwalker. I *knew*."

Jace's breath caught. "You killed him so you could become a Berserker."

Robert smiled. "Unfortunately, no. By the time I spirit-walked and learned I needed to kill our father to become a true Berserker, he was long dead. After all that time, can you believe the lucky old bastard died in his sleep? A heart attack from old age. Such a normal, boring way to go, don't you think? Especially for someone who spent a hundred and fifty years on this earth."

He flipped his knife around in his hand, admiring the gleam of light on the bloody blade. "I traveled the world for a while, perfecting my technique before I came home again. It started out as nothing but good fun—killing the women here in Rochester. The occasional wolf. But it became so much more than that."

Robert gazed down at the knife blade. "I realized I could use them to lure you to me. I realized I didn't need to kill our father to gain my abilities." He met Jace's eyes. "I just needed to kill you."

Before Jace could react, Robert threw his knife. The blade hit Jace's shoulder, lodging in his flesh. Blood gushed down Jace's arm. Pain shot through him, and he fell to his knees. His grip weakened and he dropped the gun, which skidded across the floor. The knife must have nicked an artery.

The old man died of a heart attack. His heart stopped. His heart stopped. Jace's thoughts screamed the truth at him. *Robert's not a Berserker—yet. We're both Skinwalkers.*

He scrambled for the knife. If he could stab it through Robert's heart, he might have a chance. He ripped the blade from his shoulder and launched himself at the other man. At his brother.

FRANKIE'S HEART STOPPED when she saw Robert throw the knife at Jace.

"No!" she screamed.

Her heart kicked into high gear when the blade lodged in Jace's shoulder. His blood poured out, but thank goodness the hit hadn't killed him. She would never forgive herself if he died. Damn it. She was a fool. She couldn't lose him.

"Frankie," David said, shaking the bars to get her attention. "This isn't working. Take this." He handed her the lock pick he'd been using. "Keep working at it. I need to get to Allsún, get her out of here and hand her over to Shane. She's losing too much blood. She—"

"David, it's all right. Robert is busy with Jace. It's your only chance. Go."

He threw her a grateful look and said, "When you get out, go to Shane. He's waiting outside. Don't try to fight Robert." Then he left and made his way to Allsún's side as stealthily as possible, and began working at her handcuffs.

Frankie's eyes darted to the other side of the room, where Jace was rolling on the ground with Robert, a tangle of punches and kicks. Forcing herself to look away, she shoved the lock pick into the keyhole, feeling around for the tumblers.

Come on. Come on. Come on.

She continued working at the lock. The hell with

David's instructions. She needed to help Jace, She would be damned if she was going to abandon him when he needed her most. Damned if she wouldn't avenge her parents, herself, Allsún.

There was a thud as Allsún's shackles opened and she fell to the floor. She tried to get up and toppled into David's arms. He hoisted her onto his shoulder and ran awkwardly toward the rear exit.

Damn it, Frankie thought. The lock wouldn't budge.

She kept working frantically, and just as she felt a small shifting as the lock yielded to her efforts, a loud bang echoed through the warehouse as the front doors burst open. Mr. Ice stepped in, followed by Blondie and Jersey. Ice's cold blue eyes locked onto her.

Shit. Just what they fucking needed.

JACE SLAMMED HIS fist into Robert's jaw with a disgusting crack. Bone crunched beneath his hand, but he knew it would heal in a matter of minutes. Robert slashed at him with the silver knife, which he'd managed to wrest back. Warm blood covered his body, flowing from multiple wounds on his chest, shoulders and arms. Heat burned through him, rushing to his wounds. He felt the skin knit together and regrow seconds after the wound had been made.

An equal playing field. It all came down to sheer ability.

With a massive shove, Robert pushed Jace off him. Jace fell back onto the floor, and Robert was on him in seconds. He slammed the knife down toward Jace's chest. Jace grabbed his wrist and struggled to hold back Robert's arm.

A tingling sensation ignited beneath his skin, and he was faintly aware of the glowing blue markings covering his body and glowing through his clothes. Electricity pumped through him. He felt stronger, faster.

But Robert retaliated, quickly channeling his own energy. Energy that was more practiced, more refined, than Jace's. The knife shifted down an inch, closer to plunging into his chest.

Fuck. He was going to lose this fight. He couldn't lose. He *couldn't*.

The image of Frankie's face clouded his mind. If he had one wish, it was to see her gorgeous smile one last time.

He needed to see her. Needed to talk to her. He couldn't die without telling her he loved her. In an instant Robert was ripped off him and the bloodied knife skidded across the floor as Jace's fellow hunters attacked the bastard. Damon's fists collided with Robert's face in an angry frenzy.

Jace grabbed the knife and jumped to his feet, prepared to fight.

As he lunged forward, a surge of power pumped through Jace's body. Without warning, he grabbed

Robert by the back of his neck and ripped him away from Damon's fists, then stabbed the knife straight into the fucker's side.

"Damon, get the girls out!" Jace yelled. He ripped the knife from Robert's flesh and stabbed him again.

Robert threw a wild punch, his fist slamming backward into Jace's kneecap, and Jace crumpled to the ground right alongside him. The bastard was indestructible. There was no way he could manage to stab him in the heart. Jace scrambled to his feet, but Robert slammed into him again, pinning him to the ground. His nails dug into Jace's wrists, and Jace could tell he was channeling all his strength in order to hold him down.

"Just let me kill you, Jace. Give up and I'll leave your bitch and her friend in peace."

Jace spat into Robert's face and snarled. "Not a chance, you murdering motherfucker."

"Don't make this harder on yourself than it has to be, Jace. I have you trapped. You have no way out."

Jace growled. Robert was right. He had him pinned. The other hunters were trying to get Frankie and Allsún out safely. They couldn't help him before Robert made his move. The bastard could strip him of the knife any time he wanted, and once he did it would be inside Jace's heart within seconds.

"It's too bad it had to be this way, brother," Robert went on patronizingly. "You would have made an excellent Skinwalker if you weren't such a bleeding heart, so weak."

Jace ground his teeth together. Weak? No. He was a lot of things: a stubborn, hardheaded smoking asshole who drowned himself in alcohol. But he was *not* weak. If he had his way, he would rip out Robert's throat with his...

Jace's eyes widened. With his teeth. He would rip Robert's throat out with his teeth.

Robert's fingers dug into the flesh of Jace's hand, and Jace felt the knife begin to slip from his grasp. He ignored that and focused on Robert's disgusting face. He thought of all the women he'd hurt, all the women he *would* hurt if no one could stop him. He thought of his dickhead of a father, who'd created the monster before him. His inner beast stirred, and he pushed all his energy into his chest, straining beneath Robert's grip.

In one massive push, Jace lunged forward, his body contorting and shifting as fur sprouted from beneath his skin.

Robert recoiled, the knife in his hand. He raised his arm, but not quickly enough.

Jace's muzzle collided with Robert's neck, and he sank his canines into the meaty flesh of Robert's throat as he ripped through the bastard's jugular.

Blood spurted from the wound, and Robert's body convulsed several times, thick red blood pouring from his mouth.

Within seconds Jace's fur folded in on itself and he lost his shift, but it didn't matter. He glanced down at his body as the claws retracted back into his hands. His shirt hung off him in shreds. He'd only managed to shift the upper half of his body, but he'd done what he'd needed to.

His eyes shot to Robert, and he realized the fucker still wasn't dead. He stared at the bloodied mangled mess that he was ashamed to call his brother. Already the skin of Robert's neck was beginning to knit together.

Grabbing the knife, Jace loomed over the killer and let out a low growl. "Say hi to Dad for me." He stabbed the blade straight into Robert's heart, and scarlet arterial blood spurted from Robert's chest.

In one last attempt to save his own life, Robert reached for Jace, going straight for his neck, but Jace simply twisted the knife. Robert's body continued to twitch for several moments until finally he fell limp. Jace's breath caught. Dead. Robert was finally dead.

He let go of the knife and leaned back. The intricate blue designs pulsated on his skin, then quickly faded. Energy trickled out of him as if he were a drained battery. Black dots swam in front of his eyes.

"Jace? Jace!" Frankie cried.

It was the last thing he heard.

FRANKIE THREW HERSELF to Jace's side and gripped his hand. Her chest heaved as she fought to catch her breath. Sweat beaded on her forehead and chest, and she blinked several times to clear her vision.

"Frankie." Jace squeezed her hand, his eyes wide. Without warning, he started laughing hysterically. "Frankie, I shifted. I shifted and I killed him."

Despite the carnage around them, she couldn't help but smile. He looked at her, and she could see him drinking her in as if she were a tall glass of Bushmills. Her heart thumped in her chest.

A moment of silence passed. There were so many things she wanted to tell him, but she didn't know how to say them. She inhaled and started as simply as she could. "I was wrong, Jace. Really wrong. I don't know how I ever could have thought you were involved with Robert. At the time, it just seemed like such an important detail that you were—"

"The same type of creature that killed your parents."

"Robert killed my parents." A lump invaded her throat, and she fought to swallow it. She was stupid. How could she have screwed this up? "I'm sorry, Jace. I'm really sorry. I need to…" She couldn't take this. She started to turn away.

"No." Jace grabbed her wrist and gently pulled her toward him. "I don't blame you for feeling that way. I would have been suspicious of me, too. I hunted your kind and took you captive when we first met. I threatened to kill you."

She stared at the floor. "And I made you lose your job and nearly your life when Robert took me. So we're even." She glanced up at him.

He nodded. "I'll get my job back—I hope. They saw me kill Robert, so I think I redeemed myself. But I want you to know that even if I'm hunting rogues, I won't lay a hand on any law-abiding member of your pack. You have my word."

She forced a smile.

Another lull passed between them, one that seemed to stretch for hours...months. She examined his body, and heat boiled through her. Damn, she loved him. And there was no way on earth it could ever work out for them.

She pointed over her shoulder with her thumb as she stood. He quickly followed suit.

"I should help David take care of Allsún, and the other hunters will have a lot of questions for you. Even if we're enemies now, it's been nice knowing—"

Jace grabbed her hand again and pulled her toward him. "Wait. Frankie, I have something I need to say."

JACE HAD NEVER felt more nervous in his life. His stomach flipped as he clutched Frankie's hand in his, drawing small circles across her tanned skin with his thumb. He inhaled a deep breath. This was it.

He cleared his throat and prepared for the worst while hoping for the best. "Knowing I caused you pain hurts me more than you can imagine. This is the thing, Frankie. I don't want to be enemies. I have to have you. I want all of you, every inch of you. If this ends right here and now, I don't know if I'll ever be capable of caring for anyone again. I know I'm not perfect, not even close. I'm more flawed than anyone I know. I'm uncontrollable, stubborn, hardheaded and proud. I smoke, I swear and I drink like a fish. It takes a brave soul to love me. I don't know how you ever managed it. I sure as hell couldn't have."

He drew her closer to him. "Whether you hate me or not, I want to be with you. I need to be with you. Because I don't care if you're a werewolf, I don't care if you're packmaster or if you were supposed to be someone else's, because I want you to be mine. The day I marry you will be the happiest day of my life. If you'll have me, I want to spend a long and happy life with you."

Tears clouded her eyes and streamed down her cheeks. He brushed one aside. He hoped they were tears of happiness. He didn't know if he could stand it if she rejected him. He sighed. "I wanted to let you know that I love you more than the world, and I think you are the most beautiful and intelligent woman I've ever had the fortune to know. I adore you, Frankie."

He wrapped his arms around her waist and pressed her flush against his body before she could protest. Leaning down, he kissed her deep, their tongues intertwining in an erotic dance. Relief washed over him when she didn't pull away. Instead, she melted against him.

When the kiss finally broke, he held her tight in his arms. "Please don't continue hating me. I want to spend forever with you. I want to be your destined mate."

She buried her head in the crook of his neck. The gardenia smell of her hair filled his nose. The scent was intoxicating. He could get drunk just from being near her.

She whispered against him, her words and lips brushing over his neck, "I'd like that." She ran her hand down his chest, and his body stiffened in response. She pulled back and smiled at him, lighting up the room. "I didn't mean it when I said I didn't love you, or when I said I hated you. I *do* love you, Jace. I'll always love you. I've wanted you ever since we were first together in your apartment. Since then, I haven't dreamed of anything else, haven't wanted anyone else. I don't want to be enemies again, either."

He snaked his hand down to her lower back and pushed her hips against his. A soft moan escaped her lips. Before she had time to protest, he scooped her up into his arms and held her close.

A grin spread across his face. "Let's get you cleaned up before I show you the true meaning of Skinwalker."

* * * * *

ACKNOWLEDGMENTS

Wow. I can't believe I'm already getting to write another one of these—not that I'm complaining. Who doesn't love to write acknowledgments? I'd like to give huge thanks and my deep gratitude to the following people:

Foremost, thanks to my friend Britt Marczak: thank you for pushing me through the first drafts of this book. You were the very first person to read about Jace and Frankie, and you loved them and this series before anyone else did. Without you, I don't know if I would've pushed through this. You encouraged me every step of the way. I can't thank you enough for being my friend, my mini-editor, my personal cheerleader, and for dishing out the tough love when I needed it. You're going to make a fabulous editor someday.

To my friend and agent, Nicole Resciniti: for giving me a chance when no one else would and for making this novel the best it could possibly be. Nic, you changed my life with a single phone call, all because you fell in love with Jace the same way I did.

You believed in his story immediately, and there is no way I could ever express my gratitude for all you've done to ensure that this book and this series would make it to publication. There aren't words to express how truly grateful I am. It is a blessing to have you in my life and to always have you by my side, fighting for my best interests. Thank you.

To my editor, Leslie Wainger, and to Tara Parsons, the former head of the HQN line: thank you for pushing this debut author and her little manuscript through acquisitions and for believing in this series. Leslie, thank you for all the hours of work you've put in to make sure *Twilight Hunter* debuts at its absolute best and for guiding me through the ups and downs of the publishing process. I'm looking forward to having you in my corner for many books to come.

To my fellow authors and friends Kate SeRine and Cecy Robson: thank you for being the best BFFs around. Thank you for all the support, all the love, and all the shared cursing, hehe. Love you both.

To my whole family: thank you for always being supportive. To my mom and dad: thank you for investing both time and money in the future of my writing career before it could even be called a career. Thank you for always believing in me even in the face of rejection. I love you.

Thank you to my amazing husband, Jon. Writing this book while we were dating was a challenge, but you were the best kind of distraction. You influenced Jace's character in so many ways, but most importantly, you kept my belief in love and happily-ever-after going strong during a difficult time and in a way no one else could. You always hold me up when I need it most, and I know you'll always be by my side. I couldn't ask for a more loving and loyal partner in life. I love you. You're a true blessing. My heart will always be yours.

And last but not least, thanks be to God, who shows me what grace is every day by treating me like a favorite child.

A sneaky peek at next month...

NOCTURNE™

BEYOND DARKNESS...BEYOND DESIRE

My wish list for next month's titles...

In stores from 15th November 2013:

❏ Dark Wolf Running – Rhyannon Byrd
❏ Nightmaster – Susan Krinard

In stores from 6th December 2013:

❏ Dark Victory – Brenda Joyce

Available at WHSmith, Tesco, Asda, Eason, Amazon and Apple

Just can't wait?

Visit us Online

You can buy our books online a month before they hit the shops! **www.millsandboon.co.uk**

MILLS & BOON®
Book Club

Join the Mills & Boon Book Club

Subscribe to **Nocturne**™ today for 3, 6 or 12 months and you could **save over £50!**

We'll also treat you to these fabulous extras:

- FREE L'Occitane gift set worth £10
- FREE home delivery
- Rewards scheme, exclusive offers...and much more!

Subscribe now and save over £50
www.millsandboon.co.uk/subscribeme